BOXER BEETLE

THIS IS A NOVEL FOR PEOPLE WITH BREEDING.

Only people with the right genes
and the wrong impulses will find
its marriage of bold ideas and
deplorable characters irresistible.
It is a novel that engages
the mind while satisfying those
that crave the thrill of a chase.

There are riots and sex. There is love
and murder. There is Darwinism
and Fascism, nightclubs, invented
languages and the dangerous
bravado of youth.
And there are lots of beetles.

IT IS CLEVER. IT IS DISTINCTIVE. IT IS ENTERTAINING.

WE HOPE YOU ARE TOO.

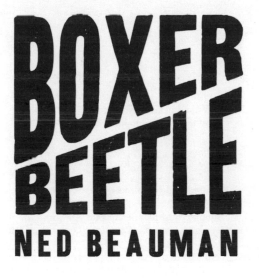

BOXER BEETLE

NED BEAUMAN

SCEPTRE

SCEPTRE

First published in Great Britain in 2010 by Sceptre
An imprint of Hodder & Stoughton
An Hachette UK company

1

A CIP catalogue record for this title is available from the British Library

Hardback ISBN 978 0 340 998397
Trade Paperback ISBN 978 0 340 998403

Typeset in Sabon by Hewer Text UK Ltd, Edinburgh

Printed and bound by Clays Ltd, St Ives plc

Hodder & Stoughton policy is to use papers that are natural, renewable
and recyclable products and made from wood grown in sustainable forests.
The logging and manufacturing processes are expected to conform
to the environmental regulations of the country of origin.

Hodder & Stoughton Ltd
338 Euston Road
London NW1 3BH

www.hodder.co.uk

... we are all accustomed to believe that maps and reality are necessarily related, or that if they are not, we can make them so by altering reality.

Jane Jacobs, *The Death and Life of Great American Cities*

Dissonance is the truth about harmony.

Theodor Adorno, *Aesthetic Theory*

1

In idle moments I sometimes like to close my eyes and imagine Joseph Goebbels' forty-third birthday party. I like to think that even in the busy autumn of 1940, Hitler might have found time to organise a surprise party for his close friend – pretending for weeks that the date had slipped his mind, deliberately ignoring the Propaganda Minister's increasingly sulky and awkward hints, and waiting until the very last order had been despatched to his U-boat commanders on the evening of Tuesday, 29 October before he led Goebbels on some pretext into the cocktail lounge of the Reich Chancellery. A great shout of *'Alles Gute zum Geburtstag!'*, a cascade of streamers, some relieved and perhaps even slightly tearful laughter from Goebbels himself as he embraced the Führer, and the party could begin.

All this is conjecture, of course. But what is certain is that at some point on that day Hitler presented Goebbels with his birthday present: an exquisite fifteen volume illustrated edition of the complete works of Goethe, published in Stuttgart in 1881 by J. G. Gottafchen, bound in red Morocco leather with a gilded spine and marbled edges.

One can't help feeling sorry for the soldiers of the 101st US Airborne Division who, nearly five years later, broke into a boarded-up salt mine near Berchtesgaden and splintered the schnapps crates piled inside to find not gold bullion, nor the Holy Spear of Destiny that pierced Christ's side, nor even a single consolatory bottle of schnapps, but instead Goebbels' personal library, stashed there in haste when the war began to turn against the Nazis. None the less, somebody was dutiful enough to make sure the books escaped the bonfires, and they were shipped back to the Library of Congress in Washington. (Meanwhile, the vast majority of Hitler's sixteen thousand books, along with his skull and Eva Braun's underwear, were captured by the Red Army and to this day lie mouldering in an abandoned baroque church on the Uzkoe estate near Moscow, which I can only assume is, by some distance, the spookiest building in the entire world.)

The book collection wouldn't even be unpacked until 1952, when the job was given to a college student on work experience who probably wished he was helping out at a summer camp. By then the Gottafchen Goethe, with its fond inscription by Hitler and scattered marginalia by Goebbels, had escaped on to the open market. And some fifty years later it passed into the hands of Horace Grublock, the London property developer who until his violent death earlier this year was an irregular employer of mine.

Between 2002 and 2007 Grublock gave me three volumes (from *Prometheus* through to *Iphigenie auf Tauris*) in exchange for errands, promising that one day, if I were loyal, I would collect the whole set. It was humiliating, but Grublock said he'd never sell – and even if he did, the sort of dealers who could handle the Goebbels Gottafchen Goethe wouldn't have taken so much as a telephone call from the likes of me, Kevin Broom – and even if they would, I could never have afforded it – so I had no choice. That's why, one day in September, when Grublock called at ten o'clock on a Thursday night, back when I'd never even heard of the town of Roachmorton, I ran for my phone with toothpaste still dribbling from my mouth, knowing it had to be him.

'Fishy,' he said.

'Yes, Horace?'

'You remember that private investigator who's been doing a spot of work for me? Zroszak?'

'I think so.'

'He's supposed to check in every evening by telephone. But he's missed two nights now, without any warning. I've tried to call him myself and there's no answer. Drive over and see if he's all right.'

'To his office?'

'He doesn't have an office. He works out of his home, like a suburban palm-reader. It's in Camden. It'll only take you ten minutes.' He gave me the address.

'What's he doing for you?'

'You know perfectly well I can't tell you, Fishy. As contingently loyal as you may be to me, I know your real allegiance is to your internet friends. Unless by any chance you've heard of a fellow called Seth Roach?'

'I hadn't.'

'That's that, then. Off you go.'

I am often asked the question, 'Why would you become a collector of rare Nazi memorabilia unless you are yourself a secret Nazi?' Or, anyway, I expect I would often be asked that question, if anyone knew about my hobby beyond Grublock, my former cleaning lady Maria, and (as Grublock calls them) my 'internet friends'.

I'm not a secret Nazi. I feel sick when I think about what they did. So do you, probably. And if just the thought can provoke a spurious little shiver of survivor's guilt, imagine what it's like to pick up an SS dagger in your hand. I don't know of any experience like it: you feel as if you're doing something terribly wrong, and yet you know it can't be wrong because you're doing no harm to anyone. It's stupid and exhilarating and revelatory. Normally you can't get a proper look at your own conscience because it only ever comes out to gash you with its beak and you just want to do whatever you can to push it away; but put your conscience in the cage of this paradox, where it can slither and bark but it can't hurt you, and you can study it for as long as you wish. Most people don't truly know how they feel about the Holocaust

3

because they're worried that if they think about it too hard they'll find out they don't feel sad enough about the 6 million dead, but I'm an expert in my own soul.

I should also add that prices for Nazi memorabilia can go up 10 or 20 per cent a year. Try getting a return like that on the stock market. I trade on internet auction sites, exploiting the stupidity and laziness of dabblers who don't realise or don't care that they could get a better price from a real dealer. Like all capitalists, I treat the free market like a rich old grandmother, insisting I adore the bitch, calling her sprightly, but more than happy to exploit her lethargy and dementia for profit. If she tries to grope my business interests with her Invisible Hand I just give her a slap. In my day job I specialise in the Allied forces from the Second World War, but I also do the Crimea, the Great War and Vietnam, plus the occasional Japanese samurai sword. (I would never buy or sell any Nazi stuff merely for profit.) I used to work in accounting, but I hated taking instructions from clients, and more importantly I thought it would be convenient if my employment were coextensional with my vocation – this way I can justify the hours I spend at my computer scouring catalogues and auction listings and messageboards. And that pays my rent, but I never have the liquidity to make any really big deals, and often I have to save for months just to afford, say, one of Ilsa Koch's cigarette cases.

So, among collectors, I am a worm – and particularly so in comparison to Stuart, my best friend, who rivals even Grublock. Every once in a while a week will go by when I'm too angry to speak to Stuart because he has refused to bid for some irresistible treasure, letting it fly away to Tokyo, never to be seen again. He could afford almost anything: the only child of a hedge fund maestro, he supplemented his inheritance with a considerable legal settlement after an accident with an office coffee machine left him paralysed from the waist down. I often wonder whether I'd give up the use of my own legs in exchange for, say, the gold fountain pen with which Adolf Hitler and Rudolf Hess wrote *Mein Kampf*, and I'm fairly that sure I would. It's not as if I leave the house very often, and Stuart always seems perfectly cheerful despite his disability (adding weight to my persistent suspicion that his paid carer will take extra for giving him hand jobs). Conversely, I also often wonder whether I'd give up such a prize in exchange for a cure for my trimethylaminuria; and, to tell the truth, as much as I hate my trimethylaminuria, I think I'd be willing not only to live with the disease, but to inflict it on Stuart too, if I could get my hands on that pen.

I mention all this only so that you can understand that I am not like Grublock. Not like him at all. Once, I heard my former employer explain his vast collection to an investor from Russia. 'In a sense, I suppose, I am a Nazi,' he said thoughtfully. 'I admire their ambition. Their courage. Their style, in the Nietzschean sense. They allowed no exceptions to their vision, and that is a lesson we should all learn. And of course I love the architecture, although sadly most of it only exists as blueprints.'

'But you also hate Jews?' said the Russian.

'Certainly not. As I said, I have great respect for certain aspects of Nazism, but not for their odd, embarrassing phobias. All that is irrational, and I'm no irrationalist. You can easily tell the collectors with those leanings. They have the books purportedly bound in human skin and the bars of soap purportedly made from human fat. Idiotic. It's almost impossible to tell tanned human skin from tanned pig skin, and the soap myth is simply that. But they so want it to be true that they will waste their money anyway. That is, if they're not deniers – in that case, you'll find none of the nasty stuff but probably some contemporaneous documentary "evidence" proving that Dachau was just an experimental vegetable garden, or some such rot.' He drained his gin and tonic. 'No, I certainly don't hate Jews. I feel sorry for the

Nazis' victims, in as much as it's possible to feel sorry for a mass of proletarian foreigners who died decades before one was born. And I admit that Hitler was probably mad, or evil, or an utter bastard, in as much as there is any difference between the three, and in as much as it makes any more sense to apply those words to a dead dictator than to apply them to an earthquake or a hurricane. And I think it was wrong to try to take over Europe, in as much as any one man's chosen political aims can be any more or less legitimate than any other's.'

The absurd thing, by the way, about Grublock's collection, which occupied the upper floor of his triplex penthouse, was that it outdid the Nazis themselves: never in the history of the Deutsches Reich would half so much finery have been gathered together in one room. It was more as if some Las Vegas entrepreneurs had started a casino in the eighties called Hitler's Palace. The centrepiece of the simulacrum was a glass case containing the Luftwaffe uniform of General Walter von Axhelm, including his Knight's Cross and his emerald-encrusted ornamental hunting dagger with a blade that belonged originally to Napoleon. Beside it was Grublock's most valuable treasure, a gorgeous porcelain falconry chest made for Hermann Goering. The rest of the room was crammed with more uniforms, medals, weapons, torture devices, ornaments and paintings, all lit by small dim spotlights. The walls were draped with long red silk banners with black swastikas on white circles. It was a wonderland. So when Grublock wouldn't even give me a hint of what Zroszak was doing for him, I could be sure that the detective was on the trail of something truly extraordinary.

I changed back out of my pyjamas and went downstairs to the car. Happy Fried Chicken, over which I live, was full of drunkards as usual – its popularity used to baffle me until I found out one of the cooks sells cannabis. It was a cold night, and as I drove over to a block of flats near the canal London felt like a whispered conversation between street lights. I wanted to listen to the radio (there's a pirate station I like called Myth FM) but I could find nothing on my crippled car system but shreds of white noise. The London air must be heavy with static, I always think, the electromagnetism rising from cars and microwave ovens and telephone wires – another thin dead residue of the city, like rust and dust and soot – I have no doubt the rats and pigeons and cockroaches have learned to navigate by it.

When I got to Zroszak's flat I buzzed his intercom but no one answered, so I waited in the cold until a girl in a grey dress came out and I grabbed the outer door as it swung shut behind her. She wrinkled her nose as she went past. Upstairs, the door of 3B was slightly ajar. The lock was broken. I knocked, but again there was no answer, so I said 'Mr Zroszak?' and pushed the door open.

Inside the small, sparse flat I saw Zroszak kneeling behind a desk as if he were praying, with his head slumped forward so that his face was hidden. There was dried blood on the edge of the desk and a dark stain where it had dripped on to the carpet. As I moved closer I could see the greenish black veins bulging on his forehead, and smell the rot already coming on like an old dull blade being slowly sharpened. All this was quite familiar from the many television dramas I watch about glamorous forensic investigators – the ones which almost make one want to be murdered just to have such a sexy woman hold your lungs in her soft hands, the ones where they primp the crime scene like an ageing film actress, with powders and tweezers and respectful murmurs – but I wasn't a detective and I just wanted to turn around and run away.

Shaking, I dialled Grublock.

'Fishy.'

'He's dead,' I said.

'Oh, fucking hell. How?'

'Shot, I think. With a gun.'

'Fucking hell. Bloody Japanese, I bet. One of those awful little consortiums. They get up to vulgar nonsense like this all the time. Well, thank you, Fishy. Go home. I'll send someone over who knows what they're doing.'

I hung up. Looking around, I realised that the place had been ransacked. The drawers of Zroszak's filing cabinet were open but empty, and there were no books on any of the shelves. On the desk, next to the murdered man's head, were a sketchpad, a pencil, a rubber and a book called *How to Draw Dogs and Cats*. Apart from that, if there had ever been even the slightest trace of Zroszak's personality in his comfortless flat, it was missing now, like the moral of a story forgetfully told.

If I could find out anything important, I thought, Grublock would probably buy me a Panzer tank for Christmas. But even if Zroszak's killer or killers had missed anything, there was no way I could search for clues with Zroszak's body there. Just the thought had me running to the tiny kitchen for an ice cube to suck on – my late mother's trusted remedy for anxiety.

The light in Zroszak's freezer was broken, and the ice tray was stuck to the bottom surface. I pulled on it hard, and it came away with a little cough of frost. As it did so, something dropped to the tiled floor.

I bent down and picked it up. It was a sealed foil packet, like an astronaut might have for his tomato soup. I cut it open with my Swiss Army knife. Inside was a yellowed sheet of paper, folded in quarters. I smoothed it out on the kitchen table and glanced over the typewritten text. The letter was headed with the address of the Führerbau on Arcisstrasse in Munich, dated 4 October, 1936, and directed to somebody called Philip Erskine at a street in Clerkenwell. When I saw the signature of the sender, I scrabbled desperately for an ice cube.

Dear Doctor Erskine,

I have received gifts from popes, tycoons, and heads of state, but none have ever been so singular or unexpected as your kind tribute. It is a reminder that the conquests of the scientist are every bit as important to our future as the conquests of the soldier. I hope you will keep me informed of the progress of your work – perhaps one day the Third Reich will have a position for you. How is your German?

Fond regards,
Adolf Hitler
Reichschancellor

I spent the next half hour searching every inch of Zroszak's flat. His body didn't matter any more. But I found nothing.

2
AUGUST 1934

Pock wasn't just losing to Sinner – he was being skinned, diced, erased. It seemed to Pock that this hairless runt could see inside him – could see Pock's memory of his first kiss, or his trick of wiggling his ears in time to a song, or his hatred of cats – could see it, take careful aim, and knock it out of his head like a loose tooth. Soon there would be nothing left of Pock but meat. Never had he felt punches so precise and impatient and cruel. And the other boy was impossibly clean – not a speck of blood on him – and although his bony chest did shine with sweat under the lights, it was a thin, efficient, cooling sweat, not the sour chicken soup that gushed into Pock's eyes and dripped from his chin and gathered in his shorts to make his cock feel heavier than his fists.

Premierland had once been a warehouse for Fairclough's, the butcher's, and if Pock felt like meat then so did many of the thousand people watching him, who were not just packed in together like meat but smoked like meat too, squinting through a blue cigarette fog so dense you could hardly see the steel girders that held up the roof. And if this tiny demon Yid hadn't decided to give the sell-out crowd a show then Pock wouldn't have lasted a round, he knew that. But Pock had never, ever been knocked out in the ring, and it wasn't going to happen tonight, with his husky-squeaky Myrna down there watching – he could never fuck her again if she saw him helpless on his back, fucked. So when the bell rang and Pock staggered back to his corner he didn't listen to his trainer's yammering, didn't take a gulp of water, didn't even knock his left fist on his right boot like he usually did for luck, he just swore under his breath and stared across the ring at Sinner, who stared back from his stool, expressionless, one arm draped over the ropes, as Max Frink, Sinner's trainer and manager, splashed him with ice water. Then the bell rang again, and Sinner spat twice and jumped up and skipped forward, already moving (as the young reporter from *Boxing* would put it) 'like a dozen kind admirers were trying to present him with a garland of poison ivy'. Pock was trudging along with his heels down on the canvas, while Sinner was still bouncing up almost on his toes. They circled each other, and Pock made a few tired jabs that he knew Sinner would dodge, then got a hard right hook to his kidneys in return – he'd dribble blood in his sleep tonight, wake up with stained underwear like a girl – feinted, blocked, feinted, and finally reached way down to thump Sinner in the balls.

(This, anyway, is how I'm almost sure it must have happened.)

Even Frink, veteran of a hundred Spitalfields street brawls, winced and clenched his teeth then, but Sinner, who'd actually taken the punch, merely grunted. Rage did come to his eyes, but that was nothing to do with pain: Sinner and pain were long estranged. Instead, Frink thought to himself, it was Sinner's realisation that he might be about to be cheated out of his knock-out. As the crowd jeered, delighted with this bit of slapstick, Frink looked down at the referee (who in those days stood outside the ring, surrounded by a mob of gamblers determined to make his decisions for him), hoping Mottle would have that brittle squint of a referee who knows he's missed something important but is too stubborn to admit his error – two times out of three you could stick a thumb in the other man's eye and not get caught – but to Frink's dismay Mottle was barking, 'Foul! Foul!'

'Nah, piss off,' said Sinner. 'That weren't a foul. It didn't hurt. Fight's still on.'

'Below the belt,' insisted Mottle. There was already a

scuffle starting among the gamblers behind him. Pock flung his hands in the air and shook his head as if to protest his innocence.

'It didn't even hurt,' said Sinner, glaring down at Mottle. 'Prick couldn't hurt me. Put a cobblestone in his glove and he couldn't hurt me.'

'We won't have any cheating here.' Mottle looked over to the judges' table for confirmation.

'I want to fucking fight. They all want me to fight.' Sinner turned to shout at his trainer. 'Frink, tell him! This is a piss-take!'

'You've won, son. Rules is rules.'

'Bollocks to this.'

Mottle nodded to the announcer. 'Ladies and gentlemen, Seth "Sinner" Roach!' There was a sarcastic, resentful cheer from a few of the crowd, and then they went back to hooting and booing, even louder now, no longer in mockery but in anger. They'd been cheated, just like Sinner, and before long an itchy discordant drone would start to rise up to the ceiling of Premierland, a threat you didn't hear with your ears but with your stomach and fists. Tonight there would be knives out all the way down Commercial Road, Pock thought, not just the gamblers but everyone who'd lost out on what they'd paid for. It didn't matter how good the first three fights were if someone spoiled the fourth – even worse than when you let a girl change her mind before you finished with her. He began to wonder if he'd made a mistake, but then he spotted Myrna in the third row, putting on lipstick with a compact mirror. He'd tell her that he'd been winning, that he'd been unlucky. Barnaby Pock, still technically unbeaten after nineteen matches, he thought. His head hurt.

'Hold on, hold on,' said Frink, hurrying over to where Mottle stood, pulling along with him a gangly fellow with a moustache who tonight was Premierland's house physician (a modest improvement over the days when the best you could hope for was a sticking plaster in the pocket of the referee). 'Let the doctor look at him. If the doctor says he's all right, then you have to let him fight.'

'I do not,' said Mottle.

'He wants to fight.'

'I'm afraid I can't possibly conduct a proper examination out here,' said the doctor.

'Have a feel!' shouted one of the gamblers.

'Are you wearing any sort of protective apparatus, Mr Roach?' said the doctor.

'He wears a strap,' said Frink.

'Only a strap! Perhaps you or your trainer are acquainted with my own line of Fistic Armatures? No? Because I assure you, gentlemen, if all pugilists were to be supplied with this inexpensive invention, there would be no question of halting a match simply because a blow had gone astray. They are impregnable.'

'Just have a look at the boy,' said Frink.

'It won't make any difference, Mel,' said Mottle.

'Quite comfortable, too,' said the doctor. 'Mr Roach, I dare say you would take a – my goodness – well, I dare say a size ten. And you, Mr Pock . . . I estimate a size four. Or perhaps a three.'

'Do you want a fucking knock?' said Pock.

'That is a very felicitous offer, sir, since I happen to be wearing one of my Fistic Armatures at this very moment. In fact, I challenge any one of you gentlemen to strike me in that region. Like St Stephen, I shall feel no pain.'

'I want to fight,' said Sinner in a voice like steel handcuffs. 'They're waiting. They didn't come to see a fucking pantomime.'

'Anyone?' said the doctor.

'Come on, mate, you've won,' said Pock.

'Surely you will be good enough to test out my invention, sir?' the doctor said, gesturing to the boy from *Boxing*, who had pushed his way through the gamblers with his notebook held over his head like a lantern.

Frink studied Sinner's face, hoping the boy's rage might scuttle back into the gloom behind his eyes. But Sinner was still angry – he hadn't given up yet.

'Do you think Mr Roach was winning, Mr Pock?' stuttered the reporter.

'I beseech you,' said the doctor.

'Come on, now, Seth,' said Frink. 'Next time.'

'What do you say, Mr Roach?' said the reporter.

'Let's all go home,' said Pock.

'Will no man here assault my testicles?' shouted the doctor. And that was when Sinner turned and smacked Pock in the face so hard that he tumbled backwards over the ropes and crashed into the gamblers like a bad idea into a hungry nation.

Frink had never seen such a punch, or heard such a cheer. As the boy from *Boxing* wiped a spray of blood from his glasses and his notebook, the crowd squealed and cackled and howled Sinner's name like a lover's, smashing beer bottles and flinging their hats in the air.

'You ought to be locked up!' said Mottle to Sinner, hardly able to make himself heard. He turned to Frink. 'Are you going to let him walk out of here after that?' Frink shrugged, and handed Sinner his robe as he climbed down from the ring. The doctor was trying to persuade some of the gamblers to help him carry Pock outside.

'Mr Roach, did he get what was coming to him?' said the reporter.

'We all get what's coming to us, son,' said Frink.

Dozens of men and women and children got up from their seats as Sinner pushed through towards the corridor that led to the dressing rooms, hoping to shake his hand or kiss his cheek or pat his back or pass him a cigar, but he just looked straight ahead, swearing under his breath. Although he would never have admitted it, even to himself, he liked having fans, and he really liked ignoring his fans, and he'd learnt not long ago that ignoring them just made them even more loyal, especially the women. Tonight, most of them were content to pay tribute to Frink instead. The only concession Sinner made was to put his fists up quickly for a photographer.

'You could have done him afterwards, Seth, if you had to do that,' muttered Frink.

'He hit me in the eggs.'

'Yeah, but you said it didn't hurt.'

No one remembered how a huge green leather armchair had found its way into the biggest of Premierland's dressing rooms, but by now it stank of sweat and resin and was vomiting stuffing from its cracks. Sinner sat down and picked up a bottle of gin. 'You can fuck off, I think, if you're going to moan like you always do.'

'You know I am,' said Frink. He tried to remember a time when the boy wouldn't have talked to his trainer like that. He could, but only if he remembered so selectively that it became a sort of fantasy. For a while, he'd worried that Sinner's growing local celebrity might make him harder to control, but in fact Sinner seemed to be almost immune to fame. Not, of course, because of any inner humility – exactly the opposite. The boy had an arrogance so unshakeable that any outside stimulation was basically redundant, a kick up the arse of a speeding train. If Sinner slipped further out of his grasp it wouldn't be because of fame, but because of a much more banal intoxicant. 'I need to talk to Pock's man anyway,' Frink added as he bent down to tidy away a skipping rope. His forehead and eyelids and the tip of his nose were always very pink, as if he'd once fallen asleep on a stove.

'Why?'

'He might try and get you banned.'

'I won't get banned.'

'No, not this time, and not next time, but the time after that you might.'

'Bye, then.'

'Don't finish that too fast.'

Frink went out. Seth sucked on the bottle of gin and then coughed and closed his eyes.

Sixteen years old; seven professional matches (unbeaten); nine toes; four foot, eleven inches tall. These were the numbers that made Seth 'Sinner' Roach, all of them pretty low, but what did that matter? Today – 18 August 1934 – he was already the best new boxer in London. To his opponents a fight with Sinner was like an interrogation, every punch a question they could not possibly answer, an accusation they could not possibly deny.

His nickname, like the armchair, was of mysterious origin. 'Jews don't have sinners, Seth,' Rabbi Brasch used to say, 'we just have idiots.' When Sinner was sober, there was an intensity to his expression so fixed that, if you gazed at it for too long (which a lot of people did, trying to understand how such a stunted, thuggish physique could be so beautiful), it began to seem not intense but, on the contrary, blank and inert, as when you repeat a harsh word too many times and it loses its meaning; and this changeless quality seemed to deny even the possibility of sin. But everyone called him Sinner none the less. He had oily black hair and thin eyebrows and long eyelashes and small nipples and slightly protruding ears and still, improbably, a full set of teeth.

There was a quiet knock at the door. 'Fuck off,' said Sinner. But the door opened, and into the dressing room stepped a tall blond man in a black overcoat. 'Mr Roach,' he said, extending a hand. He wore calfskin gloves with pearl buttons and had a neat moustache that did not make up for a weak chin. He carried himself as if he thought he might at any moment have to dive out of the way of a galloping horse.

'My name is Philip Erskine,' he said.

'Enchanted,' replied Sinner, without moving.

'I very much enjoyed your performance tonight.'

'Brought me some flowers, have you?'

'I'm sorry to intrude like this, Mr Roach, but I didn't know otherwise when I might have a chance to speak to you.' While Sinner's accent was east London with just a trace of his parents' Yiddish, Erskine's was the poshest Sinner had ever heard, with the exception of Danny Gaster's manager – supposedly a disinherited aristocrat – and announcers on the wireless. Seeing he wasn't going to get a handshake, Erskine withdrew his hand in a way that seemed intended to give the impression he had never really wanted one in the first place. 'I'd like to make you an offer.'

'Pretty sister you'd like me to meet?'

'Actually, I—'

'Oh, no, should have known. I'm looking at a hardened gangster. You want me to throw a fight.'

'No, it's—'

'I get it,' said Sinner, taking a swig of gin. 'You're going to be a heavyweight. Need me to find you a good trainer.'

'In fact I know nothing about boxing, Mr Roach. I am a scientist.'

'How fascinating,' said Sinner.

'May I explain?' The boy did not immediately respond, so Erskine continued: 'It's very kind of you to hear me out. I'll be extremely brief. For the last four years I've been busy with the study of insects. There is very little I don't know about beetles. But I've had enough of beetles now. I want to study human beings. And you are the human being I have most wished to study, ever since I first learnt of your very unusual physiology.'

'You mean I'm a short-arse?'

'Yet by all accounts a combatant of remarkable strength and skill. And your father, they say, is equally diminutive, and his father before him?'

'Yeah.'

'And only nine toes, if I'm not mistaken?'

'What's your "offer"?'

'May I sit down?'

'No.'

'Mr Roach, I would like to give you fifty pounds in exchange for permission to conduct a thorough medical examination and interview every month for a period of five or six months. After that, you would never have to see me again, and you would be kept anonymous in any resultant literature.'

'Fifty quid to prod me like one of your earwigs?'

'I can assure you that the examinations would not be unpleasant.'

'What the fuck is this?' said Sinner, raising his voice for the first time. 'You think I need your fucking fifty quid? I'm going to be flyweight champion of the world. I'm not on the fucking dole.'

'A hundred pounds, then.'

'Fuck off.'

'Two hundred. Mr Roach, you do not realise how perfectly you . . . . No one can take your place, sir. Wouldn't you like to accompany your sporting triumph with a scientific one? I hope that my humble work will make at least some tiny contribution to a project which will, without a doubt, be of wonderful lasting benefit to our whole race. The finest minds of Europe and the United States are coming together to—'

'What are you going on about?'

'Eugenics, Mr Roach. Have you heard of it?'

'Is this cunt boring you, Seth? Pardon me, I mean "this gentleman".' Kölmel chuckled. He stood in the doorway holding a cigar. Like Frink, Kölmel was stocky and flat-nosed, but fatter and balder than his cousin. 'That was a hint, mate,' he added.

'Is there any chance you might reconsider?' said Erskine quietly to Sinner.

'Fuck off back to your beetles.'

18

'Very well. None the less, I shall leave my card on the table, in case you should have a change of heart. Goodbye, gentlemen,' said Erskine, and went out.

'Why are you wearing a fucking overcoat on a day like this?' Kölmel shouted after him, but there was no reply. Kölmel turned back to Sinner. 'Who was that?'

'Some fucking bum-boy toff.'

'What did he want?'

'Put me in a freak show.'

'You should have someone on the door here, Sinner.'

Sinner shrugged.

'Anyway, came to give my congratulations.'

'You taking the piss?'

'You were murdering him, son. You could see his knees tremble. That's what counts. Pock joking about at the end like that, that don't come into it. You know Joe Schmeling actually won a title claiming a foul? They say his trainer had a cup with a big dent in it, kept it in his pocket every day just in case. Came good that time – slipped it in the cunt's shorts like a conjurer.'

Sinner was seven years old when he first met Albert Kölmel, helping his father pack up the vegetable stall on a Saturday night in February. Until 1927 Kölmel still made his rounds personally, but even back then he behaved as if Spitalfields Market was his alone, strolling around like a factory owner inspecting his machines. One hand held a cigar and the other was permanently clenched into a fist, and the young Sinner was thrilled to think that Kölmel was always so close to knocking someone's lights out that it wasn't even worth uncurling his fingers. Only later did he realise that inside the fist was hidden, implied, Kölmel's weapon of choice: a razor blade stuck into a wine cork, about an eighth of an inch of steel protruding a sharp tongue, enough to scar a man's face but not enough to kill him. A man like Kölmel would be an idiot to carry a knife or a gun or anything else that could get you caught and hanged if something went wrong – better, if you really had to punish a man, to hold him down and cut deep into his upper lip, so that later, when the scar tissue formed and pulled the lip upward, his mouth would be permanently twisted open. Or there were other pranks, without the blade. Once Bryan Harding had tried to make Kölmel pay full price for his portions of fish and chips, so Kölmel picked up Harding's cat and threw her into his deep fat fryer.

'This your boy?' Kölmel had said on that February evening.

'Here,' said Sinner's father, passing Kölmel five shillings without meeting his eye.

'What's your name, son?' Kölmel said to Sinner, who was sorting mouldy turnips from good ones. Around them were the scavengers: first the very poor, the very mean and the very old, who would wait until the end of the day to get the unwanted produce for the lowest prices, and then the homeless, the crippled and the mad, who would scurry along to gather up the detritus on the ground, looking for squashed fruit and vegetables, cardboard for bedding, and bits of broken wooden boxes that would help to make a fire. To Sinner, a market like this was just a ceaseless battle against decay, a mere waiting room for the huge rubbish dump on Back Church Lane: squint for long enough against that high wind of putrefaction, and surely before long it would begin to blow years from your own life, so you'd start to smell rotten yourself; better to work in a chemist's or a sweet shop, where the shiny pellets in the glass jars could be nine centuries old for all anyone knew. At the same time, there was something lovely about the market in the early mornings, when he was rarely here: everything ablaze with freshness but nobody much around, like the beginning of creation. Except that, at the beginning of creation, God had not yet even conceived of a creature like Albert Minyo, who could shout nothing but 'Saveloys! Saveloys! Saveloys! Saveloys! Saveloys! Saveloys!

Saveloys! Saveloys! Saveloys! Saveloys! Saveloys!' eight hours
a day for thirty years.

'My name's Seth,' Sinner had replied.

'You got any brothers and sisters?'

'Anna's my little sister.'

'I'd like to meet her. Well, see you again, Seth. Much
obliged, Mr Roach,' said Kölmel, patting him on the shoulder.

After Kölmel had gone, Sinner knew from his father's
expression not to ask who the man was or why he was taking
money; but a few weeks later, when Alfeo turned up on a
Sunday with plasters on both sides of his face, Sinner felt
almost sure it had something to do with Kölmel. (Sinner
didn't know that, if you had asked Kölmel, he would cheerfully have assured you of his purposes: the money would
help to prevent dirty new immigrants from setting up in the
market to compete with the established stall-holders.) Either
way, he couldn't help seeing Kölmel as a benevolent figure,
particularly since Alfeo loved to give Sinner a hard cuff over
the head whenever he went near Alfeo's cakes. And he didn't
mind seeing his father get humiliated. Intimidation was a
kind of conquest, and Sinner liked conquest.

By the time Sinner was nine, he was working for Kölmel at
the wet docks. Clutching a rinsed-out petrol can and a 'rum
pipe' (a few inches of metal pipe glued to a foot of rubber
tubing), he and another Whitechapel boy would creep down
to the creaking wooden platforms where barrels of rum or
port were being unloaded. There, with the other boy on look-
out, he would 'suck the monkey': jam the metal end of the
rum pipe under the barrel's stopper, suck on the rubber end
until liquid began to flow, fill the can, replace the lid, and
wait while the other boy filled his own can; then they'd run
off – snatching a lime or a banana or even a pineapple from
a crate on the way, dockers spitting curses as they passed –
slow down after a couple of minutes to walk panting and
giggling through Limehouse, and swap their cans with one

of Kölmel's men for a few pence when they got home. That was how Sinner got his first taste of anything stronger than the froth on his father's ale. It made you grimace, but if you drank enough it felt like discovering an entire hidden room in your own house that you'd never even known about. You wanted to do more than poke your head round the door. You wanted to take its dimensions.

When he needed someone beaten up, Kölmel didn't use anyone younger than fifteen or sixteen because they weren't strong enough and they got scared off too easily – and by the time Sinner was twelve, and everyone could see that he was already the strongest boy on his street and that he wasn't scared of anything, Frink had made his claim on him. But Kölmel had won such a fortune betting on Sinner's first few Premierland matches, back when no one but his cousin had guessed quite how good this midget newcomer was, that he still saw Sinner almost as an employee, and was officially 'taking an interest' in the boy's career. That meant his men wouldn't extort any more money from Sinner's father, even though Sinner told them they were welcome to. Kölmel really only ran his old protection racket for sentimental reasons, anyway – from what Sinner had heard, a hundred times more money now came from whores and marijuana and forged cheques than could possibly be monkey-sucked with a razor threat from the stale loaves and squishy apples and gnarled pigs' feet of the failing Spitalfields Market.

'What's next for you, then?' said Kölmel in the dressing room. Here they were, today, with Sinner slumped in his green throne and Kölmel standing there like a supplicant; it didn't reflect how things really were, but it still gave Sinner pleasure.

'I want to go to America,' Sinner said. 'New York City.'

'I mean your next fight.'

'Don't know. Ask Frink.'

'What do you want to go to America for?'

'Proper money over there. And you get treated like royalty, they say.'

'Tossers, Americans. Except my half-brother.'

Sinner shrugged again. He thought of his father, whose journey from a village in eastern Poland had ended at the Jewish shelter on Leman Street only because he'd been thrown off the ship that was going to take him to the United States.

'You're talkative tonight, ain't you?' said Kölmel. 'Got a girl waiting?' He was ugly when he smiled. 'Course you do. Give her a good hard one from me, son.' Kölmel didn't know what Frink knew.

After Kölmel left, Sinner drank a little more gin, got dressed, and then telephoned for a cab to take him from Bethnal Green to Covent Garden.

AFTER THE DAY'S ROUTINE SPEND YOUR EVENING AT
The Caravan
81 ENDELL ST.
(Corner of Shaftesbury Avenue, facing Princes Theatre)
Phone: Temple Bar 7665
London's Greatest Bohemian Rendezvous
said to be the most unconventional spot in town
ALL NIGHT GAIETY   Dancing to Charlie

PERIODICAL NIGHT TRIPS TO THE GREAT OPEN
SPACES, INCLUDING THE ACE OF SPADES, ETC.

The West End was littered now with these little cards, but Sinner had heard about the Caravan's opening straight from its founder, Will Reynolds, a gambler, boxing enthusiast and well-known Soho rake who had been determined to make the worst possible use of a £300 inheritance from a Presbyterian great-aunt. The basement club was decorated in a nonspecific oriental style, with lacquered furniture, red hanging lanterns and painted silk drapes. Tonight, as every night, it was teeming. The band played 'When I Take My Morning Promenade'. Later there would be a drag show.

Sinner liked coming here straight from a fight without

bothering to wash. All the other men were so soaped, even perfumed, but he just stank, and in the crush at the bar they couldn't ignore it. It was like walking around with his cock out. A few people greeted him, but he was already sick of talking tonight so he bought a double gin and stood at the end of the bar scanning faces. After a minute or two he noticed a good-looking boy of nineteen or twenty, with a French sort of bent nose, standing there with his thumbs in his pockets looking lost. Sinner shouldered through the crowd. He put a hand on the boy's arm and bent towards his ear to be heard over the music, lightly brushing the boy's crotch with the back of his other hand as he did so. 'You waiting for anyone in particular?'

'No.'

'Come on, then.' Sinner pulled him towards the door.

'Who are you?'

'It don't matter.'

'Where are we going?'

'Hotel de Paris on Villiers Street. I'll pay. They know me. You been before?'

'No, I don't really . . . I mean . . . .'

Sinner never had any trouble. In a club like this, even the boys as beautiful as Sinner would usually join in the flirtation and gossip. That was why you came to the Caravan instead of just hunting in the dark at the Piccadilly News Theatre. But Sinner didn't have to bother with that – there was something in the way he looked at you and the way he spoke to you. Or at least there was the first time – hardly anyone ever went with him a second time, not only because Sinner himself lost interest, but also because you were still too bruised and shaken, particularly if, like this French boy, you'd been unlucky enough to meet him on a night when he still had half a fight caged in him. Even if you'd been warned, though, you still didn't turn him down. The best you could do was to pick up another pint of gin on the way so there was a chance

24

that, after a last monochrome orgasm, he might pass out by daybreak.

They got to the door and started up the steps to street level just as a man in a black overcoat was making his way down. Sinner looked up. It was Philip Erskine. Sinner stopped.

'What the fuck do you think you're doing here?' he said.

Erskine blanched and started to stutter something.

'You followed me,' said Sinner.

'What?' said Erskine.

'You followed me here. Probably going to kidnap me. Posh cunt.'

Erskine swallowed. 'That's right. I followed you here. I'm sorry.'

Sinner knew that Will Reynolds wouldn't like it if he heard that Sinner had punched a bloke out on his steps, so Sinner just cuffed Erskine hard with the back of his hand. Erskine let out a yelp, then turned, hurried back up the steps, and ran off down Endell Street.

3
AUGUST 1934

Erskine was back at school. In the dream, he woke up one morning in the dormitory, threw off his sheets, looked down at his body, and saw with horror that during the night he had somehow transformed from an insect into a man.

When he woke up a second time, he was sweaty and glue-mouthed and he had an erection. He had only intended a ten-minute afternoon nap but it was already three o'clock. He was in a small hot room in the United Universities Club on Suffolk Street, where he stayed whenever he was in London, on a mattress packed with knuckles and sinews. The club was old-fashioned and full of awful Cambridge hearties and so dusty he couldn't stop sneezing, but his father had insisted that he join. Very soon, with a bit of diligence, Erskine felt he was certain to acquire lots of fascinating London friends with whom he would be able to dine and lodge as he wished, but so far, at twenty-four years old, the UUC was all he really had.

After changing his shirt he went downstairs to the L-shaped coffee room with its heavy maroon curtains half-closed to resist the siege of the summer day, and found Morton, Cripling and Nash sitting around cackling about something. He settled himself beside them in an armchair and tried to work out what was funny. No one greeted him, so he pretended to look over a copy of *The Times*. There was to be a plebiscite in Germany tomorrow to confirm the exciting succession of Herr Hitler.

'I think Nash himself enjoys the occasional "night trip to the great open spaces", don't you, Nash?' Morton was saying. 'Ever the "Bohemian".'

Nash raised his hands in mock-confession. 'I shan't deny it. "After the day's routine", I find it just the thing.' They all brayed again.

Erskine saw that they were looking at some sort of chit or card. 'What's the joke?' he asked.

'Oh, hello, Erskine,' said Morton cheerfully. 'Cripling found this on the floor at his barber's.' Julius Morton had matriculated at Trinity with Erskine, and had once, quite sober, held Erskine down and forced him to gargle port until he threw up into his Ovid, then chuckled about it for days afterwards as if Erskine had been in on the joke all along. Every time Erskine allowed Morton to treat him as a chum the humiliation of that episode, and many others like it, was redoubled, but Erskine didn't really have any choice – particularly since Morton had recently taken a romantic interest in his sister Evelyn, having met her by disastrous coincidence at one of Lady Molly's dances. One of Erskine's many objections to the orthodox eugenic theory of the day was that he knew of no proposed system which would put Morton down for compulsory sterilisation. Or at the very least a flogging.

Erskine's only consolation, in fact, was what he knew of Morton's beloved younger brother. At eight years old the brother had shoved a spade into the wheel of a moving car, which threw him on to his back so hard that he broke his leg and was blinded in one eye by a blow to the temporal lobe of the brain. The leg got better but he soon, unrelatedly, contracted polio. The Mortons' family doctor, a former military man, was called, but, suspecting the boy of malingering, instructed that he should not be put to bed but instead kept active. As a result, Morton's brother had lost the use of his right arm and both his legs, all of which had to be kept in heavy irons, and they itched so unbearably that he was driven almost insane: he would sometimes laugh for no particular reason in uncontrollable simian howls like a vaudeville comedian pretending to have gone mad. Nothing but acute pain could stop him, and his healthy leg ended up badly scarred because he used to burn himself deliberately with cigarettes. This episodic tragedy, which had darkened the lives of Morton's entire family, gave Erskine ceaseless pleasure, like a really good radio serial.

'What is it?' he said, taking the card from Morton and reading it over.

Erskine didn't understand – it seemed to be just an advertisement for a nightclub – but he forced a little laugh anyway, and gave it back. He sat for a few minutes as the three others began to joke about the temperaments of some of their university contemporaries. But as he tried to think of something witty to contribute, he slowly began to realise what they were really discussing, and at last, when Cripling used the expression 'a bunch of brown hatters', Erskine was sure. After that, he listened very closely.

But by then the theme was already almost exhausted, and the others soon started to talk about their plans for the evening. As much as he'd heard about the wonderful freedoms of a young bachelor in London, Erskine had found that one's movements were even more public in a little club like this than they had been in a Cambridge college, so he already had an imaginary dinner with a cousin prepared as an excuse for going out to the fight tonight. And when the other three got up, leaving the card behind, he realised nervously that the excuse could do double-duty. Shaftesbury Avenue was only a few minutes from the United Universities Club. He could easily slip into this Caravan place on the way back from the fight.

In Trinity's Great Hall he had once overheard part of a conversation along similar lines about a pub called the Marquis of Granby. Then, as now, he had carefully committed the exchange to memory, but it had contained no details of scientific usefulness apart from one crucial remark that 'at a place like that, one can never be over-dressed'. Erskine consequently concluded that he would have to put on white tie if he was to visit the Caravan, but he could hardly wear that to the boxing match. Luckily, he had already resolved to wear his father's overcoat on his trip into Spitalfields and keep it on at all times so that he wouldn't have to come back to Suffolk Street with the ineradicable stench of blood and poverty and herring and Jew on his suit. The tails would not be visible under the overcoat.

He spent the early evening finishing a book by Lord Alfred Douglas called *Plain English*. Douglas, like Erskine, had been in the scholars' house at Winchester, and Erskine had spent a term working at a desk on which the small carving of an erect penis was reportedly Douglas' work. What Erskine had read of Wilde and his panderers he found repellent, but when he discovered that 'Bosie' had written a book about racial purity he ordered it from the London Library out of curiosity. As he'd expected, it was a crude work, with nothing to say, for instance, about Pitt-Rivers' interesting but outlandish theory that, in sexual inversion, the great evolutionary consciousness of the species had found a way of hacking off its own least promising lines of inheritance before they could be propagated. Also, the book apparently lacked any of the coded allusions to immorality that Erskine sometimes found it abstractly amusing to identify in works by authors like Douglas, mentally netting and labelling each innuendo like a butterfly.

He ate steak and kidney pie at the club, changed into white tie, put on his gloves, buttoned his overcoat, and then, armoured, took a cab to Premierland. Commercial Road swarmed. The cab nearly ran over an organ-grinder's monkey pulling at its chain. He'd heard that Thomas Cook took tourists on sightseeing tours of the exotic East End. To Erskine, the urban poor seemed not much different from the rural poor, and he understood neither. Why must they be so ugly and sore-ridden, he wondered? Why must they scream at their own children? Why must they urinate in the street? Plainly no one could desire these indignities for their own sake, so they made sense only as a sort of deliberate, spiteful impudence. On an intellectual level he understood that the condition of these specimens was the result of degenerative miscegenation and insufficient selection pressure, but still, somehow, as the son of Celia Erskine, a well-known charitable benefactor, he couldn't help feeling personally insulted by their obvious lack of gratitude. Had Marx really spent all that time in London? Surely he must have realised that, if these withered grey creatures tried to rise up, the result would be unpleasant but barely perceptible, like a gust of smoke from a grate in the street.

The match was sold out, so he bought a ticket at four times the original price from a tout in a wheelchair, and found a seat. He looked around. The lights above the ring were enclosed in a black square shade printed with advertisements for an evening paper, and around the ropes were hung red and blue posters with the programme for next week's fight. Although the smelly man next to him kept jostling his shoulder, he felt secure in his overcoat. It wasn't like the theatre – the audience came and went and talked and whistled and drank and even, somehow, slept as they pleased, and boys climbed from row to row shouting, 'Nice apples, twopence' – but then Erskine himself didn't pay much attention to the first two fights. Instead, he looked around for anecdotal observations that he could one day include in a work on eugenics: a charming blonde Anglo-Saxon girl on the arm of some warty, toadlike Semite, for instance. Before Erskine had found anything of the sort, however, it was time for Roach vs Pock.

Erskine had first come across Seth 'Sinner' Roach in a copy of *Boxing* that was lying around in the coffee room of his club. Reading Sinner's statistics and looking at his picture, Erskine had been struck by two powerful blows. The first was the very idea that such exquisite sporting prowess could have

emerged from a physiological inheritance that was otherwise so wretched, like a peach tree growing from a plague
pit – Jewish boxers were not uncommon these days, but what
about an awkward, five-foot, nine-toed Jewish boxer who
was good enough to be a world champion? The second blow
was irritatingly obscure – like knowing you have forgotten
something and not knowing what – but Erskine did not
have time to pursue it because the case of Seth Roach had
helped towards maturity one or two heretical ideas that he
was nursing about practical eugenics, and soon he concluded
that a close observation of Sinner would be the best way to
put them to the test. He took out a subscription to *Boxing*,
and when one of Sinner's matches coincided with a visit to
London he was determined to attend.

The fight was thrilling. Both fighters glowed like medieval saints. Unlike many sportsmen Erskine had seen, Sinner
seemed to take no satisfaction in his own speed and grace
and power – they were too much a part of him – he was like
a fox or a deer, any creature that is more beautiful because it
cannot know it is beautiful, any creature with the courage to
contend that the world does not carry on while it is asleep.
Hitler had said that 'the German boy of the future must be
lithe and slender, swift as a greyhound, tough as leather, and
hard as Krupp steel'. Sinner was all that. Hitler hadn't said
anything about tall.

And there was something so intimate about these near-
naked men fighting their very hardest – Erskine almost
wanted to turn away in embarrassment, but he was too rapt.
Soon the cheers of the crowd seemed to fall away, and he
could hear nothing but the butcher's-counter slap of fist on
face.

Then it ended. Erskine was as disappointed as anyone by
the sheer cowardice of Pock, who by that point was wet and
blinking like someone who hadn't quite saved his dog from
drowning in a river. During the ensuing dispute over the foul,

Erskine remembered that a match like this was played by Marquess of Queensberry rules, and wasn't that Lord Alfred Douglas' father, sued by Wilde for calling him, illiterately, a 'somdomite'? Except he wasn't sure if it was the same Marquess of Queensberry. When Sinner knocked Pock out of the ring, he found himself screaming with joy. He'd wanted Sinner to win so much.

Afterwards he made his way to the dressing room, and stood outside the door for a minute or two before he had the courage to knock. The interview with Sinner was not a success. 'I've had enough of beetles now,' he told the boy. 'I want to study human beings.' This wasn't quite true. Whether or not Sinner complied with his request, Erskine knew that he would probably have to carry on herding insects as long as he lived. For one thing, his father, who funded his studies, would be unhappy at the abrupt switch from entomology to anthropobiology. But, more importantly, some of his planned eugenic experiments would require hundreds of bloodlines to be followed for hundreds of generations. That was ambitious enough with insects, but probably impossible with humans, unless you had a whole dynasty of scientists working under a whole dynasty of despots. In a truly enlightened society, of course, the two clans would soon fuse: scientists would be despots and despots would be scientists. At least with beetles it was easy enough to be both. Not long ago he'd read a book called *If I Were a Dictator*, by Julian Huxley, whom he'd once met at a cocktail party. Huxley argued that busy shopping streets should have their pavements replaced with moving pneumatic platforms and that sex should be taught in schools, but other parts of his argument were more creditable. 'The true-born Briton is rather proud of his reluctance to become a governmental "guinea-pig",' he wrote. 'In reality this attitude is the product of an irrational and suspicious stupidity on his part, and of unscientific unplanned action on the part of the State; an atmosphere should and could be created in which to be selected as an experimental object and to serve in the application of science to social progress would be regarded as an honour.'

But this atmosphere was missing from Sinner's dressing room, and Erskine left Premierland almost in tears. He had to trudge a long way down Commercial Road, jostled by passers-by, before he could find a cab. He didn't want to ask the driver to take him to the Caravan, so he got out at the north end of Endell Street and walked up and down it for nearly twenty minutes before he realised that the club was tucked below street level. He stood at the top of the steps gathering his resolve, as he had outside the dressing room, and then started down. And that was when, as in a dream, Sinner came out through the door.

'What the fuck do you think you're doing here?' said the boxer. 'You followed me.'

Actually, for a delirious instant Erskine had assumed the reverse – that Sinner had followed Erskine to Covent Garden to tell him that he'd changed his mind. But that didn't make sense. 'What?' he said, noticing that there was another boy with Sinner. A fellow boxer?

'You followed me here. Probably going to kidnap me. Posh cunt.'

How else could Erskine explain himself? He could be fairly confident that Sinner wouldn't have heard of Pitt-Rivers' Evolutionary Consciousness, or understand that the Caravan was the perfect place to test that theory. Also, it looked as though he might get hit if he tried to argue. So he said, 'That's right. I followed you here. I'm sorry.' And got hit anyway. He had found it strangely challenging to lie to the boy: there was something in his gaze that flayed you bare. He recalled that boxers had to be keen empiricists of human behaviour, so that they could always predict their opponent's next move. Erskine liked to think of himself as a keen empiricist of human behaviour, but the truth was he found it a rather confounding subject, like algebra.

One or two people laughed at him as he hurried down
Endell Street. He was suddenly unbearably hot in the
carapace of his father's overcoat. Crossing Long Acre, he
slowed down, and went into a pub on Bow Street near the
Royal Opera House to buy a brandy. He didn't want to go
back to his club yet. From the bar he could see out through
the window, and a minute later, to his surprise, he caught
sight of Sinner and the other boy going past. Even to watch
Sinner walk was fascinating: he had a sort of swaggering
bounce as if he were still in the ring. Erskine gulped down
his drink.

Outside, he pursued the two of them from a distance.
They went a long way down the Strand, then turned left
into the little mess of short streets beside Charing Cross
Station, where he knew he couldn't help being seen if they
happened to turn their heads. But neither did, and he was
able to watch as Sinner led the boy into the Hotel de Paris.
The narrow building was a scuffed, brown-toothed interloper
in a relatively smart street. Erskine stood on the corner for
ten minutes smoking a cigarette and mentally reviewing all
that he knew about perverts in case he should be obliged to
pass for one, then went inside, where a fat man in braces sat
behind a counter reading a paperback detective novel and
breathing heavily. He asked for a single room for the night
and was given a key in return for ten shillings.

'Expecting any callers later?' the man said.

'Definitely not.'

Erskine did not even look at the room number on the key.
Instead, he walked the shabby corridors of the Hotel de Paris,
wondering which room was Sinner's, hearing nothing but the
creak of his own footsteps and the intestinal groans of the hot
water pipes. (Why was he here?) When he'd paced all three
floors he chose a room at random, 39, knelt down, and held
his ear to the door. Inside he could hear grunting and panting.
Could this be Sinner and the other boy, he wondered, his

stomach hollow? But when he tried 38, he heard the same; from 37, silence; and from 36, grunting again.

'What on earth are you up to?'

Erskine looked up. A man who wore eyeshadow, rouge and no shirt was coming out of the communal lavatory. He had his hands on his hips and he spoke in a high-pitched theatrical voice that Erskine found physically nauseating.

'Nothing,' Erskine replied, and got to his feet.

'I'll be free in about an hour if you're looking for a bit of—'

'No!' Erskine shouted, and, once again, fled. That night, noosed in his sheets at the United Universities Club, he dreamed of two rabbits, one white and one black, strapped together on a surgical table and cut open so that each one's carotid artery gushed into the other one's heart. When he awoke, choking on blood that wasn't there, he wondered about the symbolism – he'd read Freud as well as Marx – until he remembered that this image was not a product of his unconscious, but rather a real experiment performed in 1870 by the great Francis Galton, inventor of the word 'eugenics', to disprove his cousin Charles Darwin's theory of pangenesis. 'It was astonishing to see how quickly the rabbits recovered after the effects of the anaesthetic had passed away,' Galton had written. 'It often happened that their spirits and sexual aptitude were in no way dashed by an operation which, only a few minutes before, had changed nearly one half of the blood that was in their bodies.' Erskine got up and took a very long bath.

4

Only six or seven hundred people in the world have trimethyl-aminuria. Because of a misprint in our genes our bodies are unable to break down trimethylamine, the chemical that gives the stink to both rotting fish and bacterial infections of the vagina. (Hence all those tiresome old jokes about a blind man wandering into a fish-market and taking it for a brothel, or vice versa, which could just as well be made about a blind man wandering into a convention of trimethylaminuria sufferers, although in truth if such a convention were ever to take place then it would no doubt be identified as a terrorist biological weapon and fighter planes would be scrambled at once.) Trimethylamine leaks out in our sweat and our urine and our saliva, curdling the air around us. There is no cure. Most of us will never have consensual sex, and many of us commit suicide by the time we are thirty. I used to spend time on trimethylaminuria support group messageboards, the closest thing we have to the aforementioned convention, but I found the tone too depressing, in contrast to Nazi memora-bilia collecting messageboards, which are brisk with shared endeavour and friendly competition.

Along with trimethylaminuria I also have asthma, eczema, cystic acne, mild irritable bowel syndrome and half a dozen other absurd non-terminal diseases. I have come to see my body as a sort of Faulknerian idiot man-child which I must drag along groaning behind me wherever I go. Stuart is convinced that within the next fifty years it will be possible to upload one's brain into a computer and live on as nothing more than sparkles on a hard disk, and I long for that day of rapture. (Funnily enough, though, Stuart himself suffers from a sort of electronic trimethylaminuria, the sheer obnoxiousness of his emails and messageboard posts ensuring that I am the only person left in the internet Nazi memorabilia collecting community who will talk to him. He once tricked several of his enemies into watching a nine-minute video clip, loosely of the pornographic genre, called 'Three Girls, Two Cups'; at least one victim has reportedly not approached a computer since.) But until that day, I will just have to go on smelling like unwashed cunt.

Consequently, you might expect that I would take excellent care of my flat in Holloway, since I so rarely feel motivated to leave it. But several months have passed since Maria quit, and things have got to the stage now where I worry that, without all the dirty socks, takeaway cartons and semen-stiffened tissues like crude artificial roses, the place might actually feel a bit empty and weird. I'm not someone who minds a bit of mess. Also, even if it were spotless, the trimethylamine smell would still be intolerable to anyone but me. Sometimes I like to think of it as a mutant power but the truth is I don't think I'd fit in with the X-Men.

When I got home from Zroszak's flat at about one in the morning, I woke my computer and wrote a post on the largest of the collectors' forums.

Subject: Philip Erskine?
From: kevin (Posts: 1,267)
Time: 1:11 GMT
does anyone know anything about a scientist and possible acquaintance of Hitler called Philip Erskine?

I opened my chat program. Stuart, as usual, was still online. He doesn't sleep much.

KEVIN: i saw a dead body today
STUART: dig her up yourself? lol.

KEVIN: i'm serious
STUART: where, then?
KEVIN: i can't tell you
STUART: well aren't you mysterious
     hey, what's this about 'Philip Erskine'?

Stuart has a browser extension that immediately alerts him to every new post on every relevant forum so that he doesn't have to click 'reload' every ten seconds.

KEVIN: just something i came across
STUART: to do with the dead body?
KEVIN: no
STUART: come on
KEVIN: no nothing to do with it
STUART: oh for fuck's sake, don't hold out on me like this
KEVIN: i'm not
STUART: so two unrelated exciting things happened to you
     in one night? right.

Guiltily I clicked away to another window and ran a search for 'Philip Erskine'. A motivational speaker, a history teacher, a town planner, a few others, but no scientists. I went back to the forum. To my surprise, someone had already replied to my post.

Subject: Philip Erskine?
From: nbeauman (Posts: 17)
Time: 1:14 GMT
> *does anyone know anything about a scientist and possible*
> *acquaintance of Hitler called Philip Erskine?*
anything to do with Seth Roach, the boxer?

Remembering that Grublock had mentioned that name, I wrote:

Subject: Philip Erskine?
From: kevin (posts: 1,268)
Time: 1:15 GMT

> *anything to do with Seth Roach, the boxer?*
> *yes. what else do you know?*

and waited, fidgeting, for five minutes, but there was no further response. I went to nbeauman's profile to see his sixteen prior posts: just short, routine contributions to a few forum arguments, some of which I'd actually read at the time without noting his name.

I spent the next half-hour running more searches on 'Philip Erskine' and 'Seth Roach', from which I didn't learn much, while debating with Stuart whether Unity Mitford could really have had Hitler's baby and whether the new two-disc special edition DVD of Godzilla vs Mothra was worth the money. At about two in the morning, I went to bed. At about five, something woke me. I opened my eyes. There was a man in my room.

He sat, because there was nowhere else to sit, on the low chest of drawers by the door. He was lean and muscular, dressed in black, and held a black semiautomatic pistol with a long silencer.

'Get up and stand beside the bed, please,' he said. 'Don't move unless I ask you to, and you won't be hurt.' He had a faint Welsh accent. I did as I was told. 'Hands at your sides. Thank you.' He did not lower the gun. 'I need you to tell me what you found at the detective's flat.'

'A letter from Adolf Hitler to Philip Erskine, dated 1936, in condition "Fine" to "Very Fine",' I said quickly. I wanted to lie but I was too scared.

'That is of no use to me, I'm afraid. I'd hoped it might be something more substantial. What else do you know about Philip Erskine?'

'Nothing.'

'The truth, please.'

'You killed Zroszak.'

'Yes.'

'Do you work for the Japanese? A consortium?'

'You were on the subject of Philip Erskine.'

'I need to go to the toilet,' I said, my voice cracking.

'Wait, please.'

'You can't imagine the smell if I piss myself,' I said. In truth, it could hardly get any worse than it already was: I sweat so much when I panic that I turn into a minor airborne toxic event.

He looked at me for a second and then said, 'Where's the toilet?'

'Off the living room.'

'Go.'

He followed me out of the bedroom into the living room. He flipped on the light, and I glanced back to get a better look at him. I knew I should probably study his calm face, but all I could look at was the gun in his hand, its shape familiar from dozens of computer games, and that was when I noticed the tattoo on his wrist: a hunting dagger atop a rounded swastika.

'You're from the Thule Society,' I whispered.

'Hurry up, please,' he said. As I went into the bathroom he added, 'Don't close the door.'

I didn't. But his view of the sink was blocked by my body. With one hand I tugged my penis out of my pyjama bottoms, and with the other I picked up my toothbrush mug. I pissed into the mug until it was almost full. Coming back out of the bathroom, I held the mug behind my back and with my free hand pointed at the letter from Hitler on my computer desk. 'There it is,' I said. 'What I took.' The Welsh Ariosophist reached to pick it up, and I threw the mug of hot piss in his face.

Trimethylamine in high concentrations starts to smell more like ammonia than fish, and is vilely corrosive to the mucuous membranes. Like a bethylid wasp who squirts venom at her enemy as she flees from a fight, it was only a distraction; but as the Ariosophist coughed and retched and rubbed his eyes with the heels of his hands, I had time to grab my car keys from my desk and get out of the flat.

I slammed the door behind me, and heard two gunshots no louder than the punch of a big stapler. I ran down the stairs, dodged a few post-nightclub drunks who stood smoking outside the Happy Fried Chicken, and got into my car. It had rained through the night, and the street lamps glistened off the tarmac, grainy golden light spreading under my wheels like daffodil blood oozing up through the earth. A helicopter buzzed in the distance.

Zroszak might just as well have been murdered by the Whig Party, I thought, as I careened down Camden Road on the way to Grublock's penthouse near Battersea Bridge. As far as I knew, the Thule Society hadn't operated for at least eighty years.

It had been founded in 1914 by Rudolf von Sebottendorff, an occultist and adventurer. He took the name from Thule, the capital of Hyperborea, a lost utopia near the North Pole identified by the American congressman Ignatius L. Donnelly as the real location of Atlantis and the birthplace of the Aryan race. Sebottendorff held meetings in a hotel in Munich and even purchased a local newspaper. In 1919 two Thule Society members, Anton Drexler and Karl Harrer, were asked to establish a political front for the organisation, which they called the German Workers' Party. Then in 1920 Adolf Hitler joined, and they changed the name to the National Socialist German Workers' Party.

From then on, not much is known. Sebottendorff moved to Turkey, in flight from the agents of the Bavarian Soviet Republic, and the Thule Society is usually assumed to have withered away like a moth's cocoon. But one meets a surprising number of people in the internet Nazi memorabilia collecting community who believe that the Nazi Party was never anything but a front for Ariosophist sorcerors. (Meanwhile, others believe that Hitler was either a British secret agent or the boss of some sort of homosexualist mafia.)

Indeed, Stuart insisted for a few months, until he lost interest, that the Thule Society was responsible for the September 11 attacks. You may already have heard that at the end of the Second World War the US military ran something called Operation Paperclip, shipping dozens of Nazi scientists to America to work on nuclear physics and rocketry. Actually, their true expertise, claims Stuart, was in antigravity, extraterrestrial life and necromancy, and many of them were hierarchs of the Thule Society. Somehow, these scientists made an alliance with their cousins at Yale University, the Skull and Bones Club, to which allegiance was owed by many of the most powerful men of the twentieth century, including Robert A. Lovett, architect of the CIA, and both Bush presidents. This 'Brotherhood of Death' saw the Third Reich as merely a practice run for the Fourth Reich, America's New World Order, and their recent dirty tricks have included the demolition of the World Trade Center towers with remote-control plastic explosives and two holographic aeroplanes. Their eventual aim is to conquer the holy city of Agartha, hidden beneath the snows of Tibet, and use its supernatural powers to dominate the earth for eternity.

Although it's perfectly obvious to me that we've been told a lot of lies about September 11, I find Stuart's account a bit implausible for reasons I won't go into here. It's funny, I suppose, that an organisation like the Thule Society, composed mostly of paranoid bores who talked about nothing but the gods of Atlantis and the Protocols of the Elders of Zion, even worse than my 'internet friends', should itself return as a ghost to haunt every modern conspiracy theory. All paranoids soon begin to imitate their enemies, and the Thule Society did so almost too convincingly. Either way, however, there was something laughable about the notion of the Ariosophists, in the twenty-first century, assassinating a London private detective. Something laughable, and something terrifying. As I crossed Vauxhall Bridge, the MI6 building just on my left,

I thought of how a city is just whatever happens to accrete around the intersection of a million secrets: a fox in your garden is a stolen kiss is a pirate radio station is a dead detective is a Welsh Ariosophist with a gun is an ounce of skunk with your greasy chips is the collection of Nazi memorabilia that my employer, Horace Grublock, keeps upstairs in his penthouse flat.

5
AUGUST 1935

Judah Kölmel, half-brother of the gangster Albert Kölmel, bent to lick Sinner's shoulder. It was as salty as a herring, so Kölmel said, 'That's all for now.' Any good coach could taste the sweat on a boxer and know if he'd trained long enough that day, but eighteen years after he painted the words 'KOLMEL'S GYM' over the door of an empty garment warehouse on Eighth Avenue, Judah Kölmel could do a lot more. He could taste if you ate kosher; he could taste alcohol and nicotine and marijuana; he could taste flu before your first sniffle. He could taste if his naked wife had faked it. He sometimes thought that he could taste bad luck, that he could taste impurity before God, and that he could taste the shadow of death. Three times out of four, he could taste if a boxer was going to win or lose his next fight. But when he tasted Sinner, he could taste, naturally, that Sinner had been skipping, jogging, and sparring for eight hours and that he'd done just about enough, but beyond that, nothing – sweat as blank as the condensation on a mirror.

So Kölmel, still a little perturbed by this even after a week's acquaintance, made no wisecrack as he handed Sinner a towel, leaving his cousin Max Frink to say, 'You worked hard today.' The three of them started up the metal stairs to Sinner's first-floor dressing room, though several customers of Kolmel's Gym (which had never, for trading purposes, rescued the umlaut) were still at their punching-bags.

'Can I go to Times Square tonight?' said Sinner. He said it sarcastically, as he had every night since they arrived in New

York, knowing the answer would be no. Frink insisted that it wasn't half as good as Piccadilly Circus, anyway.

'No need, Seth,' said Kölmel. 'We're having some fun tonight. Big dinner.'

'What?' said Frink.

'A banquet with Rabbi Berg,' said Kölmel. 'You know, like I promised in my letter.'

'In you go,' said Frink.

'I'm out of fags,' said Sinner. Kölmel handed the boy three Chesterfields and shut the door after him, leaving the two older men in the corridor.

'What the hell is this about a dinner?' said Frink quietly.

'Rabbi Berg is excited to meet the kid. I'm sure I told you about it.'

'Will there be wine?'

'Yes, but—'

'Rabbi Berg can meet Sinner another time.'

'I promised him!'

'No.'

'Max, you don't know how much the Rabbi does for us all. Or how much the guy could do for Sinner. He's like a kid himself when it comes to boxing – he loves it. And he has relatives in London.'

'Are you crackers? We're paying to keep a bloke on the boy's bedroom door at night, and now you want to throw him a nice party with wine?' said Frink, struggling to keep his voice down. 'Listen to me, Judah, maybe I don't know much about this Rabbi Berg, but I'll tell you what you don't know: you don't know how fast it can go wrong with Sinner. You've never seen it. For God's sake, he has to fight tomorrow night.' Kölmel had arranged a couple of warm-up bouts with local boys in advance of Sinner's crucial match with Aloysius Fielding the following weekend. If Sinner beat Fielding, and he ought to, it would be enough to establish him in America, and that meant bigger fights, bigger titles, bigger purses. He might not have to return to England for months. The trip couldn't have happened without Judah Kölmel, and Frink was so grateful that he would normally have gone along with anything he said, but this was too important; and if Frink was capable, once in a while, of defying Albert Kölmel, which very few men or women ever did, then he was certainly capable of disappointing Albert Kölmel's half-brother.

'All we got to do is watch him. You sit on his left, I sit on his right, and we follow him when he goes to take a piss.' Kölmel's false teeth were loose and they rattled as he spoke. He was rumoured to carry a small automatic pistol in his hip pocket at all times, and was a member of the New York Pangaean Club.

'No. Absolutely not. We're honoured by the invitation, Sinner and me, but absolutely not.'

So while Sinner washed and changed his clothes, Kölmel went into his office, telephoned Rabbi Berg and persuaded him not to serve wine at the dinner, achieving, in ten minutes, what thirteen years of Prohibition never had.

Out in the street the five o'clock sunshine seemed to rise up like dew from the cracks in the pavement. Sinner and Frink took a cab back down to their hostel on the Lower East Side next to the old Bialystoker Synagogue. Kölmel knew the owner, and Sinner had been put in a room with bars on the windows and a heavy lock on the door. Sinner drank a Dr Pepper – which he had never tasted before and found almost alarmingly delicious – flicked through a boxing comic called *The Abysmal Brute* – which despite the name made boxing appear as bloodless as cricket – and changed into a suit borrowed from a tailor friend of Kölmel's – which was both too tight and too long in the legs. Then the two Englishmen walked over to Rabbi Berg's house on Cherry Street.

Frink couldn't pretend he didn't feel guilty to be treating

Sinner like this, to be dragging him around like a convict on remand, to be denying him a single moment's unharnessed enjoyment of this extraordinary place. When Frink fought 'for England' in the war he had really fought for London, and yet he had to admit that New York felt like an even greater city. This was what he was stealing from Sinner, who would only be seventeen once. But to reassure himself, he only had to think of the times that the boy had turned up to prizefights drunk, or vomited during training, or disappeared entirely for days at a stretch – not to mention the more carnivalesque episodes, like the time he stole a police horse. Frink had known Sinner had that chaos in him ever since the day they met, but it had got worse and worse. And despite all the help Frink had given Sinner, with his jabs and his scabs and his dinners and his debts, he couldn't do the first thing to help him with this. He desperately wanted to, but he couldn't. Frink knew what it was like to want to drink sadness into the distance, and he knew the sadness that Sinner had, or some of it. But he often felt that Sinner wasn't drinking because of sadness, but rather because he looked at drunkenness like he looked at almost everything else: as a territory to be conquered, an opponent to be tested, a lover to be used up. No gouging, no biting: those were the words spoken before every fight like a harsh grace. Gouging and biting, though, were both just ways of grabbing a little bit of something that wasn't yours. And Sinner, if he could, if he wasn't stopped, would try to gouge and bite until there was no world left. Or until there was nothing left of him but fingers and teeth. Or until there was nothing left of him at all. Which was why he had to be a prisoner, as guilty as it made Frink feel.

But actually, to Sinner, as they passed a shop window advertising 'MOSHA 100% PURE PUMPERNICKEL' which just at that moment was nearly smashed by a little boy kicking a tin can, this place didn't seem all that different from

Spitalfields; except that New York had a certain deep generosity of sky which he would never forget. And, anyway, Frink wasn't wrong to be wary: Sinner wanted gin, or whatever they drank here, and one way or another he would get some. He looked back at the little boy, and thought about how the kid would soon know his name, just like everyone else in this city would.

Rabbi Berg's house was crowded with paintings and ornaments and little lamps and half-broken things. He welcomed them in saying, 'Wonderful, wonderful, wonderful.' His face was deeply and finely lined all over, as if he'd been caught in a shrimping net. 'A great pleasure to meet you, Seth. Who is your rabbi in London? Rabbi Brasch? Our paths have not crossed. Come and sit down because I cannot stand up for too long and Mr Kölmel is already here.' They went into the dining room and drank iced blackberry cordial. Within a few minutes the two remaining guests had arrived: Mr Balfour Pearl, a handsome dark-eyed man in his mid-thirties, introduced as having come straight from the mayor's office, and Rabbi Shmuel Siedelman, who was around the same age as Pearl and much more reserved than his colleague Berg.

Their host sat at the head of the table, with Kölmel and Siedelman on his left, Sinner and Frink on his right, and Pearl at the opposite end. As his maid brought out their dinner of veal sausage with minced onion dumplings and cabbage, the rabbi led his guests in a prayer for the Jews in Germany. Everyone closed their eyes except Sinner, who looked around the dining room. This wasn't the first time he'd been in a nice house: there were toffs he'd met in the Caravan who'd taken him back to grand old places in Belgravia or Knightsbridge. But this was the first time he'd been in a nice house as a proper guest, let alone a guest of honour, and the first time he'd been attended by a maid. The rabbis he knew in London didn't live like this, and they wouldn't aspire to have government officials over for dinner, either. He wondered what the difference was, really, between a man like Rabbi Berg and a man like Albert Kölmel. You knew everybody, everybody knew you, and that was the foundation of your power: before long, there was no one left who didn't owe you a favour. It was only the incantations, it seemed to Sinner, that were different.

'Tell me, Seth,' said Berg after the prayer, 'how long have you been boxing?'

Sinner shrugged. 'Since I can remember.'

'Max, tell them how you found him,' said Kölmel.

'I don't want to embarrass the boy,' said Frink, looking at Sinner, but Sinner made no response, so Frink went on, 'Well, this was when he was twelve years old. Some rich bloke in a big black Bentley – no idea why he was in our bit of town – but he'd given Sinner – Seth, I should say – he'd given Seth a shilling to watch his car for an hour, with another shilling promised when he got back. After ten minutes the boy just sidled off. Probably spotted something he could pinch,' he added, smiling at Sinner, who again made no response. 'When he got back, some pimply steamer was sitting on the bonnet, smoking. Must have been eighteen or nineteen. And Sinner wanted his second shilling. He told the other bloke to leave. He didn't leave. So Sinner just jumped on him. I seen the whole thing from the dairy across the road. Had to run over and pull him away or I don't know what might have gone off. Blood all over the both of 'em. Told Sinner he ought to be a boxer.'

After Berg had questioned Frink and Sinner a bit more, Siedelman said, 'And you are not worried that the sport is a little ... *goyishe midas*?' Sinner didn't know what that meant. 'Lashing out to shed another Jew's blood.'

'Come on now, Shmuel,' said Berg. 'You take the Jews out of boxing and there is no more boxing. We should be proud of that. And it is no coincidence, I think. We know how to keep a diet. We know how to keep a fast. We know how to keep clean. We know how to keep good habits. Of course we make good boxers. Have you never seen Barney Ross, Shmuel? I taught him for his bar mitzvah. These days he gets into the ring with the talaith on his shoulders and the tvillan on his arms. He unwinds them slowly and kisses them and puts them in a velvet bag which he gives to his trainer, and everyone in the crowd stays silent as if they were at shul. It is a beautiful thing to behold. Whereas I hear he doesn't even have the Star on his trunks, our Mr Roach?'

'We'll fix that, Rabbi,' said Kölmel.

'I love to see Jews fight,' said Pearl. 'It is not our scripture that says to turn the other cheek. We are all Darwinians now, aren't we, gentlemen? And survival of the fittest means you have to learn how to throw a punch.'

'Oh, leave Darwin out of it,' said Siedelman. 'I've found that if a gentile talks a lot about Darwin, it's a pretty good sign he hates Jews.'

'Darwin was a Jew himself, you know,' said Berg.

'He was not,' said Siedelman.

Berg laughed. 'No, he was not. But read your Talmud. Every seven years, Hashem used to change all the animals into other animals. You know that, Seth? You know that, once, boys and girls were one, and now are two?' Sinner had never heard of this but he found it interesting. Everyone else had barely started on their food, but he'd already cleared his plate and was now twirling his knife back and forth around his thumb. 'And it says in the Zohar that apes are the descendants of sinful men. We got there first, you see, as usual.'

'Moses was most certainly a Darwinian,' concurred Pearl. 'What did he want for his tribe but that they should come out on top? That their offspring should own the world?'

'The Christians, they panic,' said Berg. 'They find fossils that are older than ten thousand years, and they have to pretend they don't exist. But Jews find them, and they know it is proof that there were other worlds before our own. The Torah can get along with science.'

'You know, Rabbi, before Darwin the Christians had the Argument from Design,' said Pearl. 'They said, "Look at the beautiful butterflies in that meadow! That can only be the Lord's work." And the Hebrew just said, "What the hell is a meadow?"' Most of the men guffawed. Frink laughed nervously, knowing he was out of his depth. 'We have always lived in cities, ever since we lived in the desert,' Pearl continued. 'Everything we ever see, a man made. We never had time for the Argument for Design. We don't need it for our faith. We don't care that it's on the trash heap now.'

'And the man that made those cities will soon be you, Balfour,' said Siedelman.

'I'm not sure about that, Rabbi.'

'I hear you are doing very well, Mr Pearl,' said Kölmel.

'I often tell Balfour about Nicholas Hawksmoor,' said Berg. 'He built churches in London. You must know Christ Church in Spitalfields?'

'See it every day,' said Frink, glad for the chance to contribute. 'Lovely old thing.'

'Yes, although I hear sadly a little neglected now,' said Berg. 'Now, they say Hawksmoor worshipped the devil. They say if you draw lines between his churches on a map you get a pentagram, or some such. To Balfour I say, you must be New York's Hawksmoor. You must build your expressways and your parks so that they invoke kabbalah – perhaps the sephirot, the Tree of Life – and nobody but the Jews will know. Would that not be a wonderful thing?'

'I have enough trouble getting anything done as it is, Rabbi.'

'What exactly is your job, son?' said Frink.

'I work at the New York City Planning Commission, sir.'

'Balfour is going to clean up the Lower East Side,' said Siedelman.

'That's my ambition, at least,' said Pearl.

'Clean it up?' said Frink.

'Well, I hope that before long we can get rid of slums and the Hoovervilles. Move people into rational, modern developments, where children won't have to play out in the street, and no one will live next door to a liquor store or a pool hall, and good families will have some space and some privacy.'

'That sounds superb, Mr Pearl,' said Kölmel. 'But who pays for it?'

'The city.'

'In that case, with all due respect, aren't there a lot of guys who'd do all the same stuff without taking it out of my taxes?'

'Oh, yes, always those precious taxes that have to be protected like little babies,' said Berg.

'Who else will do it?' said Siedelman. 'We can't leave it to the celebrated "free market".'

'No,' said Pearl. 'Mayor LaGuardia and I are very much in agreement on that.'

'The Empire State Building's so empty they have to pay a college graduate to go around flushing all the toilets every day so the porcelain won't stain,' said Siedelman, 'and meanwhile in Arkansas they have families living in caves and eating weeds. When you put your faith in business, that's what you get. Soon it will be here like it is in Germany. After they lost the war, they had the inflation, the get-rich-quick schemes, the American money coming in, and then the crash . . . . My friends who live there write me to say that by now it is as if nothing is real any more. Money is a lie, a fantasy, and so it seems like everything else is too. That is why you can make a fortune there selling miracle toothpaste to aristocrats and generals. All that is solid . . . . No offence meant, by the way, Balfour.'

'None taken,' said Pearl. 'My grandfather's toothpaste formula made no claim to miracles.'

'So you think it's City Hall's job to fix things up?' said Kölmel.

'Not at all,' said Pearl.

Siedelman looked surprised. 'I don't understand, Mr Pearl. I thought we were in agreement. If it's not business, then . . . .'

'Real change,' said Pearl, 'at any scale, is the responsibility of the strong individual. Certainly not of government. And certainly not of the market.'

'The market has no morals,' said Siedelman.

'No, it does not,' said Berg. 'No values at all. And I must say that before that strong individual Herr Hitler made his entrance, I used to feel that a tyranny of values was better, at least, than a tyranny of no values. But today, it is not so clear to me.'

'When you've seen what we can achieve, I think you may reconsider, Rabbi,' said Pearl. 'Of course, the Lower East Side is only the beginning. I've seen the Jews in New York and I've seen the Jews in London, and I don't know who has it worse. Talented boys like Seth should not have to grow up in squalor.'

'I like where I live,' said Sinner. Everyone turned to him. He sat sprawled in his chair in such a way that, even though he was the smallest man in the room, he seemed, as usual, to take up the most space.

Pearl smiled thinly. 'I meant no offence.'

'I'm sure Seth ain't offended,' said Frink.

'Don't brush the boy off, Balfour,' said Berg. 'What exactly is wrong with slums?'

'They are cramped, criminal, dirty and diseased,' said Pearl. 'They are full of whites and Negroes and Puerto Ricans intermingled.'

'Lay off the Negroes,' interjected Kölmel. 'They're the only people in New York who ain't even a little embarrassed to say they like boxing.'

'They are irrational and inhuman, these places,' said Pearl.

'They are empty of space and light and order. And those are the things that men need just as much as they need bread or a place to sleep.'

'Where did you grow up, Mr Pearl?' said Frink.

'On East 46th Street. Not far from Grand Central Station.'

'You've never lived in a slum,' said Berg.

'No. Nor have I ever lived in an opium den or a whorehouse, but I know enough not to wish them upon my city.'

'This cunt hates us, Frink,' said Sinner. Siedelman flinched.

'Shut your bleeding mouth, boy,' said Frink quickly.

'He practically said so,' said Sinner, glaring at Pearl across the table.

'I'm sorry about the kid, Mr Pearl,' said Kölmel.

'Not at all,' said Pearl, glaring back at Sinner.

'But Seth makes a good point, I think, in his way,' said Berg. 'That all you wish to do is rescue these poor slum-dwellers, Balfour, we quite understand. But it is not always so easy to separate a contempt for the streets on which a man was born from a contempt for the man himself. You have heard that silly Christian expression: "Love the sinner, hate the sin." But Jews know that a sin is not something that you can cut out of a man like a polyp. And nor is the memory of his home, filthy as it may be.' Berg paused. 'You do not hate Seth, but wish he had not grown up in a slum. There are other reformers like you, I dare say, who do not hate Seth, but wish he were taller and had all ten toes. And there are still others who do not hate Seth, but wish he were not a Jew.'

'I don't quite understand what you're trying to imply, Rabbi,' said Pearl. 'I merely wish the best for the boy, and for all boys like him.'

'In the world you seek, there would be no boys like him.' Berg held up his hand to stop Pearl from interrupting. 'Let me return to Darwin. Without mutation, as I understand it, there could be no evolution. We would all still be bacteria in the soup. In our cells there are clerks charged with preventing any error in the paperwork. But it is lucky that these clerks have never done their jobs with too much diligence. If they did not open us to a sort of sin . . . .'

'So we are to rejoice when a child is born with no eyes, in case he is to found a blessed new tribe of the blind.'

'No. For human beings, I think, Hashem's work is done. But your clockwork towers, immaculately replicated one by one until they cover the earth and the bed of the sea, so that nothing at all is unplanned – how can anything ever change for the better?'

'That is a change for the better.'

'But I wonder if it is not a shortsighted one. The slums are not like a blind child. Nor, I admit, are they like a healthy child. They are like a child with a bent spine, a cleft lip and angels' wings.'

'Yes, I'm sure the slums look very romantic from up here in your brownstone.'

'I grew up in a tenement a few streets from here, Balfour, as you well know. Even there, we could never have predicted young Seth. And people are happier to live in a place where not everything can be predicted. Things arise, beautiful things, things that would not be understood, and so would not be allowed, in your spotless paradise, where they fear the angels' wings even more than they fear the bent spine and the cleft lip. You are right that a man needs light like he needs bread, but a man needs a little darkness, too, if only so that he can sleep, and dream.'

'If you could hear yourself, Rabbi,' said Pearl.

'Yes, yes, I know I am behind the times,' said Berg. Although his irony was clear, it brought the exchange to a close. No one wanted a raging argument. But from time to time, for the rest of the meal, Sinner and Pearl would still stare sullenly at one another.

The evening ended with sweet pastries that Berg bought from the local bakery because they were beyond the capabilities of his cook, and then cigars. Forgetting about Sinner, who sat blowing prodigious smoke rings, the Rabbi got up to get a bottle of cognac, and Frink had to call him back to the table on a pretext. Dinner parties on Cherry Street tended to linger on late into the night, but at half past ten Pearl made his apologies, saying he had on his desk a pile of bills from the state legislature. Leaving, he shook hands with all five men. Sinner's handshake was particularly vigorous.

'So tell me more about this clown that Sinner is fighting next week,' said Berg as the maid cleared the table for a second time. 'Aloysius Somebody.'

'Aloysius Fielding,' said Kölmel. 'Won't be any trouble. Long as our kid shows a little bit of discipline. Right, Seth?'

'You'll make your name, Sinner,' said Frink. 'Straight into the big leagues.'

'How much are the tickets?' said Berg.

'Two dollars, if you can't get an Annie Oakley,' said Kölmel.

'I think I can stretch to that.'

'Whose is this?' said Sinner. He was holding up a Bulova men's wristwatch with a black strap. 'It was on the floor.'

'Oh, that's Balfour's,' said Siedelman.

'Why would he have taken off his watch?' said Berg. 'Oh dear. Can we catch him up?'

'He'll be on the subway by now.'

'We'll telephone. His wife may be at home.'

'She's at her mother's house on Long Island.'

'His maid, then,' said Berg. He took down his huge leather-bound address book, which his friends sometimes referred to as *The Book of Life (Lower East Side Edition)* even though most of its hundreds of crinkled pages were long out of date. Sinner leaned over to watch as his finger slid down past Paliakov, Papirny, Pasternak, Patsuk and Pazy to Pearl.

But there was no one at home to answer Berg's call. He shrugged. 'I will try again tomorrow.'

They talked about boxing for a little longer, and then Sinner said, ''Scuse me,' and got up. Kölmel looked at Frink. When Sinner had gone for a piss earlier on Kölmel had waited outside the door of the lavatory, having already checked that it had no window big enough to climb out of. But now both men were sated and sluggish, so it wasn't until four or five minutes had passed that Frink got up to check on Sinner. And by that time, the boy was almost on East Broadway.

On his way out he'd snatched Kölmel's wallet from his coat, which had been hung up in Berg's hall. In the wallet was twelve dollars. And he still had the watch, although he didn't think he had much chance of pawning it at this time of night.

Before long he found a liquor store. They had real imported London dry gin but it was too expensive, so he bought a bottle of bourbon and some boiled sweets. Outside, he saw three chaffinches pecking at some cigarette butts. Did American birds eat ash? He hailed a cab.

'Where to?' said the driver.

'259 West 70 Street,' said his passenger.

Sinner was not the sort of drunk who made a sighing, squinting, groaning, chuckling performance out of how much he enjoyed his first pint of beer after a long day, and he was certainly not the sort of drunk who got shakes or sweats if he went without – and he had a lot of contempt for either of those failings. But there was still half a smile on his face as he sipped his bourbon.

'West 70th.'

'Yeah. Is Times Square on the way?'

'If you want.'

'Go through Times Square.'

The light in Times Square seemed like the light that would bleed out of any solid object in this world if you could somehow scourge away its surface. Sinner was astonished by the light, and also by the number of men promenading around outside the bars and restaurants and theatres whose dress and gestures would have fitted in perfectly well at the Caravan. A gaunt old man was out walking his rabbit, which he picked up and held under his arm as he crossed the street, its leather leash over his wrist. Sinner had heard that now during the day they ran soup kitchens here out of the back of old army trucks, but even that temporary dreariness couldn't dim this place. The taxi got caught in a clot of traffic, and spaced along the nearby pavement Sinner noticed three blokes in smart suits greeting everyone who walked past like an old friend.

'What's their game?' said Sinner. 'Pimps or something?'

'Travel agents,' the cab driver corrected him. 'You want to go to Los Angeles, they find three other guys who want to go too, and then they find a guy who's driving there anyway and they take a commission. Won't cost you more than thirty dollars. Course, that's if the guy driving don't sneak off with everybody's money and everybody's baggage while you're still eating lunch in a cafeteria in Newark. Or worse! I heard about one old lady—'

'Los Angeles?' Sinner interrupted.

'What?'

'Los Angeles for thirty dollars? Hollywood?'

'Sure.'

'Anywhere I can pawn a watch around here?'

'Sure.'

'Now?'

'Sure.'

Sinner thought about that for a while.

'What's the matter?' the cab driver eventually said. 'You still want to go uptown or not?'

'Yeah. Uptown.' He could go to Los Angeles tomorrow.

They dodged between the trams at Columbus Circle and within ten minutes Sinner was paying the driver on West 70th

Street. He smoked a cigarette, drank some more bourbon, and then knocked on Balfour Pearl's door.

Pearl opened it in shirtsleeves rolled up to the elbows. He smelt of sweat, being one of those rare men who can truly exert themselves alone at a desk.

'You forgot your watch,' said Sinner.

'You stole it.'

Sinner shrugged.

'I grew up in Manhattan,' said Pearl. 'Do you think I don't know when a boy slips off my watch as he shakes my hand? Do you think I don't have friends who could steal your under-pants as they wave to you from across the street?'

'Do you want it back?'

'Yes, I want it back. Are you expecting a reward?'

'I want some ice with my drink.'

'I share this house with my wife and daughter.'

'They're on the long island,' said Sinner. Pearl let him push past.

Most of the house was dark, but there was some weak light from up the stairs, so Sinner found his way up to the study, where typewritten papers were strewn across the desk beneath a green-shaded banker's lamp as if exhausted by their struggles with the city planner.

'You won't find ice in there,' said Pearl, behind him.

'Get me some, then.'

'Perhaps I'll call the Rabbi and let him know you're here. He must be concerned. Would you like me to do that?'

'You can do what you like after you get me some ice.'

'Once again, you seem to think your insolence will impress me, and once again, I remind you that I grew up in Manhattan. Talking of which, I remember your trainer said you were desperate to see Times Square – did you take the opportunity on your way?'

'It was all right,' admitted Sinner.

'Better than Piccadilly Circus?'

'Yeah, maybe.'

'It's best appreciated with a map to hand – the way it slashes through the grid. Have you heard of Oscar Gude?'

'He the bloke who stole your underpants?'

'Oscar Gude is Times Square. In 1879 Thomas Edison had the idea for the electric light bulb and in 1892 Oscar Gude had the idea for selling things with it: firstly property on Long Island – I'm sorry, "the long island" – and then Heinz pickles. By the end of the war there must have been ten or twenty thousand billboards in America with Gude's name on them, including a hell of a lot in Times Square. They called him "the Botticelli of Broadway". I met him once. He thought what he did was beautiful. Did you think it was beautiful?'

Sinner shrugged and sat down on top of the desk, his feet dangling off.

'By the way, I'm sure you're enjoying that brand of whiskey just as much as the average Appalachian hobo, but if you'd like to try something a touch more refined there's a bottle in the bottom drawer. Yes, on the left. And glasses on the shelf. Now, to Gude, you must realise, art and advertising were two names for the same beast. I can't imagine he'll be the last person in New York to get rich off that thuggish notion, or the last person to think he was the first. Except he also understood that you can't force people to look at art but you can force people to look at advertising if you put a hundred thousand light bulbs right there in the street. He liked that. He liked claiming his piece of the city. A form of conquest, really. I remember when he put up that Wrigley's sign on Broadway. Huge. Hundreds of feet long. I came back from my first semester at Yale and no one was talking about anything else. To make people excited about the fact that you're selling them chewing gum – that's a hell of a thing. If there was even one man in the mayor's office with that kind of genius there'd be no slums left in New York.'

As Pearl pontificated about lights, he still hadn't switched on any more in the room itself. Losing interest, Sinner got down off the desk and wandered over to the open window of the study, outside which a black iron fire escape crawled like an insect up the rear wall of the house, dustbins clustered like eggs at its base. Beside Pearl's desk he nearly stubbed his toe on a big cardboard box full of yellow printed forms. He bent down to look. They were all identical and blank. 'What are these?' he said.

'A project of mine, from when I was working at the Civil Services Commission,' said Pearl. 'A failure. I offered them a true hierarchy of merit but of course no one wanted it. Do you understand that expression?'

Sinner shrugged.

'Those forms were to grade the men,' Pearl went on. 'I spent a year cataloguing the functions and responsibilities of every job in New York government. And then I gave each function and responsibility a mathematical weight according to its relative importance. And then I gave out those forms so that every man could be precisely assessed according to how well he performed those functions and responsibilities, and according to his personality and morals and potential and so on. And once we had all those numbers we could have said exactly who was needed and who wasn't, who was being paid too little and who too much, with no need for any "human factor". But it never passed the Board of Aldermen. They weren't interested in change. Now they use those forms to pass around racing tips.'

As Pearl continued to speak – and he clearly liked to hear himself speak – he reminded Sinner more and more of somebody he'd once met, and, after a minute of thinking, he remembered who it was: that posh cunt who'd followed him from Premierland to the Caravan, the one who wouldn't shut up about how 'unusual' Sinner was. And at that moment of recollection Sinner was struck by an inexplicable rage, and he began to gather up the yellow forms in his hands and fling them out of the open window. They fluttered away like dead leaves. 'Cunts!' he shouted. 'You're all cunts!'

'What the hell are you doing?' Pearl said, grabbing his shoulders. Sinner turned, cuffed Pearl's face, bit his shoulder, bit his neck and bit his mouth. Pearl pulled Sinner away from the window and they both fell to their knees. Pearl, already panting, started to undo Sinner's belt. Then someone was hammering at the door downstairs.

'I know you're there, Sinner!' shouted Kölmel. 'Come out! I know you're fucking there! Or, er, otherwise, if you're not, I'd like to offer you my sincerest apologies, Mr Pearl.'

'Fuck!' said Sinner. He got up, picked up his original bottle of bourbon, kicked the still-kneeling Pearl in the face and climbed out of the window on to the fire escape, which was now littered with the yellow forms. It was a warm night, and as he looked out over New York he felt like an ant crawling over a cinema screen. Running down the clanging iron steps, he nearly toppled off the edge – a week of abstinence and constant exercise had let him get drunk tonight even quicker than he'd intended. He jumped down to the pavement beside the dustbins and looked around. The street was empty but for a stray cat. He wanted to be submerged in glow again, but Times Square was a long way away, and on the corner opposite he saw a delicatessen, closed, and a little bar, still open. He ran across the street into the bar. And there, sitting on a stool with a beer, was Frink.

'Come on, Sinner,' said Frink, not looking surprised to see him. 'Don't know what you wanted with that wanker, but you've had your fun now.'

'Fuck off,' said Sinner.

'Come on, Sinner,' repeated Frink. He got up from the stool and made as if to put his arm around the boy's shoulder. So Sinner smashed the bottle of bourbon on the edge of the bar and lunged with a grunt at Frink, who raised his hands to defend himself and got a two-inch gash in his palm. Sinner was about to lunge again when the barman smacked him over the head with a wooden drinks tray and he lost consciousness. The last thing he saw was his trainer looking sadly down at him, blood streaming from his dirty fingertips. He hadn't even eaten his sweets.

6
NOVEMBER 1935

By the side of the road there was a heap of burnt wood like a badger's funeral pyre. 'What's that?' said Erskine as the cart rattled past.

'A sort of shrine, I think,' replied Gittins, and said something to the driver in Polish. The driver's reply was so long that Erskine wished he had never raised the subject, but finally the driver did finish and Gittins translated.

'A hundred years ago it seems there was a monk called Jakub, who lived in the monastery up in the mountains. One day he went into his abbot's study to find him . . . well, doing something unspeakable with the daughter of the blacksmith from down here in Fluek, whose great-grandchildren still live nearby. Jakub, outraged, killed the abbot with a dagger, and then, stricken with guilt and panic, fled the monastery. Coming to this road, he dropped the dagger where that shrine is now, stole a horse and rode north towards Gdansk. Along the way, after witnessing evil and misery of all kinds and helping where he could, he met God in a tavern.'

'I see.'

'Jakub asked God why He allowed human brutality to go unchecked in all its awfulness. God replied that He merely gave human beings free will, which he could never take back. But Jakub argued that free will is a frail thing, always a slave to our animal instincts – if God wanted us to have real free will, why did he make men so hot-headed at the same time? God told Jakub that he had already heard these arguments from his angels, and he had ignored them then too. But at last, in frustration, God suggested to Jakub a pact, whereby any man who wanted to murder another man would finally have the chance to think it over without passion. Jakub would become the saint of repentant murderers: whenever one man killed another, Jakub would appear to that man, give him as long as he needed to consider properly what he'd just done, and ask if he regretted it. If he did, the man could take back the murder and it would be as if nothing had ever happened. If he didn't, then at least he would have acted with true free will. And if the scheme were successful, it would be extended to all sin. Jakub would become the second-greatest redeemer that ever lived.' In the distance Erskine spotted a thin plume of smoke above the darksome fir trees – they were nearing the village. 'Jakub agreed, of course, but as soon as he did he realised that God had tricked him. He would go years at a time, coming upon thousands of scenes of carnage, before finding a single person who would not do just the same thing if given a second chance. People kill, Jakub realised, because it suits us to, and our baser urges are just an excuse. In the end, he saw that he had been lying even to himself: he was glad he'd killed the abbot, and wouldn't change a thing about what had happened. He went to God and asked if he could give up the task, now that he had been shown how wrong he was about human nature and about his own. And God denied him his freedom, as a punishment for the abbot's murder. Rather a striking fable, isn't it? Now it seems that everyone who passes by throws a log or a stick on the pile, and every so often somebody sets light to it. The fire calls to Jakub, asking him to help the people of his village choose wisely in troublous times.'

Just as Gittins finished, Erskine was nearly thrown from the cart as one of its front wheels was sucked into a hole in the road. They both got out to help the driver and found themselves up to their ankles in mud. Because of the cold everything hurt a bit more than it should have. The smell of the horses reminded Erskine of his uncle's disastrous attempts to teach him to ride back in Claramore when he was twelve. He already wished he had never come on this trip.

And, indeed, he could hardly remember why he had ever thought it might be a worthwhile way to spend a fortnight. In November, Benjamin Percy, who'd just come back from the Ukraine, had made a rousing speech to the Royal Entomological Society in which he argued that, while people were only too happy to go all the way to Africa or Asia, there was a lamentable neglect of unexotic old eastern Europe, 'where every time you shake out your boot in the morning some unknown subgenus will fall on the floor'. Percy himself had come back with a few very intriguing new grubs. So several new expeditions had been organised, including this one to a region south of Bialystok, part-funded by Erskine's own father. There were supposed to be five men coming, but three had dropped out for one reason or another, leaving Erskine alone with John Gittins.

Gittins was a fat otter-faced bureaucrat in his fifties who for nearly twenty years had carried around a glass vial containing a small colony of cimicids – bedbugs – which every night he tipped out on to his hairy thigh so that they could feed on his blood as part of some obscure long-running experiment into mandible size versus nutritional preferences. Reportedly, when he checked out of hotels he would often forget the vial and then dash back to his room almost in tears in case the maids had smashed it underfoot. When he wasn't talking about his cimicid colony, Gittins was almost invariably talking about his feud with Francis Hemming CMG CBE, the formidable lepidopterist secretary of the International Commission on Zoological Nomenclature. The full details of the dispute were far too complex for anyone but Gittins himself to understand, but Erskine did know that, on the final day of a recent series of consultations in Lisbon, Gittins had been intending to table a revolutionary motion about mail ballots which would have shaken Hemming's tyranny, and, anticipating this, Hemming had got up first and spoken uninterrupted for nearly five hours about malarial parasite classification, so that the meeting had to be adjourned for the sake of the tired old men on the committee before Gittins could begin his revolt. Gittins was now determined to destroy Hemming by any means possible, and would be willing, Erskine suspected, to sacrifice not only his own life but probably also his wife's, his daughter's and even his cimicids' to prevent Hemming getting the knighthood to which he aspired. Gittins' only non-entomological hobby was languages, of which he could speak nearly a dozen, including Polish. He had a mole on his neck with six long wiry hairs sticking out of it, as if a spider had been shot from a catapult and embedded itself in his flesh.

Closer to the village, they passed grey fields of barley and beetroot. Fluck itself, chosen for the diversity of the nearby terrain, was nothing but some cottages, some barns, some stables, an inn and a church – whose roof had been cracked ever since the Bolsheviks came through in 1920 – all huddled together. Several of the timber buildings were patched up with incongruous sheets of rusting corrugated iron which must have been plundered from a nearby battlefield. There was something so submissive and exhausted about the place, thought Erskine, like a thin farmer munching on grass because his own fat cattle have bullied him out of his hot dinner again.

They all got out of the cart, and after the driver had hitched the horses to a post he led the two Englishmen to the inn. On the way, Erskine noticed several old women in shawls glaring at them from doorways.

'They don't seem very pleased to see us,' he murmured to Gittins. Was this the 'evil eye' he had read about?

'No, they certainly don't,' replied Gittins, and said something to the driver. Erskine cringed – he hadn't intended Gittins to relay his comment, and now the idiot was certain to cause offence. But the driver replied in a casual tone, and Gittins said, 'He said we shouldn't have arrived today. Today is the birthday of – well, I don't know the word – the "angel child", I think. The grandmothers think that's bad luck, he says. He doesn't believe it himself.'

'Who or what is the "angel child"?' The phrase made him shiver for some reason.

'He says we shouldn't concern ourselves with that.'

The inn was not quite as bad as Erskine had feared. A smudged woman in a red skirt was pouring tea from a samovar as they entered. At her feet lay a grey one-eyed mongrel, scratching at fleas and suckling a litter of tiny pups. The woman spoke a few sincere-sounding words of welcome and the driver helped them carry their baggage upstairs.

Their room contained only a double bed, a table and a chair. They didn't unpack because there was nowhere to put anything. On the wall opposite the bed was an odd hand-drawn poster.

'What's that?' Erskine said.

'I think that's supposed to be a louse, and it says, "This may you kill." And I think the other thing is supposed to be a bath, and it says, "This may you save." Meaning the bathwater? I may have misunderstood.' It was nearly five o'clock. Gittins went to the window. 'Dark soon. No point going out today.' He took a volume of Finnish grammar from his pretentious red leather book-satchel and sat down at the table.

'Don't you want to see the rest of the village?' said Erskine.

'Not much to see.'

Erskine, determined to prove Gittins wrong, went out for a walk. But, in fact, apart from some hens, he couldn't find anything to look at. Everyone seemed to be indoors. And the rain stung the back of his neck. So he went back to the room, sat on the bed, and read some of Sloane's commentaries on Darwin. At seven o'clock the proprietress came upstairs with two bowls of tolerable stew. At eight o'clock Gittins took off his trousers and, humming happily under his breath, fed his cimicids, a ritual that even Erskine could recognise as weirdly erotic in nature. He was almost sure, at one point, that he heard Gittins murmur something to the insects about Francis Hemming. At nine o'clock they got into bed together and Gittins blew out the candle.

'Goodnight,' he said.

'Goodnight,' said Erskine. Gittins smelt even worse than the horses, but Erskine still fell asleep immediately.

The next day they got up before dawn and went out to a stream near the village. They both wore oil-silk capes. Erskine kicked up some rocks at a bend in the stream and Gittins held a very fine net in the water a few feet further down. Every few hours they would leave the net on a tree stump to dry and then pick through its contents for specimens. Whenever Gittins tried to talk about Hemming, Erskine pretended not to hear. So in the afternoon Gittins began to initiate conversations which were not at first about Hemming but which were designed to be steered casually towards the subject of Hemming within ten or fifteen minutes. And by the evening Gittins, like a master chess player, was diligently engineering conversational junctures at which, although he had not yet himself mentioned Hemming, it would have been perverse for Erskine to respond with anything other than the allusion to Hemming that was so logically invited – leaving Erskine no choice but to go back to ignoring Gittins as he had in the morning. What seemed to captivate Gittins was Erskine's deliberate refusal to make clear whether he approved or disapproved of Hemming's regime. Meanwhile, Gittins didn't seem to want to discuss his cimicids too much with Erskine, much as a man will only discuss his mistress with his closest friends.

When, with night falling, they returned to the inn, there was a small crowd of boys waiting outside. Gittins greeted them in Polish. None replied, but the oldest, a crooked-toothed but handsome lad of about sixteen, held out a dented tobacco tin. Erskine smiled and shook his head.

'Come on,' said Gittins.

'I don't smoke a pipe.'

'I don't expect it's tobacco.'

So Erskine took it and opened it. It was empty but for five or six crawling black specks. Gittins got out his magnifying glass and bent over the tin. '*Anoplura.*'

'Lice? Is this a joke?'

'They must have heard from someone that we've come here to look for insects.'

Erskine shut the tin and held it out to the boy, but he wouldn't take it back.

'He probably wants money,' said Gittins.

'If we give him any now we'll have to fork out to all of them, every day, for as long as we're here,' said Erskine. But then he caught the oldest boy's eye again. There was something about his expression, cocky and nervous at the same time, and about the coal-dust stubble on his upper lip, which made Erskine reconsider. The boy reminded him of someone, someone for whom he felt a certain ardour, someone whose face he'd last seen when he was back in London, but he couldn't think who. 'Ask him how much he wants,' he said.

Gittins spoke to the boy. 'He wants ten groszy.'

'How much is that?'

'About tuppence, I think.'

'Oh. Well, let's give them all ten groszy.'

'I don't have any change that small.'

'What do they need it for? There are no shops here.'

'I think pedlars come through sometimes.'

Erskine gave all the boys a zloty note from his wallet. None of them moved.

'What more do they want?'

Gittins enquired. 'They want to give us the specimens, but they want their tins back afterwards.'

'Bloody hell. Ask the oldest if he will sell us his tin for ten zloty.'

Gittins translated, but then all the boys started to babble at once. 'Now they all want to sell their tins. This one' – a grimy child of about six years old with a strangely adult face, like a homunculus – 'is insisting very vehemently that he has the best tin.'

'If we give the money to anyone but the biggest, it will get stolen.'

So Erskine pressed a ten zloty note into the warm hand of the oldest boy. With a little bit of what sounded like swearing the argument ended, and one by one the smaller boys emptied the contents of their own tins into the tin that was now Erskine's. Then they dispersed. The oldest boy did not even look back at Erskine as he hurried off. When they were all out of sight, Erskine shook all the lice on to the ground and stamped on them.

' "These may you kill",' he recalled.

'You know, Erskine, I rather think we may have been swindled,' replied Gittins. For the first and last time on that trip they laughed together. Erskine wondered if any of those boys might be the 'angel child'. Perhaps the handsome one. But then what could he have to do with bad luck?

They'd been up in the room for about an hour when Erskine, hoping to start a friendly, non-Hemming-related conversation, made the error of saying, 'Did you know that Captain Robert Fitzroy nearly rejected Charles Darwin as a naturalist for the HMS *Beagle* in 1831 because he didn't trust the shape of Darwin's nose?'

'Really?'

'Says so here. What a turning point in scientific history.'

'What are you reading?'

'Sansom's *The Candle Flame*.'

'What's it about?'

'Oh, the theory and practice of eugenics. It's excellent.'

'You don't believe in any of that rot, do you?'

Erskine was speechless for a moment. 'I intend to devote my life to "that rot", actually.'

'The betterment of the Anglo-Saxon race. The triumph of the germ-plasm.'

'Yes.'

'Come on. There are forty-five million people in Britain, Erskine. And you plan to start breeding for pedigree. How do you suppose that will happen?'

'It's simply a matter of systematic encouragement and discouragement.'

'And by discouragement you mean the lethal chamber?'

Erskine hated that phrase. It stood for every irrational, feminine objection that the average imbecile had to the project of eugenics, saving him from having to think for even a moment about the substance of his prejudice.

'The lethal chamber is just one of a thousand methods,' said Erskine. 'There may be no need for it ever to come into use. You know perfectly well that it's just sensationalism to identify the whole project with one extreme measure. Imagine if all anyone knew of entomology was you and your cimicids.'

'Would I be entitled to procreate, then, according to your scheme?'

Erskine had of course already considered this, and the fact was that Gittins was fat, smelly, petty and tedious; not quite a superman. But he'd probably already gone much too far with his comment about the cimicids – it was only their second day, after all – so he just said, 'I'm sure you'd pass the relevant tests.'

'Oh, thank you, Erskine, that's very comforting.' Erskine had not realised that Gittins was intellectually capable of sarcasm. 'What frightens me is that perhaps one day I really will have to sit one of those tests, and it will be you who sets the questions and marks the answers, or if not you then perhaps Mr Hitler. I very much hope you grow out of all this.'

'So I suppose you'd be happy for your daughter to marry some crippled, recidivist negroid?'

'Well, if they were in love, then it's not for me to . . . ,' said Gittins unconvincingly.

'I suggest you think about that,' said Erskine, feeling that he had won, albeit not very deftly.

'I certainly wouldn't allow my daughter to marry a fellow of your sort. A fellow for whom half the world's already dead even when they seem to be walking about quite happily. I can't imagine you'll have a very pleasant time in life.'

'Love and happiness are very easy words to invoke, Gittins. But not everyone can do the easy thing. Some of us must do the hard thing if civilisation is to have any future at all.' Erskine, who knew deep down that he had never really done a 'hard thing' in his life, did his best to say this with the requisite gravity, but Gittins snorted, as if exactly the same thought had occurred to him, so Erskine blurted, 'It's utter fools like you who are holding everyone back.' He had never called anyone of Gittins' age a fool before, and couldn't look him in the eye as he said it. It wouldn't have happened but for a whole day of hearing about Hemming. Gittins did not respond, but instead just picked up his Finnish grammar, so Erskine picked up his own book too. An hour later, when the woman came up with the stew, he was still staring angrily at the same page, wishing he'd made a more creditable case than that jibe about the negroid, wondering how it was that an inconsequential argument could so often result in the same congealed adrenaline queasiness as a physical fight. Gittins, meanwhile, had gone straight back to making notes on the possessive suffix as if nothing had happened.

Neither spoke again until Gittins said 'Good night' as he blew out the candle, and Erskine stayed silent, feeling there was something subtly derisive about Gittins' tone. 'Good night, Erskine,' repeated Gittins, louder this time. Erskine stayed silent again. The next morning they went out separately into the forest. On their own they could only collect a fraction of what they could collect together, but Erskine was still waiting for Gittins to apologise.

Around noon, wading through a stream, the rain slathering its cold tongue across his shoulders, Erskine snagged his trousers on something and fell over. Splashing around, trying to regain his footing, he felt a pain in his hand and saw blood in the water. He'd got caught on a coil of rusty barbed wire. Towards the end of the Polish–Soviet War, after the Battle of Warsaw, the Poles had laid miles of it in the rivers to stop Bolshevik stragglers from fleeing their dogs. If he hadn't known that – if Gittins hadn't specifically warned him about it – he might have concluded that the countryside itself, sick of soldiers, full of scrap, had learnt to grow its own fearsome iron weeds. What other traps would he find in the grass, in the trees? What was he doing here? What the hell did anyone care about beetles, anyway? Shivering, he half-hoped he would get an infection and die, but felt better after putting on a plaster and eating some tinned beef for lunch.

Returning in the evening, he couldn't face another four hours of excruciating silence with Gittins so he went for a stroll around the village. As before, it was boring, but on his way back he saw, coming out of a stable, the handsome boy from the previous evening. The boy was probably on his way home too, he thought. And Erskine found himself following. He realised then who the boy reminded him of – the individual for whom he felt such ardour, whose face he had last seen back in London. It should have been obvious, but the conversation with Gittins had jogged his memory. It was Hitler.

He didn't have to follow far before the boy went into a cottage. He waited for a few minutes, then sidled up to the window and tried to look inside. He saw a table and a fire-place. He felt a tap on his back.

He turned. There was the boy. 'I'm sorry, I was just . . . .' The boy said something questioning in Polish. Erskine smiled and nodded, not knowing what else to do. The boy tugged on his sleeve.

There was not much light inside the cottage. 'Are your parents here?' Erskine said, pointlessly. The boy said some-thing else, and led him through another door. As he followed the boy into a bedroom with a ceiling so low that he had to stoop, in which a reek of urine overwhelmed the beetroot and the woodsmoke, his heart pounded and he tried not to think about what might be about to happen. But then he saw that the boy only wanted to show him something. Tied to the bed, awake, twitching, the boy's brother. The angel child. As he stared, it whimpered, or perhaps it said his name.

He had nearly got back to the inn before he vomited into the mud. The rain had stopped. He wiped his mouth and went inside. He now felt very much as if he didn't want to be alone in this place, so he said hello to Gittins and added, 'Find much?'

'Not much.'

'Nor me.'

Later, they went to bed. There was something about the pure anarchy of dreams that Erskine found very alarming. Dreams were bullies. In the middle of the night he crawled up into wakefulness through thickets of barbed wire, knowing somehow that the barbs were nothing but the buds of flowers, and when he felt that the sheet was damp he thought it must be blood. Then he realised with horror what had happened, and he remembered that before the barbed wire there had been the crooked-toothed boy.

He had been afraid of this ever since he'd found out that he would be sharing a bed with Gittins. He wasn't worried about the stain so much as the possibility that Gittins was not really asleep and had witnessed Erskine's murmurs and convulsions. These murmurs and convulsions were only really a speculation on Erskine's part, but given that boys in his dormitory at school had shouted and kicked in their sleep when all they were dreaming about was a game of football, he didn't believe that his body could betray itself so revoltingly without giving at least some signal. Of course, he could never know that for sure, any more than he could ever know for sure whether things like this still happened to men of Gittins' age, or whether, on the contrary, everyone else in the world but him had got their fluids under control long before they even left school. Why couldn't one just go to the doctor every month to have one's semen, this irrational fluid, syringed off like the pus from a boil? Perhaps he could ask Gittins all this and then strangle him once he had received some useful answers. In fact, he thought, that was exactly what he would do if Gittins ever acknowledged this episode in any way. At just that moment Gittins shifted, and Erskine had to stop himself from leaping out of bed. Only when the birds began to sing outside did he fall asleep again, and as the barbed wire grew over him again like vines he realised that he had not been dreaming before about the crooked-toothed but handsome boy. He had been dreaming about the boy's brother.

The next morning he woke up with an erection and could not bring himself to speak to or even look at Gittins, so they set off separately just as if they had argued again. Although they weren't scheduled to start on the caves for another few days Erskine was tired of the forest, so he set off north towards the hills. Near a pond he accidentally trod on a frog and had to scrape his shoe clean with a stick.

He'd been turning over stones at the mouth of a cave for about an hour when he heard someone coming up the gravel slope from the woods. He rose, assuming it was Gittins. But it was the boy.

'What are you doing here?' he said.

The boy said something in Polish.

'You followed me here.'

The boy looked down at what Erskine was doing.

'I'm sorry about yesterday. I didn't mean to behave like that. I shouldn't have been so rude to your brother.'

The boy smiled.

'And I forgot to ask if you wanted your tobacco tin back.' Erskine took it out of his coat and held it out to the boy, but the boy shook his head, took Erskine's sleeve as he had the day before, and led Erskine into the cave.

Inside it smelt of bat guano and mould, not entirely unlike the disused cricket pavilion at school where one had some- times gone to smoke a cigarette. The ground was rocky and uneven. Within a few yards they were in almost total dark- ness, and that was where the boy turned his back on Erskine, pulled down his trousers, and bent over. Erskine stood, paralysed, staring at the boy's arse, at the tip of his long cock hanging between his legs.

It was really happening. Everything around him suddenly felt so soft, a change in the texture of texture itself, so that even the rocks were flesh now; and it was because the unyielding world had yielded at last, yielded utterly, like a rabbit splayed open on a dissecting table, and he could see and touch what- ever he wanted, could reach inside and squeeze the rabbit's heart until it burst in his fist, and nobody could stop him. He couldn't breathe. After a while the boy looked back at Erskine, and a small part of Erskine was disappointed to see the autocratic face of this anonymous Polish youth and not, impossibly, the face of Seth Roach. His reverie broken, he stepped forward and started to undo his belt. For a moment he wondered what this boy of fifteen or sixteen years old had already done or seen that had taught him to offer himself like this, and for another moment he wondered whether he'd have to pay the boy afterwards or whether this was a sort of free gift that came with the tobacco tin. But mostly he wondered if he had the right idea about what he was supposed to do. He was just reaching out to touch the boy's goose-pimpled arse when he heard Gittins shout, 'Erskine?'

He looked up in panic. Gittins wouldn't be able to see them from the mouth of the cave, so his first thought was just to keep quiet until Gittins moved on, but then he remembered that all his equipment was still lying around outside; there could be no doubt where he was. For a moment he felt seared to his bones by bad luck and loss, like that day in Cambridge when he had been carrying a very rare enicocephalid across a laboratory to be mounted, and a breeze had blown it off its piece of cork, and they had spent the whole afternoon searching the floor with a magnifying glass.

'Erskine?' shouted Gittins again. 'I expected you might have come up here. Knew you were looking forward to the caves. Can you hear me, Erskine? You forgot your lunch. Thought I'd come and see if you wanted any of mine.'

The boy pulled up his trousers.

'Erskine, are you in there?'

Erskine got down on his hands and knees and started to crawl deeper into the cave. There were cobwebs stretched between the rocks, spun to trap the flies that came to feed off the bat guano, and he had to close his eyes. When he felt something odd beneath his right hand, he opened them again, but it was blindfold dark, so he took out his battery-powered torch. He flicked the switch, and screamed.

Leaning against the wall of the cave, throwing a monstrous shadow, was a grinning human skeleton. Although its clothes had mostly rotted away, there was a rifle across its knees, a knife in its hand, and a rusted water canteen at its side. A Bolshevik soldier. Erskine looked down, and saw that he was holding on to the fungoid toe of its crumbling left boot. In blind terror he dropped the torch and picked up a stone and hurled it at the skeleton with a strangled grunt. The stone smashed the skeleton's ribs, and there was a gush of black blood from where the skeleton's heart should have been. The soldier's ghost was coming for vengeance, Erskine thought, or perhaps, thank God, he was still dreaming. But then he saw that it was not the soldier's ghost. It was a small colony of beetles, disturbed by the stone, fleeing deeper into the cave. He knew what to do with beetles.

Trapping one in his gloved hands, he examined it under his magnifying glass. This species was eyeless, winged, and covered with spines. He was reaching for his notebook, wanting to sketch the unusual diamond marking on its back, when it flew out of his hand, and as it did so he saw something which he surely could not have seen.

Trying to ignore this little hallucination, Erskine searched through his memory. He knew beetles, but he did not know this beetle. And that could only mean that this beetle was new – an entirely novel and distinct species – the first they'd found on this trip, despite all Percy's promises. He would have to check in his reference books, but he already felt almost sure.

So not only had he beaten Gittins, but it would be his privilege to name this little troglodyte, and then to have the name ratified by the International Commission on Zoological Nomenclature that Gittins so hated, ensuring that it would keep that name for ever, or at the very least until civilisation was overrun by bigger troglodytes and all science was forgotten – a childhood ambition finally fulfilled.

The genus would be *Anophthalmus*, meaning 'eyeless'. But *Anophthalmus* what? It could be *Anophthalmus hemmingi*, to irritate Gittins, or *Anophthalmus jakubi*, for superstition's sake, or even *Anophthalmus angeli*, in tribute to the misshapen child, but he favoured *Anophthalmus erskini*, a chance to immortalise himself at only twenty-five years old. Considering this happily, he picked up another beetle, but before he could get a close look the same thing happened as before. And a third time, the same. Only with the fourth beetle did he realise what he was seeing. As the insect raised its membranous wings in preparation for flight the diamond pattern on them was disrupted, and just for an instant they flashed a different pattern, an asymmetrical rearrangement of the same four right-angles. A perfect clockwise tetraskelion. A swastika.

7

Grublock lived in a shining tower on the south bank of the Thames, designed for him by one of his pet Danish architects; a product of hermeneutics and plasticine, it resembled a curvaceous filing cabinet that had been hastily ransacked. At night, from the windows of his triplex penthouse, you could look over the ink-black river to the barges sinking into the sand of the opposite bank and, above them, the twinkle of Chelsea. Far off to the right was the Square Mile, rising in glow as if a drip of light from the stars had built into a stalagmite and then into a mountain range. The view was so spectacular that none of Grublock's guests ever bothered to examine the small watercolour hung on the opposite wall, a rather pallid and shaky attempt at St Peter's church in Vienna with the almost illegible signature 'A. Hitler' in the bottom left-hand corner.

Grublock's dream, I had long ago surmised, was to impale the city of London with a structure so grandly inhuman, so potently unreal, that it could be left completely empty for a hundred years and nobody would even know the difference, except perhaps the men who ran the sandwich shops nearby. Like a cathedral in a medieval town, it would be visible from anywhere; and yet nobody would ever be told the reasons for its shape and position, nobody would ever be allowed through its doors, and nobody would ever begin to understand the staggeringly complex financial transactions that were presumed to go on inside, night and day, like arguments between angels; so that although the lights would be on all the time, it would be impossible to say for sure if it was really inhabited or whether it was just a thousand-foot obelisk, a cryptogram with no meaning, a pure denial. Occasionally, reading about one of Grublock's projects in the newspapers, I wondered if this prank was one he'd already played. A few years before, scorning any economic pessimism, he had opened property development offices in both Shanghai and Dubai, telling me that he'd wasted too much time in London, where everyone loved to talk about the free market but no one really had the guts to unlock the last of its shackles. Except that the plains of Shanghai and Dubai were still mostly blank slates, and I wasn't sure he liked blank slates. He liked disruption. But disruption of a special sort. We think of disruption as the assault of the scribble into the grid, of the illegible on the legible; what Grublock achieved was exactly the opposite.

At about six in the morning I'd had to plead with the night porter to let me up to Grublock's annexe. ('Night porter' was a demeaning title for a man who spoke ten languages, had his own staff of twenty, earned as much as a good lawyer, and could reportedly procure you anything from a bottle of 1959 Château Mouton Rothschild to a prostitute who looked like Lyudmila Putin at thirty minutes' notice, but it was Grublock's choice.) Security was fierce, of course, but he recognised my face from previous visits, or perhaps just my smell, and seemed willing to do whatever it would take to get my trimethylaminuria out of his lobby, where, as in the lifts, twenty-four-hour financial channels ran silently on plasma screens.

'Fishy,' said Grublock, descending the curving stairs into his living room. His ruddy face, pink shirts, small pot belly and public school affability never seemed to match the vampiric Scandinavian furniture. (Or all the Nazi stuff, really.) 'What the fuck do you think you're doing here? Why didn't you call if it's so important? I might not have been up yet.'

'I know who killed Zroszak.'

'Go on.'

'He came to my house. He's an Ariosophist.'

'A what?'

'They were a German secret society.' I began to explain but Grublock cut me off.

'Fishy, I'm already quite sure he's working for the Japanese.'

'You have to tell me what Zroszak was looking for. I'm involved now. He had a gun, this man.'

'Well, you're safe here. And if you must know, he was looking for a beetle. Now, I need to make some phone calls to sort all this out – Teymur first – so if you're going to stay here I suggest you have a wash. Your bouquet is even more intolerable than usual.'

I knew Grublock wouldn't tell me any more. And I wasn't even sure if I could believe what he'd already told me. Undressing in Grublock's enormous marble bathroom, where the shower could exfoliate a block of cement, I thought about the letter from Hitler to Philip Erskine. How deliriously proud Erskine, whoever he was, must have been when he read it. 'I have received gifts from popes, tycoons, and heads of state, but none have ever been so singular or unexpected as your kind tribute.' That couldn't just be a beetle. Grublock was mocking me. Mocking me tonight, of all nights, when my life was in danger because of a job I was doing for him for free.

Still, I didn't feel so shaken after a hot shower, and as I dried myself off with a monogrammed towel and put on a monogrammed dressing gown I was looking forward to watching Grublock mobilise his forces. 'There could be clues in my flat,' I started to say as I strolled out of the bathroom. I stopped when I remembered that Grublock might still be on the phone.

He wasn't on the phone, though. He was sitting in an armchair with his hands behind his head. And the Welshman was standing at the door with his gun pointed at Grublock. He looked at me.

'Sit down, please. You needn't worry about the panic

button. I've disabled it.' He didn't sound nearly as angry with me as I probably would have been with someone who'd just thrown a cup of toxic piss in my face. How had he got in?

'You're making a laughable error,' said Grublock evenly. 'You don't know who's employing you, do you? You're paid through a blind escrow account.'

'Yes.'

'It's me. I'm paying. You're working for me. You just don't know it. Look, Zroszak was nearly there. I was fairly sure that, one way or another, I'd have what I wanted within a couple of weeks. Then I was going to sell it. Once the Japanese heard that you were on the hunt too – and as long as they didn't know you were working for me – the price would probably double or triple. I just didn't expect you to move so fast. I didn't think you'd get to Zroszak before he told me where to find the fucking thing. And I certainly didn't expect you to break into my home. I'm very rich but I'm in over my head, you see. This is just my hobby. But if you hurt me now – your own client – who else is ever going to hire you again?'

'I'm afraid I don't believe you.'

'I can prove it. Bring me my laptop and I can show you.'

'You trust this man?' said the Welshman, nodding towards me. His blue eyes were so beautifully clear and pale that he looked almost as if he had some sort of glaucoma.

'Yes, I suppose so, up to a point,' said Grublock. 'Why?'

'He can find things.'

'Yes,' said Grublock. Then the Welshman shot him through the forehead.

Grublock slumped sideways in the armchair and a trickle of blood ran down his nose and he made a noise like the click-rasp of my computer's hard drive when its gigaflops are overstrained.

The Welshman turned to me. I saw he was wearing white latex gloves.

'Don't become hysterical, please,' he said.

'Are you really looking for a beetle?' I stammered.

'Does that sound plausible to you?'

'No.'

'Precisely.'

So Grublock had been lying after all. But what about later on, with his story about the blind escrow account? Was he just trying to protect himself? I couldn't tell. Employing an assassin to drive up an auction prize was the sort of thing Grublock might very easily have done – once, to discourage a rival developer from trying to buy a site in Peckham before he could raise enough money himself, he'd planted a story in the *Evening Standard* which claimed that the children in the adjacent council estates had formed a sort of ketamine rape tribe armed with bicycle chains and samurai swords – but then where did that leave the Thule Society tattoo?

'What are you looking for, then?' I said.

'You've heard of a Jewish boxer called Seth Roach?' said the Welshman.

'Sort of.'

'I'm looking for Seth Roach's grave.'

'I don't have any idea where that is.'

'No.'

'Does that mean you're going to kill me?'

'I'm not going to kill you yet. I'm going to take you with me. You're going to help me find it.'

8
FEBRUARY 1936

The morning light peeked in through the windows of the mortuary, pasty and trembling like the sort of ghoulish little boy who would rather see a dead girl than a naked one. This mortuary wasn't like a proper mortuary in an undertaker's, with insectile steel instruments and formaldehyde; it was just a cold brick room where dead men waited on trolleys without even an out-of-date periodical to read until they could be taken off in a van to the crematorium in Hackney to which St Panteleimon's Hospital sent its departing guests. This morning, the body on the trolley didn't really look or smell dead – or, anyway, it didn't look or smell any more dead than it had the night before, when it was still talking – which made Sinner nervous, because, although he wasn't squeamish, he didn't like the thought of Ollie Renshaw waking up and grabbing his wrist as he reached into his pockets.

Until consumption of the spine began to coil him up, Renshaw had been a writer of begging letters. A tall, squinting, blond man who would respond to even the most banal statement of fact with a dribble of polite laughter, he moved from lodging-house to lodging-house carrying his private reference library: an old army bag full of telephone directories, out-of-date *Who's Who*s, annual reports of charitable societies, clergymen's lists and so on, each volume marked with dozens of careful pencil ticks next to the names he'd already tried. Constantly swapping aliases so that the police and the Charity Organisation Society couldn't catch up with him, he wrote to ask for money to buy a wheelchair for his daughter Ruth, although for a few pence he would also write letters, good ones, on behalf of other men in the spike. It was often assumed that he'd taken to this unreliable racket out of desperation, but actually Renshaw, on his return from the Battle of Passchendaele, still only eighteen years old and with no feeling in his left hand, had decided that a fellow who had survived what he had survived should never have to do another honest day's work in his life, and had consequently become a professional of sorts: back when he had money for a carriage and a clean collar, he used to pose as the earnest young envoy of a deposed Russian countess who needed somebody trustworthy to help her get her millions of roubles to London, offering 10 per cent of the gross in exchange for a bit of help with bribes and bank charges in the early stages. When he was no longer presentable enough to pull this off, he invented Ruth. Then he got spinal tuberculosis and ended up in St Panteleimon's Hospital in Blackfriars, like Sinner, and then he died of it and ended up here in the mortuary, which they didn't always bother to lock up because everyone at St P's knew that it was bad luck to go inside. The dead should be left alone – although in Poland, Sinner's father had once told him, they would cure an outbreak of the white plague by digging up the body of the first person to die of it and burning their heart.

Sinner's hands were shaking so hard that he could scarcely unbutton Renshaw's trousers to see if he had any money sewn into the lining. Although he did not have tuberculosis himself, something deep within his body seemed to aspire to that romantic disease and was now guessing haphazardly at the symptoms – so his skin was yellow, he vomited three or four times a day, and he bruised like a ripe peach. If he tripped over in a corridor he would fall to his knees and have to lean against the wall for a minute or two before he could get up.

After things had gone wrong in New York, they had never really gone right again. He recalled the day after Rabbi Berg's dinner, when he'd spoken to Frink through the locked door of his room.

'Let me out.'

'Don't worry, you'll get your dinner.'

'I've got to train. Fight's coming up.'

'The fight's off, Seth. It's all off. You know that.'

'Why?'

'Why?' said Frink. 'You're asking me why? First chance you got, you tricked us, you ran away, you stole Judah's wallet, you got wankered, and you stabbed me in the fucking hand. You think Judah's going to have you back in his gym after all that? You honestly think we're going to let you out in public again? We're going home before you get yourself thrown in jail, son. And, by the way, the Aloysius Fielding purse was supposed to pay for our ticket back, remember? That's out. So Judah's going to give me a few dollars a day to help in the gym, and he's going to lend me some more, until we've got enough. Which is more than we bloody deserve. Especially since I'll be a fat lot of use with bandages on my hand.'

'I want to fight.'

'You could have, Seth. You could have. This was your shot. You would have won, too. It would have been the beginning of something. You knew that. You've always been so bleeding predictable, but I thought just this once you might have made an exception. Because it's not just you that has to deal with this. It's me. You've fucked it all up for me, too. After everything. Do you give a toss about that, Seth? I don't suppose you do. Little prick.'

Despite Frink's anger, he seemed to soften before Sinner did; and on the steamboat home, and on the train to Euston, and even as they queued for a bus, he kept trying to strike up a conciliatory conversation. But Sinner didn't respond. He was so sick of listening to Frink that he almost began to regret not murdering the older man back in the bar. There was only one human being in the world who was allowed to make him feel guilty, and that was his sister Anna. He refused the offer of a spare bed for the night. Instead, he went straight to the Caravan.

Over the next few months, Sinner began to wish more and more that he could have stayed in New York, that he could have got a rematch against the city that had broken his unbeaten streak. All that glory Frink had talked about: he knew he deserved that. How could it possibly have escaped from him for ever in just one evening? He should still have been out there, but instead he was back in London, where every night was different. Sometimes he'd pick someone up and go back to their flat. Sometimes he'd pick someone up and the other man would pay for a room in the Hotel de Paris or another hotel. Sometimes he'd sleep in a park until the police moved him on. Sometimes he'd sleep among the tramps at Embankment. Sometimes he'd catch a few hours' kip in one of the all-night cinemas off Leicester Square before the usher woke him up with a torch, newsreels playing over and over in the distance, Mussolini and King Edward. Sometimes he'd even spend a shilling to get into a lodging-house dormitory. The problem was that Sinner did have friends, of a sort – Will Reynolds, say, who ran the Caravan – but the moment he had to ask them for help he would no longer be able to tolerate their friendship, so the only people he touched for money were people he didn't like, and although there were a lot of those, he soon ran out of likely prospects. There were his parents, but he was happy not to have seen them for three years, and if he ever did see them again it would be when he was champion of the world, not when he was broke. There was Albert Kölmel, but you didn't want to owe anything to Albert Kölmel, however small. And there was Frink, but that was still out of the question. He wished he could see Anna, but he didn't know where she was.

So before long he started to look around for posh sissies

who would not only give him a bed for the night but pay him, too. They weren't usually hard to find, although once he ended up having sex with an indifferent maid while her master watched from an armchair. He often stole cash and jewellery on his way out, because he knew they wouldn't go to the police, and with the money he began to drink more than he ever had before, because without Frink he didn't even need to stay sober for fights or training and life didn't really feel any different until one night in December he realised that something pretty awful must have happened to him because not only could he not find any posh sissies in Covent Garden who would stop to talk, but he also couldn't even get the bouncers to let him into the Caravan. And in fact he couldn't remember much of what had happened between that day and the day he'd found himself sipping tea in St Panteleimon's Hospital.

You were lucky to get a bed in St P's, one of the very few charitable hospitals of its kind in London. But you weren't expected to keep the bed for long. Every day the trolley was brought into Sinner's ward to take someone away. Last night it had been Ollie Renshaw, and that was why Sinner was here in the mortuary for the third time since Christmas. On the first two attempts he hadn't found any money on the corpses, but the schmuck Renshaw was certain to have some stashed away, and then Sinner could leave the lung house and get his first drink for several weeks. Admittedly, he didn't seem to want a drink quite as much as he had back then – in fact the thought made him a little bit sick – but since he'd been promising himself a drink thousands of times a day for all that time, he didn't really have any choice.

'I thought you Jews had rules about touching the dead.'

Sinner turned.

'Of course, we Christians do too, but we've never found it necessary to write them down.'

Connelly, one of St Panteleimon's priests, stood in the

doorway of the mortuary. He was an Irishman in his forties, so dedicated to his pursuit of contraband tobacco that he reportedly slept standing up in cupboards for no more than ten minutes at a time.

'Are you his brother, Roach? His nephew? His long-lost son, even? Is that why you're here?'

'He had something of mine,' said Sinner.

'Oh yes, he owed you some money, I expect? A silver tosheroon?' Connelly smiled thinly. 'I have always tried to be charitable with your kind. I have prayed for patience. But after a time the Lord stopped giving me patience, perhaps because you are all so disgusting. I am going to call the police. You will stay here.' Connelly closed the door and locked it, leaving Sinner alone with Renshaw.

Sinner looked around. One of the mortuary's windows was probably just big enough to climb out of, but it was too high to reach. So he pushed Renshaw's body off the trolley on to the floor, then wheeled the trolley over to the opposite wall and climbed up on it. But he couldn't lunge to break the window without the trolley's squeaky wheels slipping sideways under him, so he had to get down off the trolley, drag Renshaw's body across the floor, wedge its arm under one of the trolley's wheels like a brake, and climb back up on the trolley. By then he was too tired to break the window with his fist, so he took off Renshaw's boot and did it with that.

The rain and wind rushed into the mortuary like looters into a vault. Sinner was wearing nothing but woollen long underwear. Two years ago he could have climbed a drainpipe dipped in hair pomade, but this window was very small and he was feeling very weak. Finally he got one knee up, cutting himself badly on the rind of broken glass around the edge of the window, and then the other knee, and then he tumbled out on to the wet cobbles on the other side, feeling something crunch in his shoulder and his underwear rip at the groin.

Lying on his side, a crushed snail, he tried to look around, but the day was intolerably bright after the gloom of the mortuary and the rain stung his face. Then there was a shadow across him. He wondered if this was how his opponents used to feel at the end of a fight. The shadow said, 'Are you quite all right, Mr Roach?' Sinner groaned and wiped his eyes. He didn't immediately recognise the face of the man who stood there with an umbrella, but the voice was familiar – posh almost to the point of parody. It took him a few seconds to locate it in his memory, and then a few seconds more to shake off the feeling of disbelief. It was the cunt who'd come uninvited into his dressing room at Premierland that night after the Pock fight. Bearskin or something.

'What the fuck are . . . ,' began Sinner. He tried to get to his feet but he couldn't.

'It's really you,' said Erskine. 'It really is you. Well, well. Isn't this the most extraordinary good luck? And this is only the fourth morning I've spent in Blackfriars. I so hoped I'd find you. Although I'd heard you were in a lodging-house, not a hospital.'

'Ain't in either, now.'

'Quite. You haven't been well?'

'Middling,' said Sinner flatly.

'You certainly look as if you could do with a hot bath and a hot meal. Some good venison sausages, perhaps.'

Sinner hadn't eaten sausages in months. He was so sick of bread and butter. 'Where?'

'Since our last meeting, I've taken a flat in Clerkenwell.'

'Nice, is it?'

'Indeed, now that I think of it, there's really no reason why we shouldn't go there now. I've got a cab waiting. It's the least I can do.'

'Sounds all right by me.' Sinner had never begged for anything in his life, but he thought he would be willing to now.

Erskine looked up and down the street, looked back down

at Sinner, seemed to come to a decision, and then said in a harder tone, 'On the other hand, I think my father would be very upset if he found out he was paying for a vagrant's bed and board. I feel sure of that, in fact.'

Sinner struggled to his feet at last and stood there with rain dripping from the tip of his nose, his cock like a dead baby mouse. 'Come on, mate. No use playing about. I know what you want.'

'Do you?' said Erskine.

'I remember what you said before. You can do your experiments and I'll take your fifty quid and you and me and your dad and your earwigs will all be even, right?'

'I'm delighted that you remember my proposal, Mr Roach, but I'm afraid that as of today the terms have changed. I think I'm going to ask for rather more, you see, and I'm going to offer rather more in return. I will give you a room of your own for as long as you want it. I'll give you clean sheets and clean clothes. I'll give you as many sausages as you can eat, kosher or otherwise. I'll give you generous pocket money. I'll even let you continue to destroy yourself with drink, because I know that if I didn't you'd run off within the hour. I'll give you very nearly everything you ask for, and, with my help, perhaps one day you'll be fit enough to return to pugilism. But in return, I don't merely want to examine you every so often. I want ownership outright.' Erskine's voice here was not quite as confident as his words. 'I want to buy your body as one might buy a dog or an armchair. I won't restrict your freedom in any meaningful way, but until your death you'll submit to whatever experiments and observations I wish to perform in the service of my theories. And after that, I will have custody of your remains.'

'Fuck off, you cunt of a . . . .' Sinner couldn't find the words.

'Or I'm quite content to leave you here in the rain. It's entirely your choice. If you don't want to buy back life at a fair price.'

Sinner thought of Connelly and the police, and also of the sausages again. He could just stay a night or two and then make off with some of Erskine's money. That would be satisfying enough. He didn't like to think about how few alternatives he had, and how grateful he was for the arrival of this chinless toy soldier. 'Fair enough, then,' he said.

'Splendid. We'll shake hands on it.'

Sinner shook Erskine's hand as firmly as he could manage. Erskine led him shivering and bleeding to the cab, parked out on Bread Street. As soon as he sat down in the back seat, he fell asleep.

Later, he was awoken to be examined by a bearded doctor. He was in Erskine's flat, in a bed that seemed astonishingly soft and spacious after the cots at St Pantaleimon's. His shoulder hurt.

'Malnutrition, of course, and one or two nasty infections, but also severe alcohol poisoning,' said the doctor after cleaning Sinner's cuts. 'How long did you say he's been missing?' The doctor seemed to have been told that Sinner was a stableboy who had run away to London from a place called Claramore.

'Only about two weeks,' said Erskine, who had sat in a chair in the corner of the small bedroom and watched the examination from beginning to end.

'Well, he must have been drinking under your noses for quite a while. Not worth the trouble, I dare say.'

'I promised his father I'd bring him back,' said Erskine as he paid the doctor. The doctor gave him some packets of powder that he was to stir into a mug of hot water twice a day for Sinner. Not long after the doctor had gone, the landlady, who had evidently been told the same story, came up with a plate of liver and onions on a tray.

'You said I could have some booze,' said Sinner when he'd finished eating.

'Yes. You understand, I expect, that you are speeding your

own death? You understand that you will never be truly healthy again unless you give it up?'

'You said I could have some booze.'

'Then I take no responsibility.'

Erskine poured a glass of beer for Sinner, who drained it in one. Before the liquid even hit his stomach he felt an intense relief, as when someone tells you at the last moment that you do not have to do something that you have been dreading. It had a strange taste, though.

'What kind of beer is this?' he said, reaching for the bottle.

'It's just beer,' said Erskine, taking it quickly off the tray. 'You're probably used to cheaper varieties. Now, in a few minutes I have to go out to a meeting at the Royal Entomological Society. I'll be back in the evening. I hope you find the bed comfortable, and I suggest you stay in it, but if you wish to get up there are clean clothes in the drawer. You won't find any money or any more alcohol in the flat, and my laboratory is locked. I can't stop you from leaving, of course, but if you leave you can't come back. Do you understand all that?'

Sinner nodded. Just as Erskine turned to leave the bedroom, there was a knock at the door of the flat.

'Just a minute, Mrs Minton,' shouted Erskine.

'Phippy? Phippy, it's me!' The voice was a woman's, but not the landlady's. Erskine went white and clenched his fists.

'I'm dressing,' he shouted.

'I've seen you dressing. Open the silly door.'

'Just stay here and be quiet,' whispered Erskine to Sinner, and went out of the bedroom, shutting the door behind him. Sinner heard him open the front door.

'I thought you were dressing,' said the voice.

'And now I'm dressed. I really wish you'd telephoned first, Evelyn.'

'Well, I knew you'd be in, didn't I, brother? You never do anything.'

'Actually I'm very busy and I have to go out in a moment or I shall be late. Why don't we just have dinner this evening?'

'No.'

'Is dinner too bourgeois?'

'I wanted to see your wonderfully grown-up new flat. It's a bit poky, isn't it? Oh, at least you've brought that picture with you. The purchase of that picture is the only concession to good taste you have ever made in your life.'

'You just like it because Mother says it's horrible.'

'A horribly lazy pastiche of the Rembrandt, yes, but apart from that quite striking.' Sinner heard footsteps. 'Now, what's this room?'

'Don't go in there,' said Erskine.

'Why not?' said the voice, and the door of the bedroom opened.

Erskine's sister was twenty-two years old, pretty, with wavy brown hair pinned up behind her head to reveal a dull shine across her cheekbones like old scuffed velvet. She wore a sylphine green dress and lugged behind her a battered antique umbrella with brass fittings that could have sheltered a small village from a mortar attack. Her eyebrows were at a permanent ironic tilt, as if she were waiting patiently for the rest of the world to throw down its cigarette, abandon the charade and admit how absolutely ridiculous it was.

'Who on earth is this in your bed?' she said.

'That's not my bed. That's the spare bed.'

'Who is it?'

'Oh, he's my valet. He's been ill.'

'Phippy! How long have you had a valet? How absurd! And he looks like a Jew!' She said this with surprise, not disdain.

'He is not a Jew. His name is Roach. If one takes a flat one must take a valet.'

'Boy, are you really my brother's valet?'

Sinner waited a long time before he replied, enjoying

Erskine's pleading eyes and gritted teeth. At last he said, 'Yes, ma'am.' Erskine slackened as if shot dead.

'What's wrong with you?'

'He's got kidney stones,' said Erskine.

'What a bore. Where did my brother find you?'

'I absolutely must go, Evelyn,' said Erskine. 'Come along and I'll find you a cab.' Evelyn wasn't, of course, allowed a flat of her own, so when she was in London she usually stayed at the house of her friend Caroline Garlick near Gloucester Road. 'Let's say eight o'clock at the Ravilious, shall we? I'll book us a table.'

'I can't, I'm busy.'

'With whom? Is Mother making you have dinner with the Bruiselands? She mentioned they were up in town.'

'With your old friend Morton, actually.'

'You're still going about with Morton?' William Erskine, their father, had briefly forbidden Evelyn to speak to Morton after discovering that Morton had attached himself to the British Union of Fascists, an organisation which he believed gave fascism a bad name; but later he had relented.

'I don't know what you mean by that, dear brother, but you ought to be pleased. Remember that, whatever your pettier differences, he shares both your college scarf and your politics. Goodbye, Roach.'

They went out. Sinner got up, put on a dressing gown and looked around the flat. It was clean, well lit and not too cold, but it was also bare even compared to his parents' flat in Spitalfields: there were no ornaments and only a single picture, the one that Evelyn had presumably been talking about earlier.

Seven or eight doctors with black coats and big sideburns were crowded around a cadaver like ravens around a piece of meat. The cadaver was jaundiced but still quite well muscled, the tendons in its right thigh exposed by a hanging flap of skin and rendered in detail. A cloth was draped across its groin but you could see the bulge beneath. All around was gloom, like the morgue at St Panteleimon's, and indeed the cadaver's face did remind Sinner a little of Ollie Renhsaw. He turned quickly away from the painting, feeling that if he looked any longer the doctors, if they really were doctors, would fall upon the body and devour it. But then, strolling into the bathroom for a piss – what luxury not to be using a bedpan like at St Panteleimon's – he found himself staring into a mirror, which, if anything, was even worse than the painting. It was weeks since he'd seen his own reflection in anything clearer than a grimy window, and he understood now why the bouncers hadn't let him into the Caravan. He didn't want to look like this.

Apart from the sitting room, the bathroom and the two bedrooms, there was just a small kitchen and a mysterious sixth room with a locked door, presumably Erskine's laboratory. The lock was heavy but he could probably break the door off its hinges if he wanted – maybe not today, but certainly after a bit more rest and a bit more liver and onions. He wondered where he could go to pawn whatever it was that Erskine kept in there. Fifteen minutes later, as he stood at the window looking down at the street and thinking how strange it was that he'd ended up here, there was another knock at the front door of the flat. Sinner opened it. Evelyn had come back, without her brother.

'I got the cab to take me in a circle,' she said.

'Why?'

'Because I wanted to know if you were really Philip's valet. You're not, are you?' She had a mannish way of jutting her chin forward when she was daring someone to contradict her.

'I don't know. An hour ago I was a stableboy.'

'I knew it. If one of his servants really ever looked as deathly as you he wouldn't go within a mile of them, let alone put them up in his flat. What do you really do?'

'I was a boxer.'

'You're rather short for a boxer.'

'I punch pretty hard for a short bloke. What are you?'

'I intend to be a composer. Do you like avant-garde music?'

Sinner shrugged.

'I'm quite sure you would,' said Evelyn. 'I can almost invariably tell.' Evelyn was aware that she didn't completely convince when she made knowing remarks like this, especially to someone like Sinner with that gaze of his, but she didn't see how her repartee was supposed to gain any poise when she had absolutely nobody to practise on at home. If she tried to deliver a satirical barb at dinner her father would just stare at her until she wanted to cry. And Caroline Garlick's family were lovely but the trouble was they laughed rather too easily, rather than not at all – it wasn't quite the Algonquin Round Table. She was convinced that if she had been allowed to go to Paris she would have had lots of practice, and of course met lots of people like this boy, but as it was, if she ever met any genuine intellectuals – or any beyond their neigh-bour Alistair Thurlow – they would probably think she was hopelessly childish. For about a week she'd tried to take up heavy drinking, since heavy drinkers were so often reputed to be terrific conversationalists, but most of the time she just fell asleep.

Evelyn recovered herself and smiled. 'You know, my brother is an extraordinary character in many ways. I never would have known he had the courage. He gets through twenty-six years with such olympic diffidence and then suddenly it's an ordinary Thursday and one discovers a concubine in his bed. I don't expect you mind if I call you that?'

'What does it mean?'

'You don't, then.'

'What does it mean?'

'What it means is that I have never had any illusions about my brother's real—'

'You don't call me names, you stuck-up bitch,' said Sinner, and turned away from her. Immediately he heard a swish and felt a hard blow to the back of his head. He turned back. Evelyn had clonked him with the umbrella.

'And you don't speak like that to a woman,' she said, slightly flushed. She went out.

Sinner sat down in an armchair, rubbing the back of his head, surprised at how deeply he'd allowed Evelyn to irritate him, and knowing, really, that it was because of how deeply Erskine's sister reminded him of his own. The sister he'd once had. Anna.

The last time he'd seen Anna, he was fifteen and she was only twelve, eyes still too big for her head. One Friday night the whole family was at home in the flat on Romford Street, in the big all-purpose room which they called the kitchen. Sinner's mother was at the hob cooking chicken soup, Anna was determinedly trying to teach Sinner to knit, and Sinner's father was sitting with three or four of his old friends from his home village, grumbling about business over a Polish card game called Ocka on which they were gambling with shillings. After losing nine hands in a row, Sinner's father had stamped his foot and said to one of his friends, 'You took three cards instead of two.'

'I took two cards.'

'You took three. You thought I wouldn't notice?'

'I took two.'

'Cheating,' said Sinner's father. 'Cheating again,' he roared. Then he rose from his stool, picked up the rickety little fold-up table on which they were playing and hurled it out of the open window. There was a crash outside followed by a couple of startled oaths. Sinner jumped up, ran down three flights of stairs almost before the first ace had hit the cobbles below, and started snatching up the coins that had scattered across the street. He'd picked up nearly £2 in shillings before he turned and saw that his sister had followed him down.

'Go back upstairs, Anna,' he said.

'Are you going to buy sweets?' she said. She was wearing one of his old shirts.

His father appeared at the door of the tenement block. 'Come back here with our money, you little shits.'

Sinner ran.

When he got back that night, drunk, he found his mother in the room that he shared with Anna. (He'd slept in the same bed with her for most of his life. In the world he knew, it wasn't unusual for brothers to end up fucking their sisters, or at least to come close, and he was proud that he'd never touched her like that.) His mother was holding a cold wet cloth to a green bruise on Anna's head. Anna was half-awake and mumbling. Sinner went into his parents' room, woke up his father, and beat him until his face was all blood and he was cowering in the corner beside his mother's sewing machine. Then he went back into the other bedroom and took over with the cloth from his mother, who went out. The next morning he said goodbye to Anna and went to the gym to train with Frink. In the evening he had a match at Premierland, at the bottom of the bill, and a man in the crowd came up to congratulate him afterwards, and he lived for about a week in that man's flat; he tried cocaine there for the first time, but he didn't like the blank and cubic tone it gave his orgasms. When he finally went home again, Anna wasn't in the flat.

'Where is she?' he said to his mother.

'She's gone. Your father's out looking.' She'd been crying.

'What the fuck do you mean she's gone?'

'I went out and I came back and she wasn't here.'

'Why are you looking at me like that?'

'If you stayed with us, Seth,' said his mother. 'If you stayed with us this wouldn't happen.'

'Stay with you? Every day and night until he dies or fucks off somewhere else?' said Sinner.

'Just until she finds a husband to take her away.'

'Every day and night?'

'Why not? Why can't you? Because of prizefighting and girls? Stay with us, or just go. He hits her because he can't hit you. God above! If you weren't here at all, he wouldn't want to hit so much. If you were here all the time, he would want to hit, but he couldn't. But you come and go. You stay just long enough to make him angry and then you disappear. Do you think it helps when you come back here once a week to punish him? That just makes it worse for her. And for me.'

Sinner went out to look for Anna himself. He never found her. And when he lost Anna, who he loved, he lost more than just a sister. Because he was certain that Anna – just like, it now seemed to him, Erskine's sister Evelyn – had known something important about her brother long before her brother had really known it himself. She used to smile one way when she heard their mother blather to him about local girls and another way when she saw him stare at a handsome man in the street, neither smile her usual smile, which rose slowly in her face like a glass filling with orange juice until it overflowed into laughter. She was only twelve but she knew him in a way that no one else had ever known him. So what else was there to find out about himself that she had never told him, and could never tell him, now that she was gone? What other secrets of Sinner's had been washed away with her in the rain?

9
MARCH 1936

At twenty-two, just down from Cambridge and not very happy, Erskine had begun a three-month period of rigorous self-experimentation in imitation of his hero Francis Galton. Of the experiments he had performed in that time, four were particularly memorable.

The first was very brief. For most of his life, Erskine had wondered if the unconscious processes of the body could be subjugated more fully to the conscious mind. So one day, as a preliminary study, he sat down on his bed at home in Claramore and, for half an hour, concentrated only on inhaling and exhaling. Then he turned his attention to an essay he was planning about the genus *Ceratophaga* (the moth that eats nothing but dead horses' hooves and dead tortoises' shells) and commanded his body to go back to breathing without supervision as it normally did, rather as one might impatiently send a child off to play.

But his body ignored him, and he continued to feel as if he'd suffocate and die unless he specifically willed each breath. After several minutes of panic in which he wondered if he had permanently shut off some gasket in his brain and would never be able to concentrate on anything else again for the rest of his life, he realised he was breathing without thinking – but as soon as he realised, he stopped again – panicked, started, realised, stopped – again and again – and it wasn't until his mother knocked on his door to tell him about his sister's early return from holiday that the torture was inter- rupted. Three far more ambitious related projects had been planned – to fall asleep at will, to stop his nasal mucosa from producing unwanted mucus, and to pace his digestive system so that he could eat a huge breakfast every day and then skip lunch without feeling hungry – but he decided to postpone them all in case he did himself some sort of lasting damage.

After that, he wanted to know if the mind could ever be quite as unruly as the body. So for two weeks he carried a notebook, and every time he made a decision to do something, however unimportant, he made some rapid notes about the circumstances, then before bed he would expand on those notes in detail. And in all that time he couldn't find a single action that was, in Galton's words, 'uncaused and creative': everything he did, every so-called whim or fancy or inspiration, was a consequence of utterly predictable and conventional desires or obligations, and those in turn could probably be traced back to some banal combination of heredity and environment. This depressed him. Then, on the fifteenth day, he was passing his sister's bedroom when he saw on her dressing table a picture, torn from a newspaper, of the young French bank robber Alexandre Stavisky, known as *le beau Sasha*. He went into the room and stared at the photo for some time, then went back to his own room and took out his notebook, but he wasn't sure what to write down: he had no particular interest in crime and punishment so there was no earthly reason why he should have looked at the photograph. He abandoned the experiment.

The following month, he learnt that one of the cooks in his boarding house at Winchester had been committed to an asylum after trying to attack a boy with a skillet, and he became interested in insanity. So the next time he was in London he went on a walk from Rutland Gate in Kensington to the cabstand at the east end of Green Park, and on the way he pretended that everything he saw, human or animal, animate or inanimate, was a spy sent by a foreign power. By the time he got to the cabstand, he could divide the horses into those with pricked-up ears who were openly watching him and those with floppy ears who were pretending not to. Terrified, he ran back to the United Universities Club. He didn't feel better until the next day, when he began his fourth experiment, which was to investigate idolatry. He put a calabash pipe on his desk and stared at it, insisting to himself that it had the power to reward or punish the behaviour of all men. Very gradually, as the hours passed, he felt a sort of reverence developing for the pipe, but he had to go to dinner before he could really bring himself to get on his knees before the thing.

In the end, these experiments frightened him. He didn't like to think about how easy it was to demean and diminish the human intellect. More and more often, as he fell asleep after a difficult day, a particular image appeared before him. It was of a great noble building on top of a hill, a marvel of pillars and turrets, somewhere between a castle and a monastery and a stately home. But through every room and hall and corridor and staircase in the building ran a bloody, translucent, glistening tube as thick as his torso, with no beginning or end, that shuddered in a constant squelching peristalsis, staining the carpets and smearing the windows. And every so often, for no apparent reason, one knot of this intestinal beast would contract, tighter and tighter, until an entire tower or wing of the building cracked and crumbled and then toppled down the hill. The place could be rebuilt each time, but you never knew which section you would lose next, and if you tried to hack the viscid worm in half with an axe or a hammer it would just regrow, and the following day you would find it blocking the door to the pantry or twisting beneath your bedsheets. Even when he deliberately tried to picture the tube withered away to dust and the building unbesmirched, he couldn't hold the thought for more than an instant before he saw its red flesh again.

By the time Sinner was living in his flat, however, this image didn't come to him nearly so often, but only because now, if he was specifically trying not to think about something, it tended to be the angel child.

After that trip to Poland in November, and the terrible incident in bed with Gittins, he had for a short time returned to self-experimentation, determined that it should be possible never to ejaculate in his sleep or wake up with an erection again. Eating half a pound of liquorice a day had failed to muffle his libido, but he had discovered that if he masturbated about once every ten days he could achieve a sort of homeostasis.

Masturbation, however, was troublesome – though not, to Erskine, for the traditional moral reasons. He found the Bible unpersuasive, and the only reference his housemaster at Winchester had ever made to the male sexual urge was one short, uneasy interview in his study: Dr Paisey had asked Erskine, 'Do you understand the difference between a bull and a bullock?', and when Erskine had said, 'Yes', he had sent him away, apparently satisfied that he had done his duty. Still, Erskine had read a lot about masturbation since then, because it often came up in older books about race improvement. Joseph Howe, for instance, claimed that masturbation caused acne, pallor, dull eyes, a furry tongue, constipation, tuberculosis, epilepsy, hypochondria, insanity and, worst of all, 'debilitated sperm', which would in turn produce nothing but runts, weaklings and females. It was largely because of the influence of Howe and his faction that even the richest boarding schools in England refused to give up their open dormitories, coarse linens, doorless lavatories, cold showers and exhausting timetables of physical exercise, although of course these measures were generally now attributed to the toughening of the manly character rather than to the prevention of self-abuse. Rationally, Erskine knew there was scant medical evidence for Howe's claims, but he still couldn't help feeling that as a pioneer of eugenics he shouldn't be so careless with his procreative serum (although he often reminded himself that Galton's own marriage was childless). So sometimes he masturbated and sometimes he didn't, and when he did, it took great discipline to prevent either the bloody worm in the castle or the angel child from coming into his head uninvited, to the point where he would begin each reluctant session with the self-defeating declaration, 'I must not think of . . . .'

But of course the trip to Poland had renewed his experimentation in more ways than one. He had brought back to England dozens of live specimens of the beetle he had discovered. At first, because of the swastika, he had wanted to name it *Anophthalmus hitleri* – but then he decided that this species was not quite a supreme leader like the Reichsführer, but rather a forerunner, a John the Baptist, a hymenopterous herald. So instead he called it *Anophthalmus himmleri*, and hoped that *Anophthalmus hitleri* would come later, somehow. Five or six days a week, he studied the beetle in his laboratory in his new flat in Clerkenwell. That was also where he studied Sinner.

He could still hardly believe that the boy was here in his flat. On his return from Poland in the autumn, Erskine had noticed that Sinner never appeared in *Boxing* any more. So, even though after his humiliation at Premierland he'd promised himself that he would never try to see the boy again, he went back there, hoping to speak to someone who might know where Sinner was; but he couldn't bring himself to approach any of the seedy figures hanging around the gates, so the only conversation he had was with a newspaper hawker who stood outside a secondhand furniture shop shouting, '*London Jewish Sentry*, one penny! For Jews only! One penny! *London Jewish Sentry*, strictly for Jews!' As Erskine went past the hawker broke off his stilted patter and said, 'Would you like one, sir?'

Erskine turned. 'Is that a joke?'

'I'm sorry, sir?'

'Do I look Jewish to you?' said Erskine angrily, although he now noticed that the hawker didn't look Jewish himself and also didn't sound anything like a Cockney.

'It's only a penny.'

'Are you mentally deficient?'

The hawker just cringed and thrust the newspaper at him. Erskine took it, intending to fling it pointedly into the gutter, but instead of asking for money the hawker thanked him, turned away and resumed his shouting.

Sitting in a cab on the way back to Clerkenwell, Erskine glanced over what he'd been given. Written for some reason in English, not Yiddish, it was really no more than a pamphlet, with about half a dozen articles and no advertisements. The main headline was 'JEWISH-RUN MERCHANT BANKS FIND GREAT SUCCESS IN LONDON – Celebration across Hebrew world as permanent conquest of financial markets now assured, achieving in Britain what has already been achieved in Germany.' There was also a cheerful report on the spread of Bolshevism in certain Welsh mining villages, a leader exhorting Jewish shop owners not to give jobs or fair prices to non-Jews, and on the back page some 'frank advice' to Jewish men on how to marry a girl from a rich English family, including a warning to 'taste the fruit before you purchase the orchard'.

On any other day Erskine probably would have been very intrigued, but all he could think about then was how to find the boy. In the end, he hired a man from an agency in Camden which advertised in *The Times*, but the man could only report that Sinner was rumoured to be down and out somewhere around Blackfriars, so Erskine had resumed the hunt himself – and struck lucky. He hadn't consciously intended to bring Sinner back to his flat for experiments: he just wanted to know where Sinner was. But when he saw the boy's pathetic condition, he had realised there was a bargain to be made. And now, three days after they had met in the street, Sinner was standing naked in Erskine's laboratory while Erskine took detailed notes on his anatomy. It had been an ordeal to wait even that long, but there would have been no point in beginning his work while his subject could still barely stand.

'Turn around,' said Erskine, and Sinner did, so that he was facing the glass tanks full of soil, like inside-out coffins, in which Erskine kept his insects. Erskine studied Sinner's buttocks, comparing them in his mind to those of the Polish boy, and comparing them in his notebook to those of a normal healthy male. Did that particular part of the body belong to Sinner's stuntedness or to his strength or to the contradiction between the two? His penis certainly belonged to his strength: it would have been big on anyone, and on a boy of less than five foot was almost grotesque, particularly to Erskine, who had never quite got over the shock that real men did not resemble Greek statues in the British Museum. Back at Premierland, Sinner's muscles had looked so firm that they could almost have been the exoskeleton of an insect, and although they'd softened they were still marvellous. Several times Erskine sketched the perfect little crease between Sinner's buttocks and the backs of his thighs. He wondered if he would have to destroy the notebook later.

This went on for about an hour, although to Erskine it seemed to pass in minutes. Then he went to his club, where he found himself unable to make even the most primitive conversation. On Monday Erskine asked Sinner, just out of the bath, to assume a variety of positions: one foot up on a chair, then a boxer's crouch, then bent over. By the end, the boy seemed to be half enjoying it. 'Don't you want this one?' he asked, putting his fists up and cocking his head. 'This is what the snappers always get me to do.'

'I am not a cheap newspaper,' said Erskine.

On Tuesday, he used a tape and calipers to take measurements. He didn't allow himself to touch Sinner's goose-pimpled skin with his fingers, but while Erskine was on his knees taking the circumference of Sinner's thigh the boy's penis began to stiffen. Just as with the angel child, Erskine couldn't look and couldn't look away. But on Sinner's face was a rare half-smile, and Erskine realised with disgust that this was a deliberate attempt to goad him. As punishment, Erskine pressed the points of the steel calipers into the skin of Sinner's left calf as hard as he could until they produced two beads of blood, but the boy didn't flinch and didn't lose his erection. Erskine dropped his equipment and left the room, wondering if he ought to prepare a bucket of ice water for the next session; wondering, deeper down, if he ought to prepare two buckets.

On Wednesday, still shaken, Erskine left Sinner alone. But on Thursday, in the laboratory, he said to him, 'I need a sample of your ejaculate.'

'My what?' The boy was shuffling around in a shirt and trousers that belonged to his host, both absurdly baggy on him. Erskine preferred it when he wore a dressing gown because it reminded him of his first sight of Sinner as a pugilist, climbing into the ring at Premierland. He knew he would eventually have to order Sinner some new clothes – he already had all the measurements a tailor could possibly need – but he was reluctant to do anything that would make it easier for the boy to amble out into the world beyond the flat.

'Er . . . .'

'You want me to shoot my load.'

Erskine nodded and handed Sinner a test tube. 'I wish to study it under the microscope for abnormalities.' He had not yet had the courage to study his own sperm for signs of masturbatory debilitation.

'How do you want me to do it?'

'I'm sure you know exactly what . . . .'

'Will you do it for me?'

Erskine coughed. 'No, I will not. This is science.'

'Are you going to watch?'

'No!' shouted Erskine. Then he went out of the laboratory and stood in the drawing room humming to himself. A few minutes later Sinner called out, 'I've done it,' and he went back in. Sinner held out his cupped hand, ootheca oozing between his fingertips. The test tube was on the desk, empty.

'I specifically told you to use the apparatus,' said Erskine in a voice like glass.

'Thing was too cold.'

'You'll have to do it again.'

'Don't you want it?' said Sinner, and raised his hand to Erskine's face as if to smear the fluid on him. Erskine screamed, backed out of the laboratory again and locked the door from the outside. There was a pause, then Sinner began to rattle the door handle.

'Let me out.'

'I will in a moment.'

'Let me out or I'll smash this door and then I'll smash your face.'

'Don't threaten me! You can't threaten me! Remember your condition!' But the entire door was squeaking and juddering on its hinges. How could the boy have regained so much of his strength already? Could he really break down the door?

Then the juddering stopped. Erskine felt a moment of triumph.

'Actually, perhaps it's best if you stay in there for a few hours. You can meditate on gratitude and respect and—'

'And your precious beetles,' taunted Sinner back through the door.

'What?'

'I've been wanting to meet them properly. I think they watch me while I'm doing poses for you.'

'Do not touch them!' screeched Erskine. He rushed to unlock the door, but as soon as the key turned the door flew open, knocking him on to his back. Sinner stood over him, fists clenched, teeth bared. Then the boy raised his bare foot, ready to stamp on Erskine's face.

'For God's sake remember what I've done for you,' whimpered Erskine.

The boy brought his foot down with a thump on the floorboards just next to Erskine's head, then sneered and walked unhurriedly on into the spare bedroom.

After a moment Erskine got to his feet, went back into the laboratory and looked around for any damage. There was none, except that his notebook was open on the desk and the pages were sticky. The boy was an animal, he thought. He locked the door behind him, went back to the desk, bent down and several times inhaled deeply the smell of the notebook, which stuck to his brain like candle wax spilled on bare skin. Then he burnt the notebook in the grate in the sitting room. He felt sick, and unpleasantly alive.

The following day Sinner wouldn't come out of his room.

'Seth,' said Erskine through the door. 'Come on. You must be hungry.'

It was the first time that Erskine had called Sinner that, and indeed the first time in months that anyone at all had used the name. It made him uneasy. 'Go and grow a wooden tongue,' he said.

'Is that from the Yiddish? How charming. My point is, I'm sorry if you were upset by what happened yesterday.'

'Upset? You're the one who nearly pissed your pants.'

'Either way, let's forget it.'

'What the fuck did you say the point of all this was, anyway?' replied Sinner.

'What?'

'I know you've got some excuse for it all. I know you've got your magical fucking science.'

'Quite. I have some theories that I want to test. And you're right, you ought to understand your place in them. If you come outside, perhaps I can explain.'

112

Sinner opened the door. Erskine went to the kitchen and poured a brandy for himself and a 'beer' for Sinner, which was in fact Welch's Malt Tonic, virtually non-alcoholic, recommended for 'convalescents, nursing mothers, sufferers from insomnia and dyspepsia'. He'd ordered two cases after it became clear that Sinner, in his current condition, couldn't tell the difference. The boy had not, so far, demanded gin or whisky, and Erskine suspected that Sinner was not quite as oblivious to his own wellbeing as he pretended to be.

They sat in the drawing room.

'Do you know anything at all about racial improvement?' said Erskine.

Sinner didn't answer. He could tell that he was about to get a lecture at least as long as Pearl's in New York; here was the same pompous urge he seemed to arouse everywhere he went. Even some of the posh sissies he'd picked up in the weeks before he went to St Panteleimon's had given him monologues as foreplay. It was always boring. On the other hand, he did want to find out what Erskine's pretext was for keeping him here. He hadn't felt any gratitude to the staff at St Panteleimon's – they did what they did because their stodgy god told them to and they wanted to get to heaven – and he didn't feel any gratitude to Erskine, either. He'd known a very few truly unselfish people in his life – Anna, maybe Frink, maybe one or two others – and Erskine was no more one of them than Albert Kölmel.

'Well, you understand at least that if you want one day to produce . . . it doesn't matter what . . . say, a dog that runs very fast – then you let certain dogs breed, but not others, depending on how speedy they are? You see? Good. But what if you have one dog that is very intelligent and watchful indeed, but is born with crippled hind legs? You can let it mate with the others, but then you may set yourself back by several generations with regard to speed. Or you can neuter it, but then you may never get another dog that is so intelligent and watchful. What do you do?'

'Get a police horse instead.'

'Very droll, but no: normally, you might neuter the crippled dog, let brains be damned. You do so for the sake of the other dogs and their eventual young. Carr-Sanders puts it very well.' He'd memorised the quotation for a poorly attended lecture he'd given at the UUC, and he recited it now in a lecturer's voice. ' "It is the net effect which alone is relevant; the occasional production of a gifted individual from a defective stock, which is theoretically possible as a rare phenomenon, cannot compensate for prevalence of defect, especially when it is remembered that by eliminating defect and raising the average fitness we are really making the appearance of highly gifted individuals far more likely." Although actually he's talking about human beings there. And he's quite right, because it's the same with Jews, for instance. Jews, by and large, are greedy and traitorous and unpleasant, which is why so many great minds believe they ought to be driven out of civilised society. I know you won't be offended because those are just the facts.'

Sinner frowned. As a Jewboy in Spitalfields, you heard much worse than what Erskine was saying every time you played a game of dice with your friends. You knew to ignore it, in the same way you knew no one was sincerely alleging that you made a habit of fucking chickens in the beak. But this was different, because Erskine actually seemed to assume he had his listener's full agreement. Sinner didn't like that. He thought back to his father's stories – the ones told again and again until they were tiresome – about what had happened to the family back in Poland, long before Sinner's birth. If Rabbi Berg had been here, Sinner considered, or Pearl or even Seidelman, they would have knocked Erskine down in the debate's first round. But they weren't, and before Sinner had a chance to make a protest of his own Erskine carried on.

'The fact is, however, that Jews are also often very cunning and good with money, and I'd say very few Anglo-Saxon men are cunning and good with money in quite the same vicious way. A shame to lose that entirely. It comes in useful. So what to do? I believe that, under certain conditions, there is a way to use advanced selective breeding to separate the good qualities from the bad ones so that only the bad qualities need be sloughed off. You keep the Jew's cunning – double it, in fact – but not his general vileness. Of course, the method is exceptionally complex, and, for it to succeed, the scientist or despot in charge would need to be able to plan, in advance, every single sexual pairing over at least a dozen generations – which is what I'm attempting to achieve with my insects.'

'Couldn't you have got some other Jew, then? Lot of us about. Nearly as many as beetles.'

'I didn't choose you as an experimental subject because you're Jewish. I chose you because of your physique. If every soldier in the British Army were as strong and tough as you, then we'd be feared all over the world. But equally if every soldier was also as stunted as you, then we'd be a laughing stock. You're like the crippled but clever dog, you see, or the greedy but cunning tribe. So what to do? Let you breed, or not? The orthodox eugenicists would say that you should not be allowed to. That your bloodline should be terminated because of a silly flaw you were born with, even though you have so much else to offer. But isn't that unfair?' Erskine was talking loudly and his hands were fists. 'Very unfair? And cruel and stupid?' He quietened. 'So my theory differs. I call it lemniscate breeding, after the Latin for "ribbon", because of the way an inherited trait may curve away from the general population and then back towards . . . well, anyway, that's the essence.'

'But I wouldn't get to choose who I fucked?'

'No. But you wouldn't complain, because you'd be lucky to have the chance to take a wife at all. If you were weak as well as short – if you had nothing else to offer – there'd be no question of it. Or at least there wouldn't if things were run with any sense, which at present they are not.'

'Works out nicely for me.'

'Yes.'

'Works out nicely for you, too.'

'What do you mean?'

'Do you want a wife?' said Sinner.

'Yes.'

'Kids?'

'I am the heir to Claramore. Of course I shall get married and have children of my own. It's quite obvious what you're insinuating, Seth. But the theory is not merely self-serving. I can acknowledge that I'm not especially handsome or athletic or warlike, and it doesn't matter a jot. First of all, I have my intellect. Second, and more importantly, I come from a good family. Eugenics is a radical science, yes, but we are in England, not Russia, and no one is going to start inter-fering with England's good families. That would be against the founding spirit of the endeavour. I have nothing to fear from even the crudest programme of racial improvement. This theory is about the masses. Which is why I'm testing it first of all on the beetles I brought back from Poland. I want to see if I can breed a strain in which every undesir-able quality is eradicated and yet every desirable quality is amplified. No compromises, no sacrifices. Do you begin to understand now?'

Sinner nodded.

'I'm glad. It's not often that I have the opportunity to discuss all this.' As soon as he'd said it, Erskine realised how laughable it was to be treating Sinner as someone you could possibly 'discuss' anything with. 'I'm going to my club,' he added abruptly. At his club, he read in the newspaper about a New Yorker called Albert Fish who had been sent to the electric chair for the kidnap and murder of a little girl called

Grace Budd. At the age of twelve, living in an orphanage, Fish had begun a sexual relationship with a telegraph boy, and his homosexuality had soon developed into sadomasochism and coprophagia, and after that into murder and cannibalism. He was known as the Werewolf of Wysteria, the Brooklyn Vampire or the Gray Man. Once a girl in the crowd at the Oxford–Cambridge boat race had referred to Erskine as 'that grey man'.

The next day Erskine got a letter from his father, who for nearly a year had been planning a sort of political conference at Claramore. Now the date was set at last, for the beginning of August. Eminent men were to come from all over the world, and Erskine himself was to be allowed to give a short lecture on eugenics. Reading on, his great excitement was replaced by relief when he deduced that Evelyn had not yet said anything to his father about his suspicious 'valet'; but then his relief was replaced in turn by dismay when his father, in a postscript, threatened to cut off his son's funds if Erskine didn't keep a promise that he had made nearly two years ago. He had a tiresome project to complete, and the final deadline was now the conference. For at least a month, then, the boxer and the beetles would have to be left mostly to their own devices. It was time to write the history of Pangaean – the Erskine dynasty's greatest pride, and greatest embarrassment.

10
AUTUMN 1881

When Lydia Erskine's pregnancy became conspicuously visible late in 1881, her husband felt nervous and decided he needed a project of his own. And that was why, four months later, on the same day that the Jews were driven out of the village of Fluek, the adverbs were driven out of the English language.

'What's the use of them?' said Erasmus Erskine. 'If we set grammatical rectitude aside, is there any difference between "The horse galloped swiftly" and "The horse galloped swift"?'

(This, anyway, is how I'm almost sure that Philip Erskine was almost sure that it must have happened.)

'No,' replied Richard Thurlow. 'But there is a difference between "Coldly, he threw his wife's love letters on to the fire" and "Cold, he threw his wife's love letters on to the fire".'

The two friends sat drinking coffee in the drawing room of Claramore Hall. Above their heads, Philip Erskine's grandmother was in her seventh hour of labour, and exactly a thousand miles away Seth Roach's grandmother was dressing her two sleepy daughters while her four-foot husband waited at the door of their cottage, the smallest man in Fluek standing guard with a scythe against the smallest pogrom in Russian Poland.

'Very clever, Thurlow, I'm sure, but once again you've missed the point by a furlong. In a true philosophical language, there would be no such ambiguity because there would be no word that meant both "of a low physical temperature" and "unemotional".'

Ever since the collapse three years earlier of *Ultima Thule*, the London archaeological periodical of which he had been sole patron and publisher-in-chief, Erskine had not really known how to occupy himself; it was this that had led to his belated experiment in courtship and marriage, but after that he was still bored. Thurlow had tried to persuade him to take up poetry, but he found it to be a frivolous parasite on human endeavour, and after he was not permitted to stand in the general election as the Conservative candidate for North Hampshire he began to feel much the same of politics. As Lydia bloated, he kept returning in his mind to certain points of discussion at the last ever *Ultima Thule* editorial meeting, which was convened in March 1879 at the United Universities Club.

The explorer Ferdinand Silkstone, on his return from India, had asked to publish an article in the magazine about the legendary sunken kingdom of Kumari Kandam, claiming that on the Coromandel coast near Madras he had discovered a network of undersea caves which showed evidence of habitation by some advanced civilisation at least twenty thousand years past. At two o'clock that day, because Silkstone had not yet arrived at the meeting with his article, they were speculating with great excitement about the Tamil ancients of Kumari Kandam. How might they have spoken, for instance? Marcus Amersham, the editor of *Ultima Thule*, believed they would have had a melodic tongue of wonderful elegance, which reminded Gibbs, the treasurer, of a French musician called François Sudre who had invented an entirely new mode of communication called Solresol based on the seven notes of the scale: do, re, mi, fa, sol, la, si. Then of course they began to talk about the Royal Society of the seventeenth century, whose members were mad for *a priori* constructed languages, and Dodson, the secretary, even brought up St Hildegard, a twelfth-century abbess of Rupertsberg in the diocese of Mainz who had invented a language of nine hundred words in order to talk to angels. Then Silkstone arrived.

Silkstone was a cheerful burly man whose laughter could have torn the stitches out of a straitjacket. He spoke for about an hour. Afterwards, everyone but Erskine broke out into applause. The explorer gave his thanks and left. And then the row began.

Erskine alone thought they ought to see more evidence before they published the article: Silkstone's story had been contradictory and his sketches imprecise, and he had not brought back a single ancient artefact, supposedly because they were all too fragile. Amersham, Gibbs and Dodson, meanwhile, were convinced that Silkstone's sensational findings would finally give *Ultima Thule* the upper hand against their smug rival *The Journal of the British Ethnological Society*. In the end Erskine, unpersuaded, felt he had no choice but to withdraw his money from the magazine in protest, which meant of course that there could never be another issue. He had not spoken to Amersham or Gibbs or Dodson since that day, and almost every night for three years he had lain awake in bed wondering if Silkstone could have been telling the truth after all. Kumari Kandam's failure to make an appearance in *The Journal of the British Ethnological Society* was only partial vindication, since its editors were famously narrow-minded. Could he have inadvertently suppressed the greatest archaeological revelation of the age? Thurlow thought it was ridiculous but Erskine knew he could never be certain. And his former colleagues were still very well respected, whereas everyone had forgotten him down here in Hampshire.

These days, however, although he was still preoccupied with certain details of that meeting, it was not so much with Kumari Kandam as with the notion of a universal artificial language – a language without irregularities, idiosyncrasies or ambiguities. The point was not just to bring together men of different nations, but to clear their heads in the process: there would be no room for fallacy or paradox in a language where every word bore a perfect Adamic relationship to its object.

Excavating the past was enjoyable enough, but to construct one of these languages would be to invent the future.

'But Erskine, no one wants to speak a brand-new language for the same reason that no one wants to live in a brand-new castle,' said Thurlow in the drawing room of Claramore. 'A language needs its secret passages and bricked-up dungeons. Otherwise poets like me would have no profession.'

'A good thing too,' said Erskine. And then they heard a baby's scream.

Feeling that he could have no useful influence on his heir until the boy was at least eight or nine, Erskine began his project in earnest. He was determined to construct the language without any contaminating influences from any existing languages except perhaps Latin and Greek; but it was much harder than he'd anticipated, and he got himself in hopeless tangles with even the most basic syncategoremata, often rushing down to dinner very late to find his wife chatting happily with Thurlow. He was even forced to consider putting the adverbs back in, but concluded that he had left himself no room for them, on the same day in June 1882 that Sinner's grandfather returned with his wife and daughters to Fluek, where they were told by local officials that, according to Tsar Alexander III's new Temporary Regulations, no Jews were allowed to settle in the countryside of Russian Poland. When they explained that their family had lived in Fluek for generations and they had only been absent for a few months to escape the pogrom, they were asked to point out where they had lived – which they couldn't do because their house had been burnt down and their land taken over. So they left Fluek again and went north to the city of Bialystok, where their third child, Sinner's father, was born on the same day in January 1890 that Erskine completed the 998-page first draft of the *Pangaean Grammar and Lexicon*.

Thurlow had continued to discourage his efforts. He kept bringing up Volapük, which was at that time the most popular artificial language in Europe, with two hundred thousand speakers, and which had just held its Third International Congress at a hotel in Paris, where even the waiters and porters had conversed only in the appropriate tongue. He pointed out that Volapük had been created by a German parish priest called Johann Martin Schleyer who was not only a talented poet and musician but who also had at least a basic familiarity with eighty-three languages – whereas Pangaean was being created by Erasmus Erskine, who hated poetry, hated music and knew only English, Latin, Greek and a little French. Erskine retorted that Schleyer was a Catholic. Thurlow also noted that Volapük, based largely on English, could be picked up in a few weeks – whereas Pangaean, which had thirty participatory valences, forty derivative conflations, fifty adjunctive modalities and sixty-nine consonantal mutations, was so complex that even Erskine himself could not pretend to be fluent. Erskine retorted that the language was not intended for sluggards. Over those eight years Pangaean was the cause of many arguments, and by the time Thurlow published his celebrated verse cycle *Ischys and Coronis* Erskine was so angry with his old friend that he refused even to have a copy in the house. This upset Lydia, who was very fond of Thurlow, one of their only friends in Hampshire; she demanded that the two men reconcile in order that the handsome Old Wykehamist could carry on coming to dinner.

But far worse than his old friend's niggling was Erskine's discovery that Marcus Amersham, of all people, was working on an artificial language too. Orba, as it was called, already had a social club devoted to it in Yorkshire, whose members were at work translating the Bible. At the back of every pamphlet on Orba, Amersham included eight promissory forms. They read: 'I, the undersigned, promise to learn the international language proposed by Professor Amersham, if it appears that ten million people have publicly given the same promise.' On the other side was space for name and address. When Amersham, who was not really a professor, had received 10 million promissory notes, he was going to publish a book with all the names and addresses of the signatories. Whenever Erskine felt especially frustrated about the popularity of Orba, which sounded to him like nothing more than hissing and oinking, he would sit down with his wife for three or four hours and try to teach her the basics of trans-relative participants or sequential iconicity, but although she seemed enthusiastic about the basic premise of an artificial language, her progress was very disappointing, and he began to wonder for the first time in their marriage if he'd chosen the right bride. He bitterly regretted that he had not developed Pangaean in time to bring up his son to speak it as his first language. The same firm that had printed *Ultima Thule* was now printing thousands of copies of the *Reduced Pangaean Grammar and Lexicon* to be given away in tobacconists.

But by 1901 Pangaean, Orba and Volapük were all being swept aside by the onrush of Esperanto. Esperanto was the creation of Ludvic Zamenhof, a Lithuanian Jewish ophthalmologist who lived in Bialystok and sometimes bought his vegetables from Sinner's grandfather. One day, when Sinner's grandfather found out who Zamenhof was, he asked him why he had invented a language. 'Most of us are Jews who grew up in the ghetto,' said Zamenhof, who had written a five-act tragedy about the Tower of Babel when he was only ten. 'Russians and Poles and Germans and Jews, we all hate each other, but we must all live together. No one, I think, can feel the misery of barriers among people as strongly as a ghetto Jew. No one can feel the need for a language of no nationality as strongly as the Jew, who is obliged to pray to God in a language long dead, who is educated in the language of a people that spit on him, and who has fellow-sufferers throughout the world with whom he cannot even communicate.' The speech was clearly well rehearsed, but it filled Sinner's grandfather with excitement. He presumed that great

London Jews like Lord Rothschild and Sir Moses Montefiore had all learnt Esperanto, and decided to learn it himself, but he never got round to it because he was working too hard to make ends meet. (At that time the Jews of Bialystok were obliged to pay taxes on the consumption of kosher meat and on the lighting of Sabbath candles. The lease on the tax was held by a Jew called Solomon Kofler, whose agents would come to your house and snuff out your candles if you could not show a receipt.) Meanwhile, when Erskine complained to Thurlow that a Jew should have the audacity to invent a language, Thurlow wrote to him with a quotation from a 1712 article by Joseph Addison in *The Spectator*: 'They are, indeed, so disseminated through all the trading Parts of the world that they are become the Instruments by which the most distant Nations converse with one another, and by which Mankind are knit together in general Correspondence. They are like the Pegs and Nails in a great Building, which, though they are but little valued in themselves, are absolutely necessary to keep the whole Frame together.' Erskine wrote back: 'He is talking about languages, obviously, but I am not sure which ones "they" are. English and French, perhaps? I do not see what this has to do with Zamenhof.' Thurlow wrote back: 'He is not talking about languages. He is talking about Jews.'

The following year, Erskine discovered that a Delegation for the Adoption of an International Auxiliary Language would soon be meeting in Paris. He was determined that Pangaean should be considered, and so he embarked on the second edition of the *Pangaean Grammar and Lexicon*, addressing at least a few of the criticisms he'd heard from both its British enthusiasts and his devil's advocate Thurlow. Half-convinced that Esperanto was a cosmopolitan conspiracy, he now decided that Pangaean ought to help purge its speakers' moral sense as well as their rational sense. But he wasn't so crude as to simply take words out, as some of his competitors did

– that would only speed the language's corruption by slang. Instead, he chained up the syncategoramata so that you could perfectly well still say things like 'homosexual' and 'pacifist' and 'cuckold', but a sort of great semantic inertia would push down on your tongue. And as Erskine thundered through his own creation, the Black Hundreds thundered through the Jewish districts of Bialystok. Most of them were drunk and so the Jews were able to mount a hasty self-defence, scattering the hooligans with chains and hammers and pistols, but both of Sinner's aunts were raped, his grandfather lost an eye, and all their things were smashed. Sinner's grandfather decided the city was even worse than the country and moved the family back to Fluek, where Sinner's father would stay until he was twenty-two, saving money for a ticket to America.

In 1903 the Delegation met as planned to decide between Esperanto and Waldemar Rosenberger's Idiom Neutral. (Pangaean and Orba were never really in the running.) The Delegation appointed a Committee. The Committee appointed a Commission. The Commission dissolved the Delegation and instead appointed a Union. The Union appointed a Committee and an Academy. The Academy appointed an Association. It was all done very logically, and yet so many in the international language movement did not recognise the authority of the Delegation, the Committee, the Commission, the Union, the other Committee, the Academy or the Association that they all gave up without a final report ever being issued, just as Moscow's Committee on the Improvement of Jews had given up exactly a hundred years earlier after it could not decide whether rabbis, cantors, teachers, ritual slaughterers like Sinner's great-great-grandfather, and other functionaries should fall into the category of useful Jews or useless Jews.

(So in fact no new language, not even Esperanto, triumphed. Yet long after Erasmus Erskine's death in 1912, Pangaean maintained a small foothold in Europe. Hitler wrote in *Mein Kampf* that when the Jews had enslaved the world they would wish to establish a universal language, and later banned the teaching of both Pangaean and Esperanto throughout the Third Reich, even though arguments were advanced that they might help to purify German by preventing the assimilation of foreign words. After the invasion of Poland, the Gestapo chief in Warsaw received specific orders to imprison members of the Zamenhof family. Zamenhof's son was shot and both his daughters died in the Treblinka concentration camp, although his daughter-in-law and grandson did escape. Meanwhile, Stalin believed that a world revolution should have a world language, and tried to learn both Pangaean and Esperanto. He failed, and decided to ban them from the Soviet Union, ordering the withdrawal of the postage stamps that had already been issued in Pangaean by over-eager subordinates. Neither Erasmus Erskine nor Philip Erskine would ever hear the true story about the Pangaean, the Esperantist and the Jew who walk into a jail cell in Vilnius in 1939. 'Shalom,' says the Jew. 'Saluton,' says the Esperantist. 'Ilaksh,' says the Pangaeaphone. None can understand each other; all starve.)

But by 1905, Erskine was worrying less about the Delegation for the Adoption of an International Auxiliary Language than about some suspicions he had concerning his wife. She was behaving secretively and writing lots of letters. Twice now he had come back unexpectedly early from trips to London and heard doors opening and shutting that had no reason to be opening and shutting. And often, when Richard Thurlow was paying a visit, Erskine would come into a room and the other two would abruptly stop talking, then interrupt each other in their rush to cover it.

So one day, having announced a week in advance that he would be attending a meeting of the Westminster Pangaean Club, he went out and hid in the stables where he could watch the road up from Scranville. At about noon, Thurlow's carriage arrived. Erskine waited another half-hour and then went into the house and tiptoed to the drawing room. Pressing his ear to the shut door, he could hear his wife and his friend, just as he'd suspected, making the most revolting animal noises. He flung open the door.

There they were, on the chaise-longue. They looked up, faces full of shock and shame. Between them, thrown open indecently, was a book of Orba grammar.

He turned and walked away, holding back tears. 'I'm sorry, Erasmus,' Thurlow shouted after him. 'Lydia and I just find it such a great deal easier than, er . . . .'

Erskine went to his study, picked up his notes for the third edition of the *Pangaean Grammar and Lexicon*, went outside, threw them in the pond behind the house, and watched them sink down beneath the water to join the lost kingdom of Kumari Kandam, in the optimistic pursuit of which he spent the remaining seven years of his life.

11
APRIL 1936

Philip Erskine put down his pen and looked over what he'd written. He couldn't send any of this to his father. He would have to start again tomorrow, perhaps go back to the United Universities Club and take a second look at the papers in their library. His boxer was snoring in the spare bedroom. He got up and went into his laboratory. Although he'd been busy with the biographical essay, he had still found half an hour a day to supervise the breeding of his beetles and he was making excellent progress. Their germ plasm was improving faster than he'd dared hope. For the first time in his life he realised the contentment a project like this could bring.

But as he bent down to examine the case containing one of the most promising strains, he saw that in one place the glass was badly cracked. Angry, he went into Sinner's room and woke him up. They'd been living together now for nearly a month. The boy still slept all day like an old cat, but he seemed to be recovering from his illness. The pink was seeping back into his skin, and he wasn't dragging his feet so much as he walked – once or twice Erskine had even noticed him bouncing on his toes as if he were back in training. Also, the undershirts that Sinner borrowed from Erskine no longer came back smelling so acrid, which was fortunate, since Erskine sometimes wore them himself for a day or two before passing them on to Mrs Minton to be washed.

'Why did you do that to my equipment?' demanded Erskine.
'What?'
'You have attacked one of my glass cases. Why?'
'I ain't been in there for ages.'

128

'Don't lie to me.'

'Fuck off.'

'The damage is obvious. You've made threats on the subject before.'

'Yeah, I have, so do you think I'll be afraid to tell you when I smash up your fucking things? I ain't touched them.'

'We shall see.' Erskine walked to the door and then turned back. 'By the way, as I'm here: quite soon I must go down to my family home in Hampshire for two weeks. My father is holding an important conference.' He waited, hoping that the boy might ask if he could go too. The boy did not, so he said, 'Obviously I cannot leave you alone here for that long. If you wish, you may come with me to Claramore.'

'Come with you?'

'Yes. I can't force you.'

'Expect it's a bit posh for me.'

'You could come as my manservant.'

'Manservant? Think I'm going to dress you every morning?'

'Good God, do you really think I would want you to? No. Nothing of the sort. You would have no actual responsibilities in private. You would just have to play the part in public. And I think you could do a plausible enough job. Of course, you would be fed and watered as part of the bargain. And you would be witness to history. Albeit witness through the keyhole.'

'Supposed to be a treat for me, is it?'

'I'm merely extending an opportunity. An opportunity you will never have again.'

'Why do you want me there so much?'

'It's only that my observations are proving very fruitful. It would be a shame to halt them entirely.'

Sinner shrugged. 'Oh, what the fuck does it matter, then? Long as there's better grub than the old bag downstairs brings up.'

'Very well. In that case you'll need to be my chauffeur as

well as my valet. I'll arrange for some driving lessons. And some more new clothes.'

Erskine went out happy. He had been beginning to worry that the conference wouldn't be much fun. Earlier that day, on the telephone to his sister, he had said, 'By the way, has Father made a mix-up over the dates? In my diary it's the same week as the Olympics. That can't be right, can it?'

'Oh, dear, you'd better not mention the Olympics in his earshot.'

'Why not?'

'He didn't realise, and then Mummy saw it in the newspaper and told him, and of course now he's too stubborn to postpone. He says the Olympics are a waste of time.'

'But all the important fascists are going off to Berlin for them.'

'Yes, exactly, but luckily Daddy hates all the "important fascists" – and by the way it's rather laughable the way you utter that phrase with such reverence. Although he's heard Mosley isn't going to the Olympics, so he might still come.'

'But he hates Mosley in particular.'

'Yes, but he's having to invite everyone he can think of now, otherwise there will only be about three of us at the "conference".'

'I must say, I rather wish I was going to the Olympics too.'

'Don't be silly, Phippy, you hate sport.'

Erskine did hate sport, but he loved watching athletics, and also he desperately wanted to meet Hitler. 'Not always, Evelyn.'

'Oh, you'll never guess who else might come.'

'Who?'

'The Bruiselands.'

'Leonard Bruiseland?' said Erskine. This was their father's second cousin.

'No, I mean the whole family.'

'All of them?'

'Not the wife, of course. But all the rest. It's an utter disaster.'

It was, indeed, an utter disaster. But at least now Sinner's presence would more than make up for his father's inevitable bad mood and for the terrible Bruiselands. He went into the laboratory, and remembered that there was still the problem of the cracked glass. Could it have been Mrs Minton? But the door to the laboratory was always locked when she came up. As he stood there, puzzled, he became aware of a loud, repeated clicking. It was coming from the very same case. He bent down again, and could hardly believe what he saw. A beetle was smashing itself again and again against the glass, its movements jerky and unreal like the skip of a gramophone needle. Each time, the glass shuddered and the crack grew wider. And just then, as he watched, the beetle shot out of the case with an explosion of glass and soil and flew straight for the opposite table, on which there was a sack of live earthworms that Erskine had ordered from a fishing shop in Richmond. It punctured the bag with a meaty thud and then the bag began to shiver. Erskine screamed.

'Roach! Roach! Come, for God's sake!'

Sinner came in and stared at the bag.

'Get it out!'

'Get what out?'

'The beetle. Get it out of there before it gets away. But don't kill it.'

'How am I supposed to do that?'

Erskine wasn't sure. A better solution occurred to him. 'Get the big box from my bedroom and shake out all my clothes on to the floor and then bring it in here.' This was his tuck box, a heavy oak casket with a lock in which he had kept sweets and biscuits and money while he was at Winchester, where he had often fantasised about locking himself inside until term ended. It had once belonged to his grandfather.

Sinner, following Erskine's frantic orders, put down the

tuck box, took the lid off the broken glass case – 'Oh, so I'm allowed to touch this bleeding thing now, am I?' – picked it up, tipped the soil and the other beetles into the tuck box, picked up the sack of worms, stuffed it down on top of the soil, shut the tuck box, and sat down heavily on its lid.

'What was that, then?' said Sinner afterwards.

'That was *Anophthalmus hitleri*,' said Erskine, going to get the key to the box. He saw that a sliver of glass was still embedded in his palm. 'The first of the species.'

Erskine knew he ought to perform some proper tests on the specimen, and tomorrow he would. But in his heart he already knew that he had succeeded. In so little time, he had done it. With the help of his theories, his experiments, and also, in some less tangible way, his nightly examinations of the boy, he had bred this beetle as mighty as a rat or a dog, this Seth Roach among insects, this creature of snuffed candles and iron railings and dried blood crushed up in the fist of science, and it still had the deconstructed swastika on its wings, prouder than ever. He had proven his genius. He imagined vast maternity wards named after him, babies doing calculus and callisthenics in their first weeks of life. He imagined himself dictating his autobiography to a diligent male secretary. He imagined his eighty grandchildren, free of even the faintest smut on their characters. He imagined himself inside the tuck box with the worms and the beetles. He hurried into the kitchen for a glass of water.

That evening, a tepid April rain fell on London with all the sincerity of a hired sales gimmick for umbrellas, he cleared his desk of pamphlets on Pangaean and sat down to write a letter to Herr Hitler in which he would enclose a single preserved specimen of the beetle. Hitler, of all people, would understand Erskine's work: this magnificent leader for whom hunched shoulders, spindly legs and slack mouth were all an irrelevance, a spelling mistake that could not obscure the meaning. In fact, thought Erskine, Hitler might have no personal use for his theories: when the Führer impregnated some ravishing blonde before breakfast he could probably push the zygote to apotheosis by sheer force of will. But he would still see the importance of lemniscate breeding to a rational future, and would surely smile at the tiny tribute that Erskine had paid by giving his name to this beautiful new species, uninterested in the inevitable quibbles from the International Commission on Zoological Nomenclature about whether *Anophthalmus hitleri* was distinct enough from *Anophthalmus himmleri* to have its own official classification. So Erskine didn't care that there was only a remote chance that such a busy statesman would find the time to sit down and read some Englishman's obsequious letter, let alone reply. He would write anyway.

12

When I am in a stressful situation, I often like to ask myself: what would Batman do in my place? I find Batman so inspiring – his intelligence, his tenacity, his self-sacrifice – that it sometimes makes me slightly tearful. But the trouble is, it's hard to imagine Batman in a Little Chef.

I don't mean that flippantly: it's a fundamental problem. Most of the places where I spend most of my life – NHS doctors' waiting rooms, the local twenty-four-hour corner shop, Happy Fried Chicken, my ex-council flat, the tarmac playground down the road where I go when I want to sit down in the fresh air – seem to distill their peculiarly English ambience from that feeling you get when your mother wipes snot from your nose with her sleeve on the bus. In fact, both the shipwrecks of stained municipal concrete that dominate my neighbourhood and the shabby little concerns that grow like mould in their interstices might have been deliberately designed to exclude my vengeful hero.

On a practical level, people forget that Batman doesn't just look cool next to art deco architecture, he is closely adapted to it. It's a lot easier to scale a building covered in cornices, spires, arcades and geometric gargoyles than one whose sole bit of ornamentation is a supermarket shopping bag snagged on a weatherproof plastic anticlimb Prikla Strip. (Superman, by contrast, has his famous power of flight, which has long since skipped the jurisdiction of Newton's laws; consequently, he is serenely indifferent to niggling physical context. This is the second reason why he is closely harmonised with Corbusian architecture; the first, and more obvious, being his not-quite-human faith in human perfectibility. And that's funny, in a way, because of course if there's one man who really could build the Radiant City, it's Lex Luthor.)

But that's not really the point. The point is the total lack of glamour. These places aren't even dirty in quite the right way. Batman would look ridiculous. He would get chewing gum stuck on his boots. That can't happen. And meanwhile Grublock's lustrous developments are for people whose main form of villainy is complicated campaigns of perfectly legal tax avoidance, so they're no use either.

All in all, then, you will understand how happy I was when I escaped from the Welshman in my flat, doing exactly what Batman would have done, I think, if he were one of the world's six or seven hundred trimethylaminuria sufferers rather than one of the world's six or seven greatest martial artists; and you will understand how happy I was when I measured up to Batman for the second time in a row as I sat there in the Little Chef.

We had been driving west on the M3, past great drizzly industrial estates where men in overalls tended economies of scale like oxpeckers on a rhino. I was handcuffed to the dashboard cup holder. The motorway reminded me of the block of flats where I live, the way the brawny concrete seemed designed specifically to resist the mortal urge to modify one's own surroundings. At an intersection near Winchester we slowed for a moment beside a fenced-off triangle of waste ground, and I saw a man in a bloodstained suit limping through the tall grass.

'Hey, we should stop for him.'

The Welshman didn't even answer. He hadn't spoken for hours. I thought about Winchester College. Grublock had once told me it was the happiest time of his life, even though he wasn't so rich then. 'People assume that one is taught at public school to be callous towards the common man, Fishy, but that's not true,' he had once said to me. 'I am only callous towards the common man because the common man is so callous towards me.' In fact, as we both knew, it was for heartfelt Nietzschean reasons, but he happened to be in a self-justifying mood. 'These days, if you blamed the world's problems on a "conspiracy of international financiers", you'd naturally be put down as an atavistic crackpot and most likely a Jew-hater, but it's perfectly acceptable for good liberals to talk about "rich property developers" as if we were all united in evil. All those people who say they don't like property developers, I suppose they live in houses they built with their bare hands on unclaimed soil. I suppose they would rather live somewhere like where you live, Fishy. A place which is to architecture as a parking ticket is to literature.' I had wanted to defend my home, especially as Grublock had never actually seen it with his own eyes, but it wasn't easy. Whatever I may have said about Batman, I like a lot of sixties' buildings. Just not the one I live in. Perhaps I would like it better if it didn't feel so much like no one was ever really supposed to live in it.

Later, as we drove on, I said to the Welshman, 'You don't work for anyone, do you? You don't work for Grublock. You don't work for the Japanese. You don't work for the Ariosophists. You're just a collector, like me, and you're on your own. I should have guessed. What's your best piece? I collect the Goebbels Gottafchen Goethe – well, I did, until what happened to Grublock. Have you heard of it?'

The Welshman still didn't answer. But when we passed a big blue sign that predicted a knife and fork two miles down the road, he said, 'Are you hungry?'

'Yes, but I don't want to go to Little Chef.'

'I eat there quite often.'

We pulled over into the car park and the Welshman unlocked my handcuffs.

'I don't have to worry about you making a fuss,' he said.

'No.'

'Because if you do, then you will be my brother-in-law with paranoid schizophrenia and we will be stopping for breakfast on the way to a clinic in Southampton. I will apologise to the waitress and take you out of the restaurant, everyone will forget about it, and then I will shoot you and bury your body in the New Forest. I've done it before. It's very easy.'

'Right.' The Welshman always sounded so reasonable – it was something about the accent.

We went into the purgatorial café and sat down. I ordered smoked haddock on toast, as I sometimes do in the hope that passers-by might mistake my smell for a preternaturally pungent lump of fish. The Welshman ordered a full English breakfast, which I wouldn't eat because of all the phosphatidyl-choline in the baked beans. At the next table was a mother with three small children, bawling and brawling. I noticed that her mobile phone was lying unattended at the edge of the table.

'Are you going to tell me where we're going?' I said.

'A place called Claramore. There's evidence that Seth Roach attended a political conference there in the summer of 1936.'

'What is it? A country house?'

'Yes. Until soon after the Second World War the property belonged to William Erskine, the Ninth Earl of Claramore. Then the title, house and land were sold to an American film producer. In the eighties it became a private hospital for women with eating disorders. And now it's a hotel.'

That was when I did exactly what Batman would have done. You see, just as our food arrived, one of the children knocked a cup of blackcurrant squash off the table, spraying the Welshman's trouser leg. There was a moment of confusion as the waitress and the Welshman and the boy's mother all fumbled with napkins, and that was when I reached across to grab the mobile phone. Praying that nobody had seen, I hid it between my legs.

If the Welshman went to the toilet or something I could call 999, but of course he wouldn't leave me alone in a public place for even half a minute. Could one send a text message to the police? I had no idea. I decided to text Stuart. Luckily, I know his number off by heart from the rare occasions that we speak, and with the help of the little finger-orienting bumps on the '5' button I was able to type and send the message almost without looking down at the screen. 'stuart its kevin being held hostage irl by man w gun taking me to place called claramore need help not a joke dont try to call thanks.' Normally I find correct punctuation very important, but there was no time.

I knew Stuart would believe me – he has spent his whole life waiting for something like that to happen to him – and about fifteen seconds later the phone vibrated with a reply: 'omfg ok will call police.' My heart pounding, I dropped the phone between the tables. It clattered on to the sticky tiles. The mother picked it up without even looking at me and began to remonstrate with her children again.

An hour later, at about eleven o'clock, we were turning north off the A303. The Welshman made me map-read as we wound through the woods. Since a trip to Epping when I was fourteen years old, the only dense woods I had experienced were the ancient forests through which I hunted trolls and goblins as a battle mage, and the sheer quantity of leaves and shadows here seemed to speak of unimaginable reserves of computing power.

'What are we going to do when we get there?' I said.

'I don't know exactly. We will look for clues. And I hope that with your expertise in finding things that have been lost for a long time – your expertise in which Mr Grublock put such trust – we should have a good chance of finding out what really happened here in 1936.'

'What do you mean, "what really happened"?'

'Claramore was the site of a well-publicised murder,' he

said as the house itself came into view about a quarter of a mile down the road, a squat hulk of red brick and marble. There was something presciently functionalist about its blocky front elevation, and I felt as if we were approaching the giant processing core that simulated the forest around us, or the generator that powered the birds and the insects and the swaying wild grass. 'The police believed they had solved the case, but their suspects had already disappeared and were never seen again. There are two points to note. The first is that everyone who knew anything about the case seemed to be convinced that the police had got it wrong. The second is that, apart from those two suspects, and apart, obviously, from the corpse, there was another fellow who was never seen again after the incident at Claramore. Seth Roach. I think he was the real murderer. And I think he died here, too.'

13
AUGUST 1936

In the last years of his life, Erasmus Erskine began to treat Claramore as if it were little more than a rusty barge conveying him towards the coral harbour of Kumari Kandam. Busy sponsoring a series of expeditions to the Coromandel coast, he made no serious repairs or improvements to his decaying ancestral home, nor did he take any notice of his wife's increasingly pressing suggestions. But when he died in 1912 Claramore passed to his son William, who thought servants should have better things to do than shore up a ruin. Fascinated by a three-ton hand-cranked tide-predicting machine he had seen at Admiralty Arch in London, he decided to modernise the place so thoroughly that it would still be modern in a hundred years.

By the time William Erskine left Hampshire for Flanders in 1915, a typical room would be connected to the bowels of the house in at least six different ways. You could post your dirty clothes, for instance, through an engraved letterbox inside the wardrobe and they would drop down a chute to the motorised laundry; you could pick up the telephone to speak to a girl at a switchboard who could patch you through to any other room in the house or its grounds; you could plug a nozzle into an outlet in the skirting board and suck a stray moth down into the centralised vacuum pump beneath the scullery. Erskine was also very proud of his pneumatic luggage lifts, ice-making chamber, galvanic baths and motor house. The radical Belgian architectural digest *Béton* devoted an entire issue to the mechanisation of Claramore, including a well-received essay by its master in which he argued that only the worship of science could avert the dark tidings of Spengler's *The Decline of the West*.

But by the time William Erskine left Flanders for Hampshire in 1918, he had seen a man's legs crushed to paste by the treads of a tank, and worse besides; so although in public he argued that the war had vindicated beyond question his belief that nothing was now more important than technology, he couldn't prevent a certain cowardly ambivalence creeping into his private opinions. Also, during his absence, there had been problems at Claramore. By some mischance, for instance, the steam turbines in the power room and the hydro-extractor in the laundry resonated at the same electrical frequency, like a Tesla coil, so that when they were both running at full pelt the narrow corridor between them would sometimes crackle with arcs of lightning, jolting the cardiac muscle of any maid who happened to be carrying a silver jug or candlestick. Clothes sent down to be washed would be sent back up two or three weeks later, usually to the wrong room, perfectly spotless but also ripped at the seams and stinking of petrol, with the result that guests began to hoard their muddy riding breeches under their beds. One male visitor had to be driven to hospital after an accident with a vacuum nozzle that was never satisfactorily explained. William Erskine was willing to ignore all this, but then one day in 1919 his favourite footman was electrocuted by the plug chain of a galvanic bath, and suddenly, just as his father once had, he lost all interest in the details of Claramore's functioning, leaving his wife to take charge of a house which now needed an additional cadre of servants merely to compensate for the erratic behaviour of its machines.

At only one other time in his life did William Erskine feel a spasm of optimism about the automated future. In the same week in 1928 that his son went up to Cambridge, he read in *The Times* that several companies were now manufacturing 'brass brains', the sophisticated progeny of the tide-predicting machine he had observed sixteen years earlier. Temporarily gripped by exactly the ardour that had first inspired the reinvention of Claramore, he sold some stocks and paid for a top-of-the-range brass brain to be shipped over from Binghampton, New York and installed in the library. For several months thereafter William Erskine seemed to have an endless supply of arithmetical problems that urgently needed solving, often during dinner or in the middle of the night, and the house would vibrate for hours at a time with the grinding of the beast's polished teeth. (The library was no longer a very popular place to sit and read.) He went as far as sacking his estate manager, presuming that he basically just did a lot of sums, and a short while later was forced to write a curt note to his wife asking her to rehire the old man. His entire personality somehow rejuvenated by his purchase, he would now often ask Philip and Evelyn what they and their friends got up to for fun, embarrassing them by chuckling complicitly over even the tamest jokes and stories. But the effect couldn't last for ever, and before long William Erskine was back to his gruff old self, with the result that there was no one there to take the slightest pleasure in Claramore's machines until the arrival some seven years later of Amadeo Amadeo, one of the guests at the conference of fascists, who had read the original report in *Béton* and was now beside himself with exultation to be caressing with his own hand the house's famous central-ised vacuum pump.

'So very superior to those puny little portable models they have these days,' said Amadeo over the roar of the pump. 'With this one you could suck the clouds out of the sky.'

'Er, quite,' said Philip Erskine.

Sinner had driven the car up from London that afternoon. By the fourth or fifth time the boy swerved merrily into the wrong lane or nudged a cyclist into a ditch as he overtook, Erskine was convinced that Sinner was doing it deliberately to frighten him; but although he wasn't sure that either he or the car would ever quite recover from the ordeal, he could not deny that they had made astonishingly good time, arriving quite early in the afternoon to find his mother standing on the lawn in front of the house talking to a xanthomelanous gentleman in a bright yellow suit of a radically asymmetrical cut, seemingly made of some sort of shiny wrapping paper, fastened by just one large steel button halfway down the jacket.

Sinner parked near the stone griffins and they got out. Erskine's mother came over. 'Darling! You're here. And who is this?'

'Hello, mother. This is just my valet, Roach.'

Sinner doffed his cap in the way that Erskine had insisted he practise. In his waistcoat, stiff collar and pressed trousers he looked quite respectable – comically so to Erskine, who had taken some satisfaction in picking out the clothes.

'You've brought your own valet with you to visit the house you grew up in?'

'Yes.'

'That's a pity. I was expecting my son, not Prince Francis Joseph of Battenberg, but I suppose we shall have to muddle through.' She embraced him, and then quietly added, 'Isn't he a bit . . . I mean, what does he do if he needs to reach something on a high shelf?'

'He's an excellent valet.'

'Very well, then.' Philip Erskine, it will be possible to deduce by now, had not been an easy child to raise, and his mother assumed that he had finally found a manservant who knew how to deal with his absurd squeamishness and pickiness. She herself was not at all like her son. Very beautiful as a debutante, and indifferent to politics except when she wanted to justify her large donations to the poor, she had realised soon after her wedding that she hadn't married a man so much as married a house – a house which, even before the slow dwindling of the Erskine family's income and even before the damned machines, had been known for hatching troubles at a rate disproportionate to its moderate size. And at first it had all felt utterly impossible, but by now she quite enjoyed herself and sometimes wondered whether, after her husband died, she could go and manage one of the great European hotels.

Her son, for his part, liked his mother, but there were still various obstacles to a warm relationship between the two, not the least of which was his secret disgust at the very notion of family resemblance. Whenever he saw a pair of relations who looked very much alike, each face seemed to stand in relation to the other as the smell of rotten fruit does to the smell of fresh fruit, or as a caricature does to a photograph, the copy exposing the latent ugliness of the original. He hated to catch himself and his mother or father or sister reflected in a mirror. Just then, Sinner was no doubt looking at the two Erskines and thinking that Philip looked like a grotesque masculinoid parody of his mother while his mother looked like a grotesque feminoid parody of Philip.

'Now, I must introduce you to Signor Amadeo,' said the feminoid parody.

Amadeo smiled and stuck out his right hand so that his arm was exactly perpendicular to his body. Erskine awkwardly shook it, momentarily dazzled by the bright August sunshine gleaming off the Italian's steel button. 'A great pleasure to make your acquaintance,' said Amadeo.

'Signor Amadeo very much wants to see all the contraptions downstairs – why don't you show him?'

'All right,' said Erskine. 'Take my bags upstairs, please,' he said to Sinner. Nowhere in the luggage was *Anophthalmus hitleri*; he had decided it would be better to leave the tuck box safely in the flat, stuffed with enough chicken bones to last the hungry beetles a month.

'Go inside and ask for Godwin,' added his mother. 'He'll show you Philip's bedroom, and everything else. I'm afraid the luggage lifts have broken down again.'

Sinner went inside with the suitcases, leaving only the precious valise containing the bowdlerised second draft of the history of Pangaean. Erskine picked this up before going downstairs with Amadeo, who he now remembered was one of the lesser Italian Futurists. Like many others in the movement, Amadeo had called for a war to reinvigorate Europe. After war did obligingly arrive, most of his colleagues, who had not expected to get what they wanted quite so quickly, started to call for other, different things, but Amadeo just called for more war – longer, bloodier, and even more thoroughly mechanised. He thought of himself, in fact, as the most dedicated of all the Futurists, because he had not altered a single one of his aesthetic or political positions in over two decades, leaving them proudly in place like the machines of Claramore. At fifty years old he still wouldn't eat pasta, he still used an alternative punctuation system of his own invention, he still had all his clothes made at the only 'dynamic' tailor left in Milan, he still fed poison to seagulls, and he still occasionally shampooed with engine oil. Like many of the speakers at the conference that summer, he had few friends.

They moved on from the vacuum pump to the hydro-extractor. 'Its shining industrial vectors recapitulate the perfect curves of a woman's thigh,' said Amadeo, and then sighed wistfully. Erskine decided to leave him to it. He still hadn't seen his father and he knew he had better get that over with. But on the way to his father's study he heard jarring piano chords and went into the drawing room.

'Hello, Phippy,' said Evelyn. 'I must admit I'm almost pleased to see you.'

'Same to you.'

'I notice you brought your "valet" or whatever he is.'

'Yes. Are you composing?' Erskine knew that his sister had only seized upon 'atonal music' (whatever that meant) as a way of disconcerting their parents, and he also knew that it wouldn't work – even their father wouldn't be dense enough to believe that she really liked all that rot, most of which sounded like something a sadistic dentist would pipe into his waiting room to frighten his patients. Alistair Thurlow, who supposedly knew all about these things, had claimed that Evelyn's compositions displayed 'so much potential it's rather staggering', and had tried to persuade Erskine's parents to send her to an academy of some kind, but Erskine felt sure he was just being polite.

'No. Practising. I can't get anything done when I'm cooped up in this house.'

'Go for a walk, then.'

'That's no use at all,' said Evelyn obscurely.

Before Erskine could ask her what she meant, a red-haired girl of about twelve years old burst into the room and shouted, 'Mr Erskine, I have just seen your friend Mr Morton brutally sodomising your dear mother!' Erskine was taken aback for a moment before he realised that the girl was Millicent Bruiseland and this was quite normal. Millicent's mother, apparently as a devious mode of retribution in some feud with her husband, had sent their insufferably precocious daughter to a Finnish psychiatrist who had packed her head with words she still only dimly understood, and the girl was now in the habit of making accusations like this one. Her parents were confident that she would soon grow out of it as long as nobody paid her any attention.

Evelyn said, 'Go away and write your novel, Milly.' Millicent tutted and went out. 'I really don't understand why anyone is interested in children,' she added.

'No.' Then Erskine looked up. 'Wait a minute, is Morton actually here? Was that much true?'

'Yes.'

'My God, of all the blasted people,' said Erskine. 'Why?'

'Well, Mosley's not coming – not that anyone but Father ever really thought he would – and Bruiseland insisted that there be some representation from the Blackshirts.'

'Then why Morton? He's not much of a "representation". As far as I know he's only vaguely associated with that gang.'

'It also happens that Julius and I have become engaged,' said Evelyn, not meeting his eyes but staring past him at the atrocious green wallpaper.

'Are you joking?'

'No.'

'When?'

'Last week.'

'Evelyn, for heaven's sake, you don't even know the man.'

'Yes, I do. And we're both from good healthy stock. Isn't that all you care about?'

'I do have some concern for your wellbeing, sister.'

Then their mother came in clutching a flower pot.

'Angels, go upstairs and pay a visit to Casper Bruiseland. He's up in the observatory and I'm sure he'd be pleased to see you both.'

Philip and Evelyn began a shrill duet of protest. Their mother was too busy to argue so she said, 'All right, all right, Casper can wait. But your father can't, Philip.'

'Where is he?'

'In the library. Off you go.'

Erskine did as he was told. The door to the library was closed. As he reached for the handle he heard voices inside, and paused. One voice was his father's and the other was Leonard Bruiseland's. He pressed his ear to the wood. He had always loved eavesdropping.

'How many letters have you got from this thug?' said Erskine's father.

'Just one,' said Bruiseland.

'Did you recognise the handwriting?'

'No. Did you?'

'No. I think it was deliberately disguised.'

'Probably.'

'And it contained the same threats?'

'Yes,' said Bruiseland. 'It's very alarming.'

'It's not alarming. Any fool can write a nasty letter.'

'We'll see.'

Erskine heard muffled footsteps and backed away from the door of the library just before it was flung open.

'Aha, the Erskine boy!' said Bruiseland. He was a cheerful muscular man with a peeling red nose who would often, mid-sentence, perform a totally unselfconscious symphony of snorting, barking and choking sounds to dislodge some particle from his sinuses. 'How is our young scientist?' Bruiseland, devoted to his three farms, disliked most scientists, but he liked Erskine because Erskine studied what Bruiseland understood to be a sort of advanced branch of animal husbandry.

'Very well, thank you.'

'You're mostly in London nowadays?'

'Yes.'

'You'll snargh snargh hargh snargh soon grow out of that, I'm sure. And, er, how is your sister?' said Bruiseland, his broad smile shifting to a look of apprehension.

'She's recently engaged,' said Erskine, discreetly wiping spittle from his forehead.

'Oh.' To Bruiseland, Evelyn Erskine was an object of profound terror. Since most of his stereotypes were at least fifteen years out of date, he placed her somewhere between the opium-smoking flapper and the Ibsen woman who instead of children has 'soul-conflict'. He felt sure that her unlucky future husband would discover on her naked body the wounds of at least three (apparently contradictory) sexual tendencies, each on its own enough to prevent her from ever giving him a healthy heir: the bruised pustulent genitals of a dizzy aristocratic whore; the sinister buttock tattoos of a lesbian cultist; and the pancake breasts of a neurotic Modernist androgyne. Her sarcasm, her impetuousness, her music, her (presumed) sexual degeneracy and half a dozen other terrible qualities made her, to

Bruiseland, not only a summary of everything that was wrong with post-suffrage women, but also a culprit in the decay of his own marriage. He didn't believed that his wife would ever have thought of sending their daughter to that Finnish amoralist, for instance, without a bit of a push from Evelyn Erskine and her comrades, nor would she have thought of running off to Florence to spend all his money. Still, he acknowledged that ultimately the nobility of England had no one but themselves to blame for the condition of their wives and daughters – no one but themselves, foreigners, and the free press.

Erskine finished his conversation with Bruiseland and went into the library. His most unpleasant interviews with his father had always taken place there, and even after three years at Cambridge he still couldn't help feeling that the smell of old books had a certain malevolence.

His father nodded in greeting and said, 'What's that you're carrying?'

'My monograph on Pangaean.' Erskine had not got used to his father's hair being so grey. Other than that they looked quite alike.

'I hoped it might be. Out with it, then.'

Erskine's father sat in the armchair beside the brass brain while Erskine stood and read from his handwritten pages. When Erskine had finished, his father said, 'That's not absolutely inadequate. May as well have it typed up and bound.' Erskine smiled with pride. 'Now, what's this your mother says about your bringing a bloody valet with you?'

Erskine stuttered something.

'First of all, I don't hand over all that money every month so that you can pay someone to iron your newspapers. And, second, to bring your midget valet from London up to visit your own family home, which has perfectly good servants, some of whom have been taking care of you since you first soiled yourself as a baby, is a good distance beyond the pale. Is that understood?'

'Yes.'

'You'll send him home.'

'I'd rather not,' said Erskine.

'You'd rather not? Well, I'm afraid there isn't a bed for him downstairs. If you don't send him home, he'll just have to sleep in your room.'

Erskine gulped. A door from the library led out to the pond at the back of the house and part of him wanted to run outside to join the ducklings. His father, of course, had not made the prior threat with the slightest expectation of it being carried out – it was just a way of making clear that Sinner wouldn't be allowed to stay – but Erskine said, 'All right.'

' "All right"?'

'I'd rather that than send him home. I find him indispensable.'

Erskine's father raised his eyebrows. Erskine knew he would be too stubborn to go back on his offer. 'Very well, then. Tell your mother to tell Tara to make up a cot in your room. Let's see how long you can maintain this charade. But I don't want you complaining to your sister that I've punished you. This is your ridiculous choice.'

'Yes.'

'Your speech is ready for tomorrow, at least?'

'Yes.'

'Good.'

Erskine went out, leaving his manuscript. He decided to go upstairs to see if Sinner had bothered to unpack his luggage. On the stairs he met Morton, who was looking well fed.

'Hello, Erskine.'

'Hello, Morton.'

'Lovely house.'

'Yes. How is your brother's health?'

'Fine.'

Each of them felt they should make some comment about the engagement but neither wanted to endure a whole conversation on that subject so they just stood and looked at each other until finally Erskine lifted his empty valise and said, 'I'd better take this upstairs.'

'Right.'

'What about that time you kicked a football into my head so that I fell over, came and helped me up, apologised at such length that I got embarrassed and laughed it off, waited for me to walk on, and then immediately did it again, in front of the whole of Trinity College First Eleven?' Erskine wanted to add. 'Will you still do that sort of thing when you are my brother-in-law?' But he didn't. Instead, he walked on up the stairs, thinking about what 'threats' anyone could possibly make to his father and Bruiseland. Violence? Even if that were likely, he couldn't bring himself to feel any concern.

Sinner was dozing in Erskine's bedroom, although of course he had not bothered to unpack the luggage. When a fox wanders into the streets of London, Erskine had often wondered, does it notice a change, and does it care? Is there some deep quality of wrongness, as in a nightmare, to cement and glass, to straight lines and right-angles, or is the beast's ontology as rugged and graceful as the beast itself? In the same way, he now asked himself, did Sinner feel out of place in Claramore, or would Sinner have sneered at the very possibility of feeling out of place, and the weakness it implied? He stroked the boy's shoulder for a few seconds and then, when Sinner stirred, hurriedly turned the stroking motion into a vigorous shaking one.

'My father says you're to sleep in here with me.'

'Oh?'

'But there's no reason for you to be up here during the day. You'd better go downstairs. Ask Tara about a cot.' Then, as Sinner left, Erskine said, 'By the way, if that arsehole Morton asks you to do anything, even so much as take a telegram, you aren't to do it, all right?' He'd never said 'arsehole' before in his life.

'Who's Morton?'

'My sister's fiancé. He's an absolute bacillus. I can't tell you how much I wish something terrible would happen to him.'

Erskine already felt tired of humanity, so rather than going back downstairs he lay on his bed with a book until the telephone rang at half past seven. He picked up the receiver and heard the tinny sound of a gong being struck. It was time to change for dinner.

On his way back down he came across two big-eared men arguing in German on the landing. Seeing Erskine, the older man broke off and said, 'How do you do? You are Philip Erskine, I expect. I am Berthold Mowinckel and this is my second son Kasimir.' As he shook Berthold Mowinckel's hand, Erskine was thrilled to recall that Berthold Mowinckel had probably once shaken Hitler's.

A decorated lieutenant-colonel in the Austro-Hungarian army, Mowinckel had found himself in Munich soon after the Great War. After being introduced at a lecture to an ex-soldier and art student called Walter Nauhaus, he became a member of the Thule Society. At the third meeting he attended he stood up and announced that he had discovered in himself a rare mystical gift: ancestral-clairvoyant memory, which meant that he could remember the whole history of his tribe, passed down from first-born son to first-born son since the dawn of the human race, as clearly as if he had been present himself.

His chronology began around 228000 BC, when there were three suns in the sky and the earth was populated by giants, dwarves and aquatic centaurs. After a long period of strife his Mowinckel ancestors, the descendants of a union between the air gods and the water gods, helped to restore peace and soon founded grand colonies as far afield as Agartha in Tibet. Then around 12500 BC a war began between the Irminist religion of Krist and the corrupt Wotanists. The war raged on and off until 777 AD, when, by some treachery, the arch-Wotanist Charlemagne managed to capture the Irminist temple at the Externsteine rocks near Detmold, so the Mowinckels had to flee to Russia. Berthold Mowinckel himself had for his entire life been persecuted by the Wotanists, the Catholics, the Jews and the Freemasons, who, collectively, were also to blame for Germany's recent defeat and the collapse of the Hapsburg empire, injustices only slightly greater than the conspiracy's sabotage of the hairbrush factory in which Mowinckel had invested most of his wife's savings.

Mowinckel became a hero to the Ariosophists and wrote several books of prophecy and poetry. In 1931 Richard Anders, a member of the Thule Society who had also joined Hitler's Schutzstaffel, introduced Mowinckel to Heinrich Himmler. Himmler became fascinated with Mowinckel's chronicles and later appointed him head of the Department of Ancient History within the SS's Race and Settlement Main Office in Munich. That very week, however, tragedy struck. His two sons, Gustav and Kasimir, were walking down Sparkassenstrasse in Munich when Gustav pushed his younger brother out of the way of a chunk of falling masonry. Gustav himself was hit in the head and died in hospital three days later. And with the death of a first-born son, the flame of the Mowinckels' ancestral clairvoyant memory was snuffed out for ever. For several months afterwards Berthold gave Kasimir regular tests on Irminist history, but whatever he tried – berating him, slapping him, hypnotising him – his son couldn't seem to remember a single detail. Then one day Kasimir told his father that his brother's spirit had appeared to him in a dream and passed on the power, but the details he timidly offered were never quite consistent with his father's recollections. 'Why did your brother have to give his life for you?' Berthold asked over and over again.

Eventually, on the brink of wringing his son's neck in frustration, he went to Himmler and persuaded him to fund an expedition to Tibet to find Agartha. On his return three months later he claimed to have drunk the blood of a talking panda that he'd shot, met a tribe of women who carried magical stones in their vaginas, and seen the ruins of a gigantic monastery the size of a city. Himmler was fascinated, but the two men fell out over a disputed cocktail recipe and Mowinckel was never again part of the Nazi inner circle. Now he travelled Europe giving lectures and selling books of his poetry.

Erskine chatted with the two men for a few minutes, failing to find a polite juncture to ask for gossip about Hitler, and then went downstairs to find his sister, hayfeverish, blowing her nose in the hall. He accompanied her into the north dining room, where he was dismayed to see that only ten places had been laid out. He'd known the Berlin Olympics would disrupt the conference, but he'd never guessed that attendance would be quite so poor. Were these the only fascists in Europe who didn't yet despise his father? Perhaps the rest were too embarrassed to admit that they hadn't been invited to the games either and were sitting at home with the curtains closed and the radio on. That is probably what he would have done in the circumstances.

Circling the room, he counted off the guests on his fingers. 'You, me, Father, Mother, Bruiseland, Mowinckel and his son, the mad Italian—'

'He may be mad but he does have some interesting ideas about music.'

'—and your noble fiancé, which makes nine. Who does that leave?'

A placecard revealed the final visitor to Claramore to be Edgar Aslet, who was a Tory MP and the most boring human being Erskine had ever met – so boring that he had never been able to fix in his mind even a single detail about the man's life or achievements. Erskine's father sat at the head of the table, and he preferred to dine with men he already knew, so he had Aslet on his left and Bruiseland on his right. Erskine's mother sat at the other end, and she liked to keep an eye on the foreign guests of honour, so she had Amadeo on her left and Berthold Mowinckel on her right. Between them, in the middle of the table, was a more youthful quartet: Erskine next to Morton, and, opposite, Kasimir Mowinckel next to Evelyn. As the wine was being poured, Erskine's mother said, 'Now, Mr Morton, is it true that as a Blackshirt you smoke nothing but special Blackshirt cigarettes?'

'Morton's not a proper Blackshirt,' said her husband.

'I'm afraid that's right,' said Morton. 'I've been to a lot of the meetings and I know a lot of the top men. But I've decided not to join.'

'Good thing too,' said Bruiseland. 'Those "top men" as you call them – I know one or two myself and before they were Blackshirts they were all rubber planting in Malaya, sheep farming in Patagonia, mining in Kenya . . . . Failed in England, went abroad, failed abroad, came back to England, cast around for something to do. And then they're supplemented by a rabble of taxi-drivers and cabinet-makers flinging potatoes full of razor-blades.'

'My reasons are more to do with their political ideas,' said Morton. 'The British Union of Fascists talk a great deal about revolution and dictatorship, which is one thing in Italy, as you know, Signor Amadeo, but quite another thing in England. The English like solidity, stability and banality. Most of the Blackshirts are too young to realise that. But if they carry on behaving with such crudeness and aggression they will set fascism back ten years.' Erskine noticed that whenever Morton was not speaking Bruiseland seemed to stare very aggressively in his direction, but whenever Morton was speaking Bruiseland seemed to stare very aggressively at a spot on the wall behind Evelyn's head.

'Oh, come on,' said Erskine's father. 'All that is beside the point, which is that Mosley is not only an incurably frivolous nightclub-going popinjay, but also a Jew-lover. For a long

155

time he wanted us to believe that he saw sense about the Jews but was too polite to come out and say it. But my patience is exhausted and so is my credulity. I think he'd be happy with a Jew as his deputy.'

'Attacking the Jews in public does bring trouble,' said Aslet.

'You don't have to attack them, you just have to state the facts,' said Erskine.

'For example: that Jewish blood is like a black fog obscuring an Aryan's knowledge of the magical powers of the runes,' said Berthold Mowinckel. 'Interbreeding is the problem.'

'Well, I'm not sure about runes, but, yes, interbreeding is the problem, as I trust my son will explain in his lecture tomorrow,' said Erskine's father.

'The worst are the aristocrats,' said Bruiseland. 'They spend all their money on trinkets and horse-races, their houses start to crumble, so they marry some rich Jewess just for the dowry. And once the Jews have got their claws into the noble families, we're all buggered. It's precisely what happened to the Roman Empire.'

'If a Jew takes a woman's virtue, but then she finds a good Aryan husband afterwards, their children will still be Jewish,' said Kasimir Mowinckel.

'*Halt die Schnauze*, Kasimir,' said Berthold as Bruiseland looked at Evelyn with horrified concern.

'Fascists are as bad as you, Mother,' said Evelyn, ignoring Bruiseland. 'They spend all their time disapproving of other people's marriages.'

'Evelyn!'

'Yes, Evelyn is quite right, and I think there are more important things to worry about,' said Morton. 'You know, Bismarck once remarked on how well the children of Jews and Germans seemed to turn out. He said a Semitic mare wasn't a bad consort for a German stallion and he'd be happy for one of his sons to marry a Jewess. Nietzsche said the same thing. For any Junker type who knows how to obey and command but doesn't have any real intelligence, he prescribed a daughter of Israel.' Erskine examined his wine glass.

'Oh, to hell with Nietzsche,' said Bruiseland.

'He does seem to be a favourite of Herr Hitler's,' said Aslet.

'Do you think Hitler has really read Nietzsche on race?' said Morton as Battle, the head butler, served the soup. 'Or Gobineau or Wagner or Chamberlain? Of course not. It's quite obvious that he has read nothing but a handful of cheap pamphlets, the publishers of which he thereafter proceeded to jail.'

'Nietzsche is indispensable,' said Amadeo. 'He shows us that Christianity is just a tumour of Judaism.'

'What rot,' said Bruiseland.

As Aslet reached past his steaming bowl for the pepper, a button flew off his shirt and plopped into his soup. Embarrassed, he reached in and then whipped his fingers away with a grunt of pain. 'It's like boiling oil!'

'Oh, I'm sorry, sir,' said Battle. 'If you'll allow me.' Calmly he plunged his hand into the green liquid and fished around for the button. When he'd retrieved it he dropped it into a napkin and picked up the bowl. His hand had gone bright red but he hadn't flinched. 'I'll dispose of this and get you another portion of soup, sir.'

'He is a warlock!' was Berthold Mowinckel's shrill cry.

'Oh, no, don't be alarmed,' said Erskine's mother. 'It's just how Battle is.'

Battle had been born with a rare neuropathic disorder called congenital analgia which dulled his sense of pain. As a child he had inadvertently bitten off the tip of his tongue and his speech was still slightly indistinct. He was particularly useful at Claramore because he was effectively immune to both powerful electric shocks and accidental discharges of superheated vapour.

'Do you really not think breeding is important, Morton?' said Erskine.

'Of course it's important,' said Bruiseland. 'What breed of sheep, what breed of horse, what breed of chicken could have been abandoned as modern man has been abandoned – to random, promiscuous mating – without falling into disarray?'

'Morton, have you heard of the Kerangal family of Brittany?' said Erskine. 'It's in Saint-Brieve. Between 1830 and 1890 they were found to have produced seven murderers and nine prostitutes, and most of the rest were blind or deaf.'

'Yes, I have heard of them, and I recall that in that time they also produced one painter, one poet, one architect, one actress and one musician.'

'But Galton says—'

'Remind me what that fellow said about the Royal Family,' said Bruiseland.

'He proved that they aren't any healthier than the rest of us, even though millions of people pray for them every Sunday, which is, er, a bit odd,' said Erskine.

'Exactly. The man is an idiot,' said Bruiseland.

'As bad as Nietzsche?' said Evelyn.

'As bad as Nietzsche and Wagner and Gobineau and Chamberlain and Ibsen and Rodin and Verlaine and Mallarmé and all the rest of them.' Bruiseland had learned the latter set of names from his wife. 'Cripples and clowns.'

'Wagner was a titan,' said Kasimir Mowinckel.

'*Halt die Schnauze*, Kasimir,' said Berthold. 'Although, yes, he was a titan.'

'Pitt-Rivers said that, "Only the Jews will deliver us from the Jews",' said Erskine. 'What he meant was that the Jews have guarded their own racial purity better than any other nation on earth, so we ought to learn from them.'

'Oh, for heaven's sake, what is all this about purity?' said Morton. 'Britons are mongrels – part Norse, part Celt, part Roman, part Norman. Everyone knows that. Even Chamberlain said we weren't as good as the "pure Aryans" from the frozen north.'

Then Millicent Bruiseland skipped into the room. She had so many freckles that Erskine wondered if she might have stolen some from other children.

'You're supposed to be in the nursery, Millicent,' said Erskine's mother. 'Have you even had your tea yet? Where's your nanny?'

'I'm too old for the nursery, and anyway I must speak urgently to your son.'

Conversation resumed as Millicent went up to Erskine and whispered, 'Mr Erskine, I have the most shocking news. Your friend Mr Morton has asked me to deliver this to your sister.' Millicent then passed him a crumpled note, quite obviously in a child's hand, that read: 'DEAR MISS ERSKINE, I WISH TO HAVE AFTERNOON TEA WITH YOUR PUDENDA, YOUR'S FAITHFULLY, MR. MORTON.'

'Dispose of this at once, Millicent.'

Millicent tutted and went out. Kasimir Mowinckel asked his father for the salt and his father ignored him.

'Morton, you've done nothing this evening but snipe at our morals and mock our beliefs,' said Erskine's father later on. 'Why on earth do you call yourself a fascist if you're not interested in cleaning up the race?'

'Because, as I said, there are more important things to worry about. Capitalist democracy is exhausted. It is grinding itself away. We're told we live in a free country, but any freedom which allows a man who cannot afford food to own a newspaper or initiate a legal action is meaningless. Pure decadence. Something must be done. And we have two choices for the renewal of our society. One is communism, which is godless and anyway would never work. The other is fascism.'

'So what exactly are you proposing?' said Erskine's father.

'I don't want to bore everyone.'

'Come on, Morton.'

'Well, to be brief, the whole adult population would be

divided up into twenty-four corporations: Agriculture, Chemicals, Transport, Banking and Insurance, and so forth.'

'Would there be a corporation of Music?' said Evelyn.

'I'm afraid not, my dear, because, to the great relief of most of us around this table, twelve-tone music is not one of Britain's foremost industries. You might be put into Professional or into Miscellaneous Manufactures. And of course there would be a corporation for Married Women. Now, above all that there would be a National Corporation, made up of elected representatives of each lower corporation. No one would be elected any more on the back of slogans or speech-making or good looks, because men would vote for colleagues in their own trade, based entirely on competence. The National Corporation would take control of profits, hours, working conditions and so on, adjusting consumption to production by the control of wages. An end to poverty and unemployment and exploitation.'

'Sounds like Jewish socialism to me,' said Aslet.

'Oh, are Jews socialists?' said Evelyn. 'That's funny, I'd heard they were all haughty financiers. I must have misunderstood.'

'Same thing – it's just that the head of the serpent is in Moscow and the tail is in New York,' said Berthold Mowinckel. His lips were stained with wine and it made him look vampiric. 'They're all Jews and they all want to bring civilised Europe to its knees, so what does it matter what we call them?' Erskine heard 'bring civilised Europe to its niece', which sounded quite benign.

'Jews love currency so much because it is abstract and homeless and slippery, just like them,' said Amadeo. 'They feel at home with market capitalism because their whole religion is based on a contract. And because of the desert, too. The beating sun and the clear moonlight encourage soulless intellectualism. The senses and the emotions wither, and gold is all that's left. At the same time, in the desert, you never know whether your flock of sheep will double in number or die out from hunger and disease. So you become obsessed with unlimited acquisition and production and speculation. Such a thing could never happen in a decent, settled farming community.'

'Oh, are Jews soulless intellectuals?' said Evelyn. 'That's funny, I'd heard they were all dissolute and oversexed. This is far too complicated for me.'

'Admittedly, what I propose is not entirely unlike what Roosevelt is doing,' said Morton, trying to return to his subject. 'But a great deal sterner.'

'Morton, it seems to me that you just want to replace Parliament with something even worse,' said Bruiseland. Although he was sitting to Morton's immediate left, this was the first time that evening that he had directly addressed the younger man. 'What is the point of Parliament – what has it ever been – but to prevent the government from governing? Bit by bit it broke the monarchy, it broke the Church, and finally it even broke the country squire. Then, having broken everything that could keep the country in order, it left us at the mercy of the Jews.'

'Now, Bruiseland!' said Aslet.

But Bruiseland ignored him. 'A "National Corporation" would be no better. What we need is a king who's not afraid to do what needs to be done.'

'Fascism is not about pretending we live in medieval Albion,' said Morton.

'You mean to tell me, young man, what fascism is about?' said Bruiseland. 'Fascism is not about corporations and it is not about science and it is not about Britain. It is a great deal less fashionable than that. It is about time-honoured English traditions. It is about the crown and the soil. It is about noble blood and the working man's loyalty. It is about George slaying the dragon.'

'Fascism is a war as old as time,' said Berthold Mowinckel.

'That is all bunk,' said Amadeo loudly. 'You are all reactionaries. In Italy, do you see any crown or soil? Or in Germany, any war as old as time? No. Fascism is modern! Fascism is about the triumph of the machine. Fascism is about pistons and propellors. Everything else is impotence. Surely you agree with me, Mr Erskine, you who have rebuilt this wonderful house? Tell me, how long must we wait until a skyscraper is built with Buckingham Palace as its base and the dome of St Paul's as its top? How long must we wait until we can send into Moscow tanks the size of barns?'

'No offence, Signor Amadeo, but I think that sort of nonsense is half the trouble,' said Aslet as the venison arrived. 'Railways, motor cars, telephones, cinemas – "Everyone must learn to read, everyone must go to the shops!" – it's too much. The great mass of humanity is now exhausted. Life is too frenzied now for anyone to really appreciate it. Overstimulation of the senses means mass degeneracy.'

'Quite,' said Bruiseland, once again glancing darkly at Evelyn.

'Whoever uses machines receives a machine heart,' said Kasimir Mowinckel. 'The West today is a turbine filled with blood.' Then there was a loud bang and everyone jumped in their seats. In panic, Erskine looked at his father. William Erskine's face was white and a dark red stain was spreading across his chest. His fork dropped from his hand.

Only Amadeo seemed unperturbed. 'There are not enough explosions in this country,' he said, holding up a silver pocket-watch. 'As you can see, this does not really tell the time, because there is a tiny pistol mechanism instead of the normal clockwork. Calibre only two millimetres. Popular among the Nazis, I hear, and it is very useful for when I am finding a conversation boring or retrogressive.'

There was a long silence. Battle helped Erskine's father mop the spilled wine from his shirt, then went to prise the miniature bullet out of the wall with a pair of brass nutcrackers.

Erskine's mother said, 'I read in the newspaper today that now you can find out the time over the telephone. The Post Office seem very proud of it but I must say we've had that in this house for years.'

'Oh, really?' said Aslet.

The rest of the dinner was not a success, particularly when the women withdrew at the end to leave the men to drink their port and smoke their cigars in silence. Erskine was relieved to go to bed, declining the offer of a game of chess with Kasimir Mowinckel. He had hoped Sinner might already be asleep in the cot, but he wasn't, and although Erskine lay awake for nearly three hours, listening to the soft crackling of the faulty electrical socket in the skirting board, Sinner still did not come upstairs. Erskine wondered if his mother had overruled his father and found Sinner a bed in the servants' quarters, but when he woke up the next morning Sinner was there, asleep.

He stood over Sinner for a few minutes, watching his chest rise and fall, and gave himself a moment's amusement thinking of how Amadeo had described the Jews: 'abstract and homeless and slippery'. Sinner had been homeless, of course, when Erskine had found him at St Panteleimon's, and the boy was slippery too, but he'd never met a human being less abstract. He dressed and went downstairs. Breakfast had not been laid out and the house seemed strangely quiet, as before a surprise party. He found the head butler in the hall.

'What's going on, Battle?'

'I have some very disturbing news, sir. Mr Morton was found dead this morning.'

'What on earth do you mean?'

'The younger Herr Mowinckel discovered his body in the pond, sir. He seems to have been badly beaten. The police have been called.'

Erskine walked stiffly to a bentwood chair and sat down. He imagined the pages of the third *Pangaean Grammar and*

Lexicon swirling around Morton's body, covering his eyes, sliding down his throat. How could this have happened? Quite a few of the guests at dinner had probably ended up hating Morton but none of them, with the possible exception of Amadeo, were Mussolini types – surely they wouldn't murder a fellow fascist over a political disagreement? The most important question was, why had Sinner come to bed so late the previous night? Where had he been? And then Erskine remembered exactly what he'd said to Sinner that afternoon.

14
AUGUST 1936

There were only really two things that Alex Godwin, the youngest of Claramore's footmen, wanted out of life, and he saved every penny he could spare out of his paltry wages in the hope that one day he would be able to afford them both. The first was that Tara Southall, Evelyn Erskine's maid, should become his wife and bear his children. The second was a top-class conjugal safety coffin.

As one of only nineteen remaining subscribers to *Burial Reformer*, the quarterly magazine of the London Society for the Prevention of Premature Burial, Godwin was an expert in the technology of funerary prudence, and nothing was more repugnant to him than the German *Leichenhausen* or 'waiting mortuaries' that had been popular in the nineteenth century. For three days after a doctor had pronounced you dead, you and twenty or thirty companions would lie on wooden slabs, set out in rows like a school dormitory, decorated with bouquets of flowers to hide the smell. Wires would be tied to your fingers and toes, and the wires would run up along ceiling rails and down to the levers of a harmonium, so that a note would sound, and the attendants would hear, if your limbs began to twitch. Every night the attendant would be obliged to play a short waltz on the harmonium to prove that all the reeds were still functional. Members of the public could tour the mortuary for a small charge.

Perhaps that was all right in Germany or France, believed Godwin, but certainly not in England. If a man wasn't responsible enough on his own behalf to make sure that he wasn't accidentally buried alive, why should he expect the state to do it for him? That was socialism at its most childish. Godwin could look after himself, and consequently he planned to invest in a reliable safety coffin.

Before he met Tara, he would have been quite happy with one of the standard models. These came with an air tube up to the surface, a flask of water, and a string you could tug to let off a firework from the headstone. Quite enough for a bachelor. But what if, after Tara finally agreed to marry him, the two of them were stricken by the same cataleptic disease and buried simultaneously? How cruel if, separated by only a few inches of oak and soil, they couldn't share an embrace as they waited to be rescued!

The solution, obviously, was two adjacent chambers with a collapsible shared wall. He often thought of the happy time they might spend there together – perhaps even choosing not to let off the firework straight away. And in the horrible event that Tara really was dead and only he was still alive, then at least he would have a proper chance to say his farewell. This seemed a perfectly obvious precaution, and yet, in the 144 years since Duke Ferdinand of Brunswick had invented the safety coffin, no one had published a plan for a conjugal model, so Godwin would have to have it designed and built himself at great expense. But it would be worth it, for the pain of separation was the greatest pain of all – a principle that came back to him as he stood in the darkened corridor outside the servants' kitchen, squinting at Tara through the crack in the door as she served Sinner a plate of kidneys and mushrooms.

'Miss Erskine says you ain't really a valet,' said Tara.

'Oh, yeah?' said Sinner.

'Don't need anyone else to tell me that, pet.'

'What am I doing wrong, then?'

'What are you doing wrong?' Godwin loved the way Tara screwed up her big eyes so tightly when she giggled, as if momentarily blinded by a bright light. 'Tell you what: next time I've got a few days' holiday, I'll sit down and make you a list.'

Then Millicent Bruiseland ran into the kitchen through the other door. 'Will you act in my play, Mr Roach?' She tried to pass a sheaf of typewritten pages to Sinner, but Tara snatched it out of her hands.

'Let's see,' said Tara, and began to read.

Enter MR. BRUISELAND and MRS. ERSKINE.
MRS. ERSKINE: You have the most exquisite frenulum I
  have ever seen.
MR. BRUISELAND: You are too kind, madam.
  They combine savagely, then have tea.
MRS. ERSKINE: What a nice day to be ravished.
MR. BRUISELAND: Shall I put it in your ear next time?

'Oh, my sainted aunt, Milly!' said Tara, throwing down the script. 'There'll be no more of this. You'll shock our guest.'

'I ain't easily shocked, darling,' said Sinner, overconfident for the first time that evening.

'Do you know all about sex, Mr Roach?' said Millicent.

'I know a bit about it.'

'What's the most revolting thing you've ever done?'

'Sure you want to hear?'

'I am no shrinking violet, Mr Roach.'

Before Tara could stop him, Sinner leaned over and whispered something in Millicent's ear.

'I'm not at all surprised,' replied the twelve-year-old. 'That is what Dr Karjalainen told me old-fashioned people used to do before they had the imagination to . . .' and then whispered something to Sinner in return.

Sinner's eyes widened. 'No fucker has ever done that!'

'Don't listen, lad,' said Tara. 'She don't know what a single one of them words means. Now, clear off, Milly, so Sinner can have his tea in peace.'

'No!' said Millicent.

Then Godwin sneezed. Tara looked up. He tried to cover his blunder by striding straight into the kitchen as if he had just been on his way there instead of hiding outside, but Tara still swore under her breath and hurried out through the other door. She had to squeeze past Battle, who had come to look for Godwin.

As soon as she saw Battle, Millicent snatched up a carving fork from the sideboard and started to stab him in the buttocks, humming a tune as she did so.

'Please don't do that, Miss Bruiseland,' said Battle, concerned for his trousers.

While Battle was giving some instructions to Godwin, Millicent, reluctant to put down the fork, tentatively poked Sinner in the shoulder instead.

'Careful, girl,' said Godwin. 'The lad isn't the same as Battle. You'll hurt him.'

'I ain't easily hurt, mate,' said Sinner, overconfident for the second time that evening.

'Aren't you, Mr Roach?' said Millicent.

'Used to be my profession not to get hurt.'

'Oh! Can we play a game?'

And so, after a few minutes' cajoling, Sinner and Battle were standing side by side with their backs to the sideboard, on which Millicent herself stood holding a heavy copper frying pan with a rounders player's two-handed grip.

'Ready, Battle?'

'Yes, miss.'

Millicent swung the frying pan as hard as she could into the back of Battle's head. There was a loud clang, but Battle merely bent his knees slightly and coughed.

'Ready, Mr Roach?'

Sinner, concluding that the girl was even punier than she looked, kept his hands in his pockets and didn't bother to brace himself.

'All right.'

168

Millicent swung.

When he awoke, Sinner found himself lying on the sideboard with a cold damp towel wrapped around his aching head. At the kitchen table sat Tara and her mistress.

'And none of them said a word for the rest of the meal,' said Evelyn. 'They're all such infants. We haven't even got to the speeches yet – if world war isn't declared before Friday we shall have made a lucky escape. Oh, look, the young pugilist has been roused. I hope you weren't too uncomfortable, but we just weren't quite sure what to do with you after your mazzatello. Now, Sinner – as Tara tells me you like to be called – you must promise me that you will never listen to another word that awful little girl says.'

'I think you might have knocked me on the head once yourself.'

'Yes, but I had a point to make.'

'That butler . . . .'

'Oh, butlers can't feel anything.'

'I'd best be off, miss,' said Tara. 'There'll still be a fair bit to do upstairs.'

'All right, Tara, I'll see you in the morning.' Evelyn gave Tara a goodnight kiss on the cheek and then Tara went out.

'You're nice and familiar with your girl,' said Sinner.

'Yes. I can tell from your infinitesimally elevated eyebrow what you're trying to imply, and it's nothing at all like that. We are great friends. I've known her since we were both quite young and she is the only person with any sense in this whole house. She tells me when I'm being a fool and she tells me when I'm being a coward. I can't tell you how much I'm looking forward to taking her off to London so she never has to see that ghastly slug ever again.'

'Which one? Lot of slugs around here.'

'Godwin. The footman. He's been oozing after her ever since he got here. She sometimes finds him standing outside her room at night. My father once caught him menacing her in the library, and of course he got the wrong impression, and now he thinks they're having a secret love affair when in fact she can't stand to be near him. He talks about nothing else but coffins. Although, actually, I can't admit this to Tara, but I did have one fascinating conversation with him. Do you know anything about waiting mortuaries?'

Sinner shook his head, so Evelyn explained them to him. 'And naturally it's supposed to be that the harmonium only plays a note if someone has woken up and is wiggling their toes,' she finished. 'But Godwin says a corpse will keep bloating and stiffening for days, so the wires will be yanked over and over again, and the harmonium will be sounding practically all the time. Can you imagine the music? Such unearthly dissonance. I should love to go there and transcribe it. And Godwin says that gas builds up in the corpse's stomach and sometimes when the gas escapes through the mouth the corpse will groan almost as if it's singing. Like a Webern lieder about putrefaction. I've tried to write down what I think it might sound like, but I can't quite . . . . Why don't I play it to you?'

There had once been a shabby upright piano in the servants' dining room for carol-singing at Christmas, but soon after he bought the brass brain William Erskine had replaced it with an ondes Martenot which nobody knew how to play, so Evelyn and Sinner had to creep upstairs to the drawing room. The more he saw of the house, overflowing as it was with antiques and trinkets and tassels, not unlike Rabbi Berg's but somehow with none of the same cosiness, the more Sinner understood why Erskine had wanted to keep his own flat so empty.

Evelyn sat down and played for a few minutes and then said, 'What do you think?'

'You ain't much good at the piano,' said Sinner, who sat on the floor beside her.

'It's supposed to sound like that. Didn't you like it? That's a shame – Brecht insists the working classes love avant-gardism,' she said, half-serious. 'I'll play it again.'

She did.

'Sounds wrong.'

'It sounds wrong! That's exactly it – in a manner of speaking. You see, everyone says atonality is a perversion. Serial music is supposed to be foreign and sinister and subversive. All those fools think the tonal system is God's law, so if you cast it aside you must be mad or bad. And they're right that the tones pull towards triads and triads pull towards tonality, but the whole point of life is to resist whatever pulls on you – you must know that even better than I do.' She played a few more bars. 'Schoenberg says, "What distinguishes dissonances from consonances is not a greater or lesser degree of beauty, but a greater or less degree of comprehensibility." But he's wrong. Beethoven is no easier to understand than Berg. It's not about beauty or comprehensibility. It's about life. Dissonance is the sound of life in the twentieth century.'

'All the fighting,' ventured Sinner. When Pearl or Erskine had tried to instruct him he'd been bored and irritable, but as Evelyn talked on he found himself thinking back to all the times that he had sat and listened as Anna gave him a lesson: knitting, hopscotch, cracking eggs without getting your fingers gooey. He was never a good pupil, and he had nothing to teach her in return; she did like him to tell her stories, but he never had many that she was old enough to hear.

'Very good try, but, no, it's not as simple as that – wars are as unequivocal as mountains. Very tonal. It's about the horror of peacetime! All capitalism's lies and illusions and hypocrisies and suppressions and denials and analgesics. People are afraid of dissonant music because they recognise in it, deep in it, the truth about their own condition. It's not that they don't understand it – they understand it much too well. Dissonant music is honest, whereas tonal music buys a sort of silly superficial unity at the price of annihilating all resistance.

171

When you understand that, you realise that consonance is a great deal uglier than dissonance because consonance is the sound of bloodless tyranny.'

Sinner looked at her blankly. She smiled.

'I don't know why I'm telling you all this. I just never have anyone to talk about it with, now that Alistair Thurlow's gone abroad.' Sinner remembered the similar admission that Philip Erskine had made to him a few weeks ago. 'I found out there's a man called Ronald Slater at the BBC who's "sympathetic to modern music", so I made up a parcel of a few scores and sent them down there. I thought he might at least write me a letter. But I just got them sent back to me about six months later with a printed card that said they were "unsuitable". It was obvious they hadn't even been opened. Made me feel rather pathetic. It'll be easier when I'm in London all the time. I can meet the right people.'

'How long until then?'

'Morton and I are getting married in the spring.'

'Your brother seems to think that bloke is a bit of a cunt.'

'Yes, well, Morton did bully Philip terribly at Cambridge. But I was a perfect little bitch myself when I was at school. He's not so bad, really.'

'He's not so bad?'

'No. I was very impressed with him at dinner tonight.' She shut the lid of the piano and then opened it again. 'You mean to say, why am I getting married if that's the best I can find to say about him?'

Sinner shrugged.

'When I'm in London I always stay with Caroline who is my best friend from school,' said Evelyn. 'Her parents live in Kensington. But now she's getting married to an absolutely lovely Scottish chap and they're off to Edinburgh, so I will have nowhere to stay unless I stay with my brother, and now that he's got you I would feel terrible about putting a damper on . . . you know. So I shall be trapped down here all the time. And I can't write anything here. I can practise, but I can't compose. I need to be in town. I need the noise and the grime and the maze. London's so inscrutable, and there's something so erotic about the inscrutable, isn't there? I'm useless in the country. If I marry Morton I shall be able to live in London for the rest of my life, and Father won't be able to threaten me about his will – and what's more, Morton does always seem to have the most interesting people coming to dinner, despite being a stuck-up fascist. I know he'll let me do whatever I like, and I can have a lot of glorious affairs and so on. And he's handsome, although not nearly as handsome as you, in your odd way. The alternative is to sit here in Claramore going mad until I meet some jowly squire's son at a hunt ball and end up living somewhere just like this, married to someone just like Father, or, worse, just like Philip. I know one is supposed to marry for love, but that's not a very realistic proposition when you're . . . .' She realised she was about to cry, and she couldn't stop herself. After a time she looked up at Sinner, hoping he might try to comfort her, but he didn't move. She sniffed. 'Aren't you going to say something, at least? A friend of Caroline's once told me that homosexuals make the most wonderful confidants but I'm not finding you very wonderful.'

'Sorry,' said Sinner.

And then Evelyn reached for his hand and hauled him up towards her, clamping her mouth over his.

Sinner was surprised, but he thought he might as well do what she wanted – he still felt an unusual fondness for this demanding girl. He could taste the wine on her breath and feel her tears on his cheeks. Like rotten fruit, women's bodies were too soft, yielded too easily.

'Please . . . ,' she said, looking into his eyes, and lifted the hem of her dress. He got the sense that she hadn't known that she wanted this even one minute earlier but now that she did know she couldn't wait even one minute longer.

She was too low on the piano stool, so he picked her up and moved her awkwardly on to the piano itself, her arms wrapped around his neck. As he undid his flies, she pushed her knickers down to her ankles and spread her trembling knees, still kissing him as if she were trying to steal a piece of chewing gum out of his mouth.

(At that moment Leonard Bruiseland was walking past the drawing room. He wondered who was so thoughtless as to practise the piano after most of the house was already in bed, and then realised from the ugly, thudding chords that it could only be Evelyn Erskine. He was about to go in and reproach her, but then reasoned brightly that at least if she was playing the piano she couldn't be off fornicating.)

Abruptly Sinner entered her, and she gasped and bit into his lip. The angles were wrong and he had to stand on awkward tiptoes, feeling a bit as if he were doing some special exercise in Frink's gym, sharply aware of the moon-drowning purplish night sky outside the drawing room windows and of the piano's cold rosewood against the skin of his forearms. 'Are you going to . . . ? You know that you mustn't . . . . Not now,' Evelyn murmured uncertainly, but Sinner knew he was in no danger of that, so he kept going – trying to be gentle, but thinking about some of his favourite boys from the Caravan to keep himself hard – until Evelyn had what she wrongly took to be an orgasm and went slack in his arms. She winced again as he withdrew and a trickle of blood chased him down her thigh. He helped her down to the carpet, where she lay on her side, panting; he sat beside her. The whole thing had only lasted three or four minutes.

'Have you ever been with a woman before?' she said after a long time.

'Yeah.'

'How many times?'

'A few times.'

'Do you hate it?'

'No.'

'Good. You know, it's lucky you are how you are, most of the time. Imagine if you made it your business to go after people's wives. Think of the jealous husbands. Legions of them. You'd have been shot dead a dozen times by now.' She stroked his hand. 'Well, that's that. Now at least I have a proper secret from my dear fiancé. He'll never have the whole of me. And even if I don't have all those glorious affairs, I can say I was deflowered on a piano in a country house by a foul-mouthed Jewish boxer. How fantastic. And all my babies will be Jewish according to that German oaf.' She laughed, but he didn't laugh with her, so she looked up at him and said, 'Oh, come on, doesn't it get dull being so surly and serious all the time? Never even smiling? I bet you wish you could. I bet you would if you knew no one would see. I mean, I know I do a good job of being blithe and ironical and all that, but it doesn't mean I'm utterly without . . . .' When he still didn't reply, she scowled. 'For Christ's sake, say something to me. Instead of just grunting and shrugging all the time. Say something you mean. Once. Please. Or can't you?'

There was another long silence and then Sinner said softly, 'I don't want that prick to get my body.'

'What do you mean?'

'Your brother.'

'What about your body?'

'I sold myself to him.'

'Philip?'

'He owns me. For ever. For his experiments and everything else. I made a bargain.'

'My God, I thought you were with him because—'

'I don't give a toss what he does with me now. But after . . . .'

'After?'

'After I'm dead. He's going to keep me. Probably wants to measure my bones or something. Like in that picture of his. I don't want that. I'd rather be buried alive like your slug.'

'You want a Jewish burial?'

'I don't give a toss about any Yid burial. I just don't want him to have me for ever. I want to be buried in a hole with no name on it so he can never find me. I could run away now, but if I'm in a hole with my name on it then he'll find me and dig me up. He'll take what belongs to him.' Then Sinner got to his feet. 'I need a drink.'

'Please don't. I must go and wash, but it's too depressing to think about you getting drunk on your own.'

'Who the fuck am I going to drink with around here?'

'There's always Casper Bruiseland,' said Evelyn.

She'd suggested it as a joke, but Sinner said: 'Will he have booze?'

'He invariably does.'

'Where is he?'

'Locked up upstairs.'

But when Sinner arrived at the door of the observatory, which Erskine's father had installed at the top of the east wing in 1914, he found it ajar. Inside were Millicent Bruiseland, on the sofa, and two unctuous costly pale limp shiny things, one of which was a silk dressing gown that contained the other.

'Hello, Sinner,' said Millicent.

'You're Erskine's boy,' said the unctuous costly pink limp shiny thing that was not a silk dressing gown. 'I watched you arrive.'

'Who are you?' said Sinner.

'Didn't they tell you about me? I'm the monster in the attic.'

'Casper's not allowed downstairs,' said Millicent. 'Father says he has a chronic disease. Battle has to bring him all his meals. It's not very nice for him.'

'Yes, my father always feels obliged to bring me with the rest of the family, although I thank my lucky stars he at least bothered to find me a room with a lavatory this time. Still,

I'm happy to say that dear Millie has always been very kind to her brother. She runs errands for me,' said Casper, lifting up a fat brown bottle with Polish writing on the label.

'Is that booze?'

'Straight to the point, I see. Yes, it is. Would you like some? I've quite a lot of it.'

Sinner sat down in an armchair and took the bottle from Casper, who opened a new one for himself.

'Careful with that. It's Polish honey mead. Very strong. It's hardly the best stuff in the house, but I only ask Millie to steal what no one else would ever think to drink, otherwise Battle might notice. Before you know it you'll be absolutely desolated.'

'I ain't easily "desolated",' said Sinner, overconfident for the third time that evening. 'And my dad's Polish.'

'Oh, really? Well, then, *na zdrowie!*'

They both drank. 'You ever been to the Caravan?' Sinner croaked, wiping his mouth. He had managed not to gag but he felt as if his adam's apple were about to fall out of his neck and roll down the stairs.

'Don't torture me. I've heard so much about it.'

'You'd do all right.' Though not with Sinner, who hated Casper's type.

'I hope I would. You, on the other hand, could do a lot better than my cousin,' said Casper. 'You're a perfect vision and he's such a creepy-crawly. I made a pass at him myself once – just out of pity, I thought it would do him good – but he didn't notice, or at least he pretended he didn't. Evelyn and I have always agreed that her brother could be perfectly happy if he could just admit to himself what the rest of us already know, but he's so spineless. In fact, I'm astonished he had the courage to bring you here. Astonished, and pleased. I would certainly make advances on you myself, but I'm afraid I've been almost powerless in that respect for some time . . . .'

Casper rambled on in his damp spidery voice. About an

hour later, Sinner finished his bottle. He looked up. Millie had departed at some point, but Casper had never stopped talking: '. . . And of course they were just about to legalise buggery in Germany if it hadn't been for the silly old stock market crash.' Sinner hurled himself forward out of the armchair, then crawled to the door on his hands and knees. It was seven or eight months since he'd drunk anything stronger than Erskine's second-rate beer, and he felt like a child again.

'Oh, are you off?' said Casper. 'Well, it was delightful to meet you. Send my regards to Philip.'

'They really . . . they really keep you locked up because you drink too much?' slurred Sinner.

'Because I drink too much? God, no. As you can see, my dear, I have no trouble holding my alcohol. I've dined with all the drinking societies in Oxford. One learns.'

'Why, then?'

'I kept getting caught wanking off farmhands. Father said it was this or the sanatorium.'

Sinner staggered down the stairs. He remembered that he was supposed to be sleeping in Erskine's room, but he didn't want to go there, so he decided to find somewhere he could safely pass out until morning without anyone finding him. Doors and oil paintings and umbrellas and lamps and books swerved past him at reckless speeds; the moonlight came in at odd angles and his shadow seemed to bark at his heels like a dog.

Some while later, he found himself vomiting into some sort of complicated metal cage. He pursued the vomit inside and curled up into a ball, spikes digging uncomfortably into his ribs and shins. He dozed off; but no more than ten minutes later he was awoken by lights and voices. He already felt much more clear-headed for having voided his stomach. He tried not to make any noise, wondering where he was. Inside a torture device? An experimental piano? A very advanced safety coffin? A mechanical model of Evelyn Erskine's womb? He couldn't really see out.

'Couldn't we do this tomorrow?' said the first voice. 'I'm very tired and I'm sure there'll be time for a chat between the lectures.'

'I'm afraid privacy is of the utmost importance to this discussion,' said the second voice. 'That's why we had to wait for everyone else to go to bed. Pour yourself a drink and sit down.'

'I say, something smells a bit odd.'

'I can't smell anything.'

'I think it's coming from Mr Erskine's calculating machine.'

'Please do sit down and pay attention, Morton.'

'Sorry.'

'Good. Now, I'll get straight down to business. You're familiar, I trust, with the Protocols of the Elders of Zion?'

'Superficially.'

'Do you believe in them?'

'Of course not. They're thoroughly discredited, as every schoolboy knows. Copied from a nineteenth-century satirical dialogue about Napoleon. You don't mean to say you think differently?'

'I think they have the ring of truth, and I think it's very easy bargh glargh glargh bargh snargh to trump up evidence for a charge of plagiary. But it's not for me to say. The point is, the average man has been taught to scoff at them. They're no use to us any more.'

'To us?'

'To fascism.'

'I'm not sure they were much use to fascism in the first place.'

'Perhaps not to your brand. But to those of us who aren't in bed with the Jews—'

'Sir, I—'

'—they were once a very useful way of knocking some

sense into people.' Sinner smelt cigar smoke. 'So what can we put in their place? That is the question Erskine and I asked ourselves several months ago. We concluded that with a little bit of trickery – no more than the Jew himself uses every time he goes to the vegetable market – we could achieve something masterful. You know about the *London Jewish Sentry*?'

'I'm aware of it, yes.'

'I thought so. The idea, you understand, was to spill a few secrets that the Jews would never spill themselves, and to do it so that people would have no reason to doubt what they read. Propaganda with an honourable heart. Very effective. Now, publishing a newspaper isn't cheap, especially when it has to be done largely in secret, but Erskine and I felt that money should be no object when the future of the British Empire is at stake. We took out our cheque books quite happily.'

'You mean to say that you and Mr Erskine were funding the whole thing?'

'Don't play stupid with me, Morton. As you must know, we had no choice but to involve one or two dullards from Mosley's gang. Erskine and I don't go to London very often, and they know the lie of the land. But I always knew it would be our undoing. Those bloody Blackshirts – I'd rather entrust my secrets to a six-year-old girl. Which is how, over the last few months, Erskine and I came to be receiving letters of the most despicable kind. All anonymous. The first ones were just full of sinister innuendo. But now we've been threatened with exposure if we don't hand over cash.'

'Blackmail?'

'Yes, my boy, blackmail. That's what it is. Nothing less. I'm glad you realise that. And Erskine and I wouldn't normally give a damn. If it did get in the papers that we'd been paying for the *London Jewish Sentry*, we'd be heroes to every fascist in the world. Hitler would probably give us a medal. If we were vain men, we'd be begging this blackmailer to go to *The*

Times. But the point is, it would set back the cause. Not only would we lose influence – and before long, mark my words, Parliament will be trying to take us to war with Germany, so we will need our influence more than ever – but all our work on *London Jewish Sentry* would be wasted before it had really borne fruit. We can't let that happen. But we also don't want to give in to a common criminal. So we won't pay a penny. What do you say to that?'

'Quite right. I think you should go to the police.'

'Don't taunt me, Morton. You know perfectly well we can't go to the police. They'd start poking their noses everywhere. A disgraceful affair like this has to be settled man to man.'

There was a pause. 'You're not suggesting . . . ,' began Morton.

'I've been watching your face, my boy. You're as guilty as they come. You're not a real fascist, you're just a blasted opportunist.'

'Oh, please be serious – does Mr Erskine realise you're making these accusations?'

'Since you're marrying his daughter he's had to pretend you're a decent fellow, and by now he's spent so long pretending that he doesn't know any better. He wouldn't listen if I tried to tell him. But now you're going to come with me and confess to his face. Then you'll break off the engagement, which, by the way, is to your own advantage – I assume you didn't realise what you'd have been faced with on the wedding night – and you'll make some sort of restitution to Erskine and me. Then I expect you'll either hang yourself or go off and live amongst the wogs for the rest of your life.'

'Mr Bruiseland, I'm sorry, but this is utterly absurd. I had no inkling that you and Mr Erskine had anything to do with this ersatz newspaper. In fact, I would have thought rather better of both of you.'

'Admit it, and we can settle this.'

'It would be more sensible if we could both talk this over with Mr Erskine.'

'You're caught, boy. Don't embarrass yourself.'

'Perhaps we should just go to bed and in the morning we can—'

'Oh, you Blackshirts are scum. You're as bad as the Jews. I don't know why I even bothered to give you the chance to behave like a hargh margh nargh nargh nargh nargh gentleman. Come here.'

'Mr Bruiseland, for God's sake!' screeched Morton, and then for an instant Sinner found himself looking directly into Morton's panicked eyes through a gap in the machinery as Morton's face was smashed into the side of the brass brain. Morton seemed to recognise him, but then Bruiseland grabbed him by the hair, jerking him back out of view, and the metal around Sinner reverberated with blow after blow, droplets of blood spraying like some evil lubricant grease over the cogs and levers. There was a final thud as Bruiseland dropped Morton's body on the carpet of the library, and after that all Sinner could hear was the older man's loud phlegmy breathing. He could smell blood and tobacco and it reminded him of Premierland.

During the murder, Sinner had been too bewildered to try to intervene. He now thought of confronting Bruiseland; but the trouble was, he was still so drunk that it wasn't impossible that Bruiseland might get the better of him with a curtain rail; and it wouldn't do either Sinner or Morton any good if Sinner was discovered beating up a house guest; and anyway, Erskine had said that Morton was an arsehole and Evelyn hadn't really disagreed, so perhaps Bruiseland had basically the right idea, even if he was obviously loony himself to have gone as far as he had. Frink would have known what to do. But Sinner didn't. So he just stayed where he was, listening to Bruiseland's grunts as he dragged Morton's body feet-first out of the library. He felt a draught of cold air, and a little while later there was a faint splash from outside the house followed by some startled quacking. When it was obvious that Bruiseland wasn't going to come back to clean up the blood or even to turn the lights off, Sinner dolloped himself out of the brass brain, stretched his tingling legs, and staggered upstairs to Erskine's room.

15

Evelyn came into the hall while Erskine was still sitting there in the bentwood chair. He jumped up.

'I suppose you're pleased,' she said.

'Oh, no, Evelyn, please don't say that – I wouldn't wish what's happened on my worst enemy. Certainly not on my sister's fiancé.' Actually, he had wished humiliation, torture and death on Morton dozens of times, but he decided now that he hadn't really meant it. 'I'm so sorry, it's the most awful . . . I don't know what to say.' Gingerly he reached out to touch her shoulder but she rolled her eyes and pushed his hand away.

'You're not cut out for sentimentality, Phippy. Anyway, I'm in shock, they insist, so it doesn't really make any difference what you say now. Save it up for when I'm crying myself bald. Have you seen Tara?'

'No.'

'I must find Tara. She will know what to do. But she seems to have disappeared from the house. What about your chap?'

'Do you mean, was he, er, responsible?' said Erskine, wondering how Evelyn had already come to share his suspicions.

'No, of course not – one of those fascist fuckers did it, that is absolutely obvious to anyone with even a knitted brain. I mean, where is he to be found?'

'He's asleep.'

'Where?'

'In my room. Why?'

Evelyn smiled. 'Oh, yes, Tara told me you'd persuaded Father to let him sleep up there with you. I don't know how on earth you managed it but clap clap clap.'

'I did not "persuade"—'

'No, dear brother, of course you didn't. No. Well, I'm off to smoke a hundred cigarettes, so I'll see you at lunch.' As Evelyn started up the stairs to her room, she turned and added, 'And if you want to gawp at the blood with all the others, they're in the library.'

Out on her balcony with a Sobranie Evelyn looked down at the pond, where a stiff breeze whisked the sunlight gently through the water. It occurred to her that if she were a girl in a melodrama she would presumably take Morton's death as a punishment for her little crime with Sinner and be scared off sex for the rest of her life. But actually she had always felt it was natural that things happened all at once. Still, it was impossible to clear her head because thinking about one just reminded her of the other, as if the events were two older, taller girls throwing a ball back and forth to keep it out of her reach and she would have to run endlessly from tormentor to tormentor until she collapsed from exhaustion. What she'd done with Sinner wasn't horrible like what had happened to Morton – she felt deeply grateful for it, in fact – but it was still perplexing down to her bones. And now there began to emerge a third, kindred uneasiness, a stealthier, more complicated thorn: the guilty possibility that really she cared more about what had happened last night in the music room than what had happened (at exactly the same moment, for all she knew) over in the library – the possibility that even if she never saw Sinner again (and they had still only really met twice) she would still remember his face for longer than she would remember Morton's. She had always known that one day she would escape from the Wykehamist and all that he represented, but she had never guessed, nor truly desired, that it would happen so soon, or so drastically. The border between her past and her future, hostile countries, had been drawn in blood.

Downstairs, in the library, Erskine found Bruiseland, Aslet, Amadeo and the Mowinckels standing in a row along the smeary brown trail that led from the brass brain to the French windows. Like soldiers at a frontier they did not seem to want to step over it. He thought of Fluek, that disputed village.

'We're certain it couldn't have been suicide?' said Aslet.

Erskine noticed that a few of Morton's hairs were still stuck to the floorboards.

'Secret agents of Zion,' said Berthold Mowinckel. 'Not for years have they struck so deep into the heart of the nobility.'

'It was no secret agent of Zion who produced a pistol at dinner last night,' muttered his son.

'What are you suggesting?' said Amadeo.

'I have read some of your poetry. "The Bliss of Violence"?'

'I wonder why you would make these baseless insinuations unless you yourself have something to hide?'

'Don't be ridiculous,' said Berthold Mowinckel. 'Unlike his late brother, my son would never have the courage to do something like this.'

'Courage? No. Stupidity? Perhaps.'

'Do you wish to settle this like men?' said Kasimir.

'What do you mean?' said Amadeo.

'A duel.'

'Oh, steady on,' said Aslet.

'A duel! How laughably quaint,' said Amadeo. 'But, still, why not?'

'Choose your weapon, then.'

'Let me see. I choose. . . .'

'Yes?'

'An electric tin-opener.'

'You are mocking me!' shouted Kasimir Mowinckel. He

snatched up a brass poker and lunged at Amadeo, but the poker thumped harmlessly into the kidneys of Battle, who had entered the room without anyone noticing and interposed himself at the last moment. 'Lord Erskine would be very grateful if his guests might join him in the drawing room,' said the butler.

They did as they were told. Erskine's father waited until they were all assembled and then said, 'I'm happy to inform you that at least one part of this unpleasant ordeal is over. We know who is responsible. Battle has made a search of the house and has found various things missing. These include much of our most valuable silverware and jewellery. They also include a footman, a maid and all of their personal effects. It is all too clear what took place last night. The two servants were planning to elope and also to burgle the house while they were at it. Morton must have caught them in the act, and they decided they had no choice but to murder him. Such things happen quite often these days. The police will be on the look-out and I don't expect they shall get far.'

'Which servants?' said Erskine.

'Godwin, and that girl of your sister's.'

'Tara?'

'Yes.'

Erskine felt great relief about Sinner, but he still couldn't help saying, 'They wouldn't have eloped. She detests him. I remember Evelyn saying so.'

'I think my daughter probably has better things to do than keep up-to-date with her servants' romantic lives. Or at least I hope she does.'

'Have you told her? She'll be upset.'

'Your mother will tell her.'

'Were either of these servants Jewish?' said Berthold Mowinckel.

'If it were up to me I'd have my footmen neutered,' said Bruiseland.

'Will the conference continue?' said Aslet.

'That boy, whatever his faults, was supposed to be my son-in-law,' said Erskine's father. 'The conference will not continue.'

'Why put your trust in the police?' said Amadeo. 'We should capture these beasts ourselves.'

There was a small cheer, and soon the five fascists were rushing off to find out how many hunting dogs you could fit in a motor car. Erskine followed them as far as the hall, not wanting to be left alone with his father, and then sneaked upstairs to his bedroom and woke up Sinner.

'Something pretty bad has happened. Morton's dead. You know, my sister's fiancé.'

'Do they know who did it?' said Sinner. His face showed no reaction.

'Two of the servants here.'

'Which ones?'

'Godwin the footman and Tara the maid. They've run off with a lot of valuables. My father says Morton must have caught them and so they beat him to death and threw him in the pond. It's rather horrifying. But a relief in a way because – I won't lie to you – I did think for a moment it might have been—'

'No,' said Sinner.

'What?'

'That's wrong.'

'What do you mean?'

'It weren't them.'

'How can you possibly know that?'

'I seen it. Well, I ain't seen it, but I heard it. Last night.'

'What do you mean? Who was it, then?'

'The beefy old toff.'

'Bruiseland?'

'Yeah.'

'That's nonsensical.'

188

'I heard it,' said Sinner.

'Why on earth would Bruiseland want to murder Morton?'

'He thought he was trying to blackmail him.'

'Morton thought Bruiseland was—'

'No, the fat one thought the other schmuck was sending the fat one letters.'

Erskine's heart almost stopped when he remembered what he'd heard through the library door the previous afternoon. Still, there were other ways that Sinner might know about that – one of the other servants might have eavesdropped on a related conversation and then gossiped about it.

'I was talking to Tara last night,' said Sinner. 'She didn't say nothing about wanting to leave. And your sister says she hates that other bloke.'

'Yes, but . . . .'

'The other schmuck got done in the library, right? So how could he have caught 'em stealing? What would they be stealing from a library?'

'My father owns some important rare books,' said Erskine, but he realised how implausible it sounded that servants fleeing a house on foot would decide to weigh themselves down with a few antique folios.

'And, last, that slimy one – what's his name?'

'Godwin?'

'He couldn't knock the wings off a moth. How was he supposed to smash the other schmuck's face in on that machine?'

'Fine, fine, I admit all that, but still, Bruiseland – it's too ridiculous.' And then Erskine remembered something his sister had heard from Casper Bruiseland: that on the day Leonard Bruiseland's wife had finally left for Florence, he had strangled all five of her terriers with his bare hands.

He sat down heavily on the bed. 'Or, well, what if it is true? What does it matter? What can anyone do?'

'Tell them the truth.'

'Be serious.'

'What about the maid? What'll happen to her?'

'So you're going to go down there and say, "You're all wrong, I know what happened, arrest the Master of Foxhounds"? It's impossible. They'd start asking questions, they'd find out exactly who you are – that you're not really a valet – that, even worse, you're a Jew. They'd ignore everything you said and just insist you were part of the plot. You'd end up in the village jail on charges of conspiracy to commit murder, or something like that. That is if Mowinckel or Amadeo didn't try to stage a summary execution.'

'I know all that. I'm not a bleeding half-wit.'

'Good.'

'You'd have to come with me.'

'What?'

'If I go and tell 'em on my own, I'm fucked. If you're with me, what can they do?'

'In principle, yes, I might be able to stop them putting you in jail. But they'd ask all the same questions and find out all the same things. Am I supposed to admit I brought an East End Jew into my parents' house? This week of all weeks? How could I explain it?'

'What about your sister? What if she knew it was really the fat cunt who'd knocked off her fella, but her maid was going to get done for it? What would she have you do?'

'That's a bad example. My sister has no idea what's good for her or anyone else. What about the trouble it would cause? How could I possible carry on with my work? How could I do anything at all after that?'

'There ain't any other way.'

'It's impossible.'

Sinner looked Erskine in the eyes for a moment, then grabbed Erskine's shoulders and pulled him down on to his back so that Erskine's legs were dangling off the side of the bed. He got down, kneeled on the carpet, unbuttoned

Erskine's trousers, freed Erskine's cock, and licked it with his dry morning tongue all the way from the balls up to the tip. Erskine went bright red.

'What the hell do you think you're doing?' he whispered.

Sinner began to slide the head of Erskine's narrow cock in and out of his mouth, stroking Erskine's balls with his nails. Erskine squeaked and slapped the palms of his hands on the bed like a frustrated child. Sinner started to push the tip of his little finger into Erskine's arsehole. This was too much, and Erskine tried to sit up, but Sinner cuffed him across the face, just as he once had outside the Caravan, and pushed him back down. Before long, Erskine's trousers were around his ankles, the whole of Erskine's cock was in Sinner's mouth, and Sinner's middle finger was in Erskine up to the second joint. Erskine was making a continuous low groaning sound like the vacuum pump downstairs. Then Sinner got to his feet, took a pot of hair tonic from the dressing table, and flipped Erskine effortlessly on to his front. Outside, the hunting dogs were barking.

Although Sinner tried to be nearly as gentle with Erskine as he'd been with his sister, Erskine soon found himself biting into his own forearm through his shirtsleeve. Tears streamed down his cheeks and he struggled to stop himself from screaming. He felt almost as he had in the cave in Fluck, except that now he was the rabbit on the dissecting table, he was the one getting his little heart squeezed in a grimy fist. He'd fantasised about this moment a thousand times, but only in the most abstract terms, and now the idea was getting fucked by the reality.

But despite the pain, as Sinner thrust faster, the pinched friction of Erskine's penis against the sheets was bringing him closer and closer to climax, and at the same time he became intensely, deliriously aware of a process going on in his own cells, from his testes up to his brain. Every time a cell divided, it now struck him, a new copy was produced of its codex:

all the maps, diagrams, timetables, hierarchies, procedures. Once in a while a mistake was made, and most of the time that mistake was corrected, but if it was missed, then almost anything might happen: a tumour might sprout like a potato in the rich soil of his hypothalamus, or his sons might be born with teeth instead of eyes.

Of course, he also might grow wings from his shoulder blades, or his sons might grow up to catch bullets like conkers. In all probability, though, something would go wrong, which was why the scriveners had to be so vigilant. But, now, for the first time, he wondered: did the tiny scriveners have a choice? When they failed to correct a mistake, was that always a redoubled oversight, or was it sometimes a deliberate gamble? Could a diligent copyist, a decent, responsible man, notice an irregularity, a sin, and just leave it to perpetuate itself, not knowing whether the result would be a swoop of seraphic feathers or a suppurating goitre? As a whole library of these untrustworthy documents were gathered for their dissemination at the base of his penis, and he perceived Sinner approaching a powerful orgasm of his own, he remembered something Amadeo had said about fascism creating a 'new man' – and he realised that a new man could be conceived and born here on this bed, a new man who was nothing like the one Amadeo or any of the others wanted, a new man who could see salvation in the imprecise and the illegible – the only sort of new man worth having, the only sort of new man who was really capable of doing anything really new. Tears springing to his eyes for a second time, Erskine began to exult, and he wanted Sinner to exult with him, so that afterwards they could go down hand in hand and tell the truth about Morton's death and after that who could say what might happen? He was ready. And then he heard the bedroom door creaking open, followed by Millicent Bruiseland's voice.

'Just as I suspected!'

Erskine's heart caught like a toe in a mousetrap. Sinner showed no sign of stopping, and Erskine didn't have the strength to throw him off, so in desperation he tried to pull a sheet over the two of them, but his arms were trapped.

'I'm going to tell everyone,' Millicent said. Erskine, cringing, heard her run out of the room. And just then, with a last excruciating jab, Sinner completed his task.

The boy rolled off his owner and they lay there panting. Erskine smelled the insolent smell he knew from that incident in his lab. He wanted to suffocate himself with the pillowcase, but instead he said, 'Get dressed. Someone else might come up.'

'They ain't going to believe her.'

'You should have stopped!'

'Wouldn't have made any difference.'

'Shut up.' Erskine put on a dressing gown. 'I'm going to have a bath.' He couldn't look at Sinner. He spoke in a monotone. Something inside him had drowned like kittens in a sack. For a second time he remembered the cave in Fluek. Why must he be interrupted every time? Were Gittins and the girl in league? 'If that . . . act was intended to persuade me of something, then it failed. I'm not one of your nightclub boys.'

'You liked it.'

'Shut up.'

'You think I can't tell?'

'Shut up.'

'What's that, then?'

Sinner pointed. Erskine looked down. There was a damp patch on his shirt tails and white sap oozing from the pubic hair on his belly. He had been so wrenched with horror by Millicent Bruiseland's arrival that he had been oblivious to his own choked pointless orgasm. Quickly he closed the dressing gown and tied the cord in a tight complicated knot. He thought of the Australian orchid dupe wasp, which is tricked into ejaculating on a flower because it mistakes it for a female, and even comes to prefer the flower when given a choice.

Two hours later he got out of the bath and went back to his room. Sinner was gone but it still stank. He got dressed. Outside in the corridor he found his mother. She looked as if she'd been left in somebody's trousers while they went through the wash.

'Your little man drove off in your car,' she said.

'Er, yes, I asked him to.'

'Why on earth would you do that, Philip?'

'He – there was some urgent business for him to take care of in London.'

'At a time like this?' Her eyes were very red.

'Yes.'

'Mrs Erskine!' said Millicent Bruiseland, who had appeared at the end of the corridor.

'Not now, Millicent.'

'But I have the most important news about your son.'

'You often do.'

'But I utterly utterly promise that this time it's—'

'For heaven's sake, girl, even you are old enough to realise that this is not the time for your interminable filth,' barked Erskine's mother. 'You and your parents should be ashamed of yourselves. Go to your room.'

Millicent Bruiseland looked angrily at Erskine and then ran off. Erskine's mother took a moment to calm herself and then said, 'If the car's gone, how are you going to get home?'

'On the train,' said Erskine.

'You hate the train.'

'Oh, what the hell does it matter, Mother?' he shouted, and pushed past her to the stairs. He wondered what Sinner was laughing most heartily over as he drove back to London – how easily Erskine had been overcome, or the disgusting unmanly noises he'd made in the process? But in fact as he passed Camberley Sinner was not thinking about Erskine at all, but rather about a remark that Casper Bruiseland had made in the observatory last night; a remark that had been submerged in the Polish honey mead until that pre-coital conversation with Erskine had jogged his memory; a remark about a clever new scheme that Casper had developed to get some money out of his father.

16

As I sat sipping tea on Tara Southall's comfortable sofa, this is what I thought: Kevin, you need a bit of focus. If you hadn't been chatting to Stuart at the same time as you ran a search for 'Philip Erskine', you might have realised that the scientist who got the letter from Hitler and the planner of a town in Berkshire weren't necessarily two different people. If you hadn't got used to skim-reading Wikipedia pages, you might have been able to remember whether the latter man had a confirmed date of death. And if you hadn't been so obsessed with Ariosophist conspiracies, it might not have taken you quite so long to come to the conclusion that it was Philip Erskine himself who, at the age of ninety-eight, had employed a murderous Welshman to track down Seth Roach's body.

In 1957, shortly before his second, fatal stroke, Edgar Aslet was appointed to the committee of the East Berkshire Regional Plan. Asked to suggest some talented young men to carry out the committee's recommendations, he chose the fellow who he thought was most likely, of all his friends' sons, to impose a calming conservative influence on the dubious notion of socialised housing. But when Philip Erskine arrived for his first meeting, Aslet hardly recognised this bright-eyed evangelist for the government's New Towns policy. Erskine couldn't stop talking about the ideas of an American called Balfour Pearl, who had become his friend and mentor after a chance meeting at a black tie gala in Manhattan in 1949. (Neither *The Perception of Harmony: A Life of Philip Erskine* nor *Look Upon My Works: Balfour Pearl and the Fall of*

New York is able to pinpoint exactly which black tie gala this might have been.) Pearl had been forced out of government and now spent most of his time in Los Angeles; but his ideas were as influential as ever, and Erskine was determined to apply them in the south of England, where even after a decade of rapid house-building there was still, as he wrote in one report, 'a desperate need to rescue good families from our dark, overcrowded, morally ruinous cities and install them in rational new communities which combine the most desirable qualities of rural and urban life'. Though Erskine, now forty-seven, still had little or no hands-on experience of town planning, his enthusiasm and knowledge were so impressive that the committee soon put him in charge of a New Town that was to be built south of Hungerford. After consultation with local historians (*The Perception of Harmony* is, again, unable to say when this took place) Erskine decided to name the new settlement after a little-known medieval village called Roachmorton.

Drive into Roachmorton, as I did with the Welshman three or four hours after our visit to Claramore, and the first thing you will notice is the quantity of giant roundabouts, which so dominate the landscape that it is difficult to believe that the road system has been built for the benefit of the town and not the other way round. But there is a lot more to Roachmorton than roundabouts. Despite a projected population of under fifty thousand, Erskine was determined that Roachmorton should have a little of the shining grandeur of a city like New Delhi, the designer of which, Edwin Lutyens, Erskine admired almost as much as Balfour Pearl. (Erskine regretted that he had not had the chance to meet Lutyens before his death in 1948, but at least by then he was acquainted with Lutyens' daughter Elisabeth, who had become great friends with Erskine's sister Evelyn.) Consequently, Roachmorton is almost unique among British towns for having its public facilities arranged in classical fashion, like entries in a grammar table, along a wide tree-lined boulevard. And while many postwar estates were notorious for lacking anywhere to socialise, Roachmorton puts in pride of place a boxing ring (Premierland), a pub (the Caravan), a working men's club (the UUC), and a hotel (the Hotel de Paris), all named with the help of those same diligent local historians to give a sense of what later eras would call 'heritage' and 'continuity'. Nearby are St Panteleimon's Hospital, the Gittins Museum of Entomology and Philology, and a town hall built of red brick and marble in a distinctive country-house style, incorporating the well-stocked public library, from which visitors can look out over a large artificial lake, colloquially known as 'the Pond'. Like Oscar Niemeyer, the designer of Brasilia, Erskine had declined to visit the site before making his plans, so he didn't set eyes on Roachmorton until 1961 when it was nearly half-complete. By then, his ambitious vision had already received special praise from both the Minister of Housing and the leader column of *The Times*. But within only a few months of the arrival of the first optimistic residents, while the town was practically still under manufacturer's warranty, the complaints began.

In Roachmorton it was impossible, for instance, to vary your route to school. For every one of the town's thousands of detached houses there was a specific mathematically optimal path towards the larger thoroughfares, and to make the perverse choice to reject this path would often require a ten-minute detour. So it was rare to bump into anyone near your home but your immediate neighbours. But it was even rarer in the centre: trudging to the town hall across the gaping boulevard, you might, like an Arctic fisherman, catch sight of a friend in the far distance, but a face-to-face chat would require, like the town itself, a detailed plan. To get lost even a few streets from your front door took only a moment's inattention, since every little close looked exactly alike, and the flashers who took day trips to Roachmorton because of its many blind underpasses would often find themselves wandering like minotaurs in a maze until long after they'd missed the last train back. With many houses, for privacy's sake, facing the blank side wall of the next prefabricated house, there was not much pleasure to be taken in looking out of the window, yet at the same time almost every family could point out some glitch in the sight-lines which meant that they could see directly, for instance, into the upstairs bedroom of the house round the corner. Naturally, all this was pretty claustrophobic, but no one wanted to get on the bus just to go for a pint in the enor-mous Caravan, and there were hardly any pubs or shops out in the residential areas because the generous provision in the centre was supposed to have negated any need for them. As every day brought new problems that Erskine had never anticipated and had no particular interest in addressing, many of the first residents of Roachmorton reported that they felt as if they'd been sent into exile; and on our visit to Tara Southall's house – around which the streets were so lifeless that one expected cobwebs the size of football nets – I could see why.

Back at the Claramore Hotel, I had been almost sure I was going to die. After all, as soon as I wasn't useful to the Welshman any more he would stub me out under his heel, and we'd been hunting around for ages without finding even a spectre of a clue. (Certainly, there was no evidence for the Welshman's contention that Seth Roach was buried some-where in the grounds.) Finally, though, we wandered into the bar, expecting it to be as thoroughly corporatised as the rest of the old house, only to discover that the original bookshelves had been retained, in the brochure's words, as an 'evocative period feature', much like the framed archive newspaper clip-pings about the murder of Julius Morton. While a crowd from a marketing convention chatted over their mid-morning tomato juice, I searched through a shelf of heavy marbled visitors' books which went all the way back to the nineteenth century. And that – just as Batman, the world's greatest detective, probably would have done it – was how we learnt that somebody called 'T.S.' from 'Roachmorton, Berkshire' had paid a visit to Claramore every summer from 1951 to 1999. Back then, of course, I hadn't heard of Roachmorton and I didn't know it had anything to do with Philip Erskine, but the Welshman knew all that, along with the name of Evelyn Erskine's fugitive maid.

First, we tried directory enquiries. But Tara Southall was still, in theory, wanted for murder, so she plainly couldn't be living there under her real name. Indeed, there was no reason to think she was even still alive. Still, it was the closest we had to what on television they call a lead, so we left the hotel and set off east down the motorway to Roachmorton.

On the way, it occurred to me that if Tara Southall was really living in her mistress' brother's town, then, for some reason that was so far unfathomable, Philip Erskine himself must have pulled some strings to put her there. I knew from my late great-aunt, who lived in Cumbernauld, that when someone involved in a New Town pulled some strings to get a friend or a relation a house, then the friend or relation would be among the very first residents to move in. And the very first residents to move in would all, for obvious reasons, have been put in the same little district. So if we could identify that district, we might be able to find out if there were any nonagenarian women who had been living there ever since the town's original designation. To find all this out would probably take a bit of what hackers call 'pretexting' – which was far beyond me, but not, I expected, beyond the Welshman; and indeed he had only been in the office of Roachmorton's junior housing manager for ten minutes before he came back out to the town hall's car park, where I was still handcuffed to the steering wheel of the car, and told me that there was a ninety-one-year-old called Tara Smith who had lived opposite Galton Primary School for forty-seven years. (There had been no more opportunities to escape, and I hadn't stalled the Welshman for long enough to give the police time to arrive at Claramore. To be honest, for much of the time I had forgotten that I was even supposed to be stalling him – more than once I caught myself taking pleasure in the progress of our investigation, as if we were partners, not captor and captive. I think he may genuinely have been impressed with some of my insights. I don't know. Anyway, afterwards I had hoped there was at least a chance that the police might have been able to track his car on motorway CCTV, or something like that, but they weren't waiting for us when we got to Roachmorton. Perhaps Stuart was so childishly overexcited to be part of a real adventure, I thought, that they hadn't believed him when he called?)

'Are you Tara Southall?' said the Welshman when a woman opened the pink front door. It was about four o'clock.

'Yes,' she said. 'Who are you? And what's that smell?' She wore her hair long, and the tall masts of her cheekbones saved the rigging of her face from the androgyny of the very old. Behind us were faint playground noises.

The Welshman had told me, for once, to do most of the talking, because there was something about my cravenness to which he thought an old woman would probably warm. 'My name's Kevin, and this is, er, my friend. We're here because we hoped you might be kind enough to tell us something about Seth Roach. And that smell is me, I'm afraid. It does linger for a bit, but after I've gone you can use one of those sprays.'

'You know, it's been years since anyone called me by my right name. Southall. No one since Battle passed over. Didn't think anyone else knew.'

Inside, she sat us down and made tea. The room smelt of

slightly sour milk and there was a skulk of little porcelain foxes on the mantlepiece. The first thing I could think to say was, 'We were at Claramore earlier today.'

'I used to go back every year until my back got too bad to sit on the train. Wish it would burn down.'

'What happened there?'

'A lot happened there.'

'But what happened in 1936?'

She looked surprised. 'What do you mean? I thought you must have found out. I thought that was how you found me, finally.'

'We hardly know anything.'

'Well, you know about poor old Morton.'

'Yes.' I'd read the newspaper clippings.

'Bruiseland did it. I never found out why. I was tucked up in bed when it happened.'

William Erskine, Tara went on to explain, had woken her up at about two in the morning, stood there while she got dressed, and brought her quietly down to the library, where Bruiseland and Alex Godwin were already waiting. There was blood everywhere. The two servants were told that they were going to have to leave the house and go to London and live together under different names. They would be allowed to take all their things with them, along with some jewellery which they shouldn't sell straight away. If they made trouble, they would certainly both be hanged for the murder of Julius Morton.

Tara, frightened and confused, had worked up the courage to say that she would rather go separately from Godwin, but Erskine explained that they weren't to be allowed to live apart in case either of them should decide to tip off the police anonymously about the other, and, since they had clearly been plotting to elope anyway, it shouldn't be any hardship. Godwin looked delighted. Erskine went upstairs to pack their bags for them, then came back down, put them in the car and drove them all the way to London, emphasising several times on the way that Bruiseland and he knew every judge and senior policeman in Hampshire. When they arrived, he gave them money for a couple of weeks in a boarding-house until they could find new jobs and a place to live, then set off back to Claramore, where he planned to arrive before dawn. But it was too late to find a room, so they decided to skipper in a park – except that Godwin immediately tried to force himself on Tara, rubbing her thighs with fistfuls of damp soil as he did so, and she fled with nothing but the clothes she was wearing. After walking until her heels blistered she arrived at the Garlick house in Kensington, outside which she waited until she saw Evelyn's friend Caroline going out later that morning. Tara ran up to Caroline and begged her to get a message to Evelyn about where she was. She wouldn't explain any more because she was terrified of retribution from Erskine and Bruiseland.

'So that was how I ended up back in London. For years I was still living in a little flat in Spitalfields, calling myself Tara Smith. I even met a lad during the war and we got engaged, but he found out about who I was, or he nearly did, and I had to break it off. He wasn't even snooping. It was just bad luck. Anyway, by the time this awful place got built old Lord Erskine had copped it, so Evelyn came to me and asked me if I wouldn't rather live somewhere a bit nicer. She said it was something to do with her brother, but it might still be all right. She didn't know any better and neither did I, so I said yes, and she wrote a letter to her brother, and he got me a house. Left all the friends I'd made, moved here. Regretted it ever since.' She seemed relieved to have told the story.

'What happened to Philip Erskine?'

'He got married to an American girl. I can't remember her name. Rich, though – family made a fortune in toothpaste, they said.'

'No, I mean . . . .' I glanced nervously at the Welshman. 'Where is he now?'

'The old bugger's been dead about thirty years, pet. He's buried near here.'

Could Erskine have faked his own death? No, I decided, that was preposterous even by the standards of the past twenty-four hours. But in that case I'd run out of theories completely.

'And what happened to Evelyn?'

'Got together with a lovely man from the wireless called Ronald Slater. They didn't have much money, though, so things were a bit difficult by the end. Then she died, too. I'm the only one from those days that's lasted this long.' In fact, as I later learnt from *The Perception of Harmony*, the 'dodecacophonist' Evelyn Erskine struggled in her career as a composer, often forced to make ends meet by writing scores for Hammer horror films, before ending up at the BBC Radiophonic Workshop, where she did things with synthesisers that apparently no one has been able to replicate since. Around that time she began a long affair with Kasimir Mowinckel, who had fled to Gibraltar in 1942 with a suitcase full of his father's secret diaries, been picked up by a British ship, endured six months of internment on the Isle of Man, and eventually started a new life in London as a sculptor.

'And what about Seth Roach?' I said. My voice cracked as I asked the question, because I realised at that moment that as soon as the Welshman knew the answer it might not just be Kevin Broom who would become fatally superfluous – it might be Tara Southall, too.

'Oh, yes, that was what you wanted to know about, wasn't it?' she said. 'The boy. You know, when Evelyn met him for the first time, that spring before what happened to Morton, she came back to me and she said, "That handsome little thug is going to change all our lives. I'm sure of it. He's already changed my brother's, and I don't know how but he's going to change mine, too." But he didn't, really, in the end. He didn't really change anything for anyone. Such a pity what happened. We had to keep it all a secret, of course. Such a pity.'

17
OCTOBER 1936

For the third time in his life, Erskine stood outside the Premierland Boxing Club on Commercial Road. Two years ago, the first time he had come here, there had been what he had thought of, back then, as a very dense, noisy crowd – but what, in truth, had just been a timid and diaphanous rumour of human presence, a ghostly and almost imperceptible nuzzling at the elbows, a sort of cheap alternative to a lengthy rest cure on one of the lonelier banks of Lake Geneva in winter. Today, as he found himself compressed to the width of a cigarette by the amalgamated force of five hundred million vengeful Cockneys, he understood what a crowd really was. Ever since the indignity at Claramore Erskine had felt even more revolted than usual by the heat of other human bodies, and now he was being poached in that heat: an infinite merciless crush of Irish dockers and barefoot schoolboys and toothless drunks and purulent spivs and ludicrous Hassids, all howling, 'They shall not pass!' and 'Down with Mosley!' and 'One, two, three four five, we want Mosley, dead or alive!', as if Cadmus had taken the teeth from the poorest, filthiest, ugliest imaginable dragon and sown them in the grey compacted mash of shit and rags that in Whitechapel was what passed for pavement. Red flags and bedsheet banners fluttered in the air, children slithered up lampposts for a better view, and pregnant mothers leaned from the windows of the sooty tenement blocks on either side. As he shouldered his way desperately down Commercial Road towards a stretch that was merely unpleasantly packed, Erskine thought of how absurd it had been to come here. The previous week, when he had first read in the newspaper that the Blackshirts were planning a march through the East End, he had realised that a lot of Jews would come out looking for a fight; and he knew one East End Jew in particular who, despite his ignorance of politics, would surely never pass up a brawl of that size; so he had come back to Whitechapel, hoping he might just bump into that Jew by good luck. Well, he might have been an imbecile, but at least there was not even the remotest possibility that he would see anyone here that he knew.

'I never forget a face.'

Erskine turned. Before him was a stocky man with scars on his cheeks and plump wet lips like slices of raw calves' liver. The man wore an ostentatious cheap suit and brandished what must have been a chair leg. 'You're the posh cunt what was hassling Sinner that day after the match that night. Year or two ago.'

'Yes – I suppose you must be right,' said Erskine nervously.

'Did you get what you wanted?'

Erskine coughed. 'Not quite.'

'Lost, are you? Your lot are down the road.'

Now one or two other men were looking at him with suspicion. Erskine imagined himself getting strung up by his toes. 'No, no, I'm on your side.'

'Oh, yeah?'

'Yes.'

'You sure about that, mate?'

'Absolutely.'

'Splendid. Can't remember if we were properly introduced last time. My name's Kölmel.'

'Philip Erskine.' They shook hands.

'If you're on our side, you won't mind helping out, will you?' said Kölmel genially, slapping the chair leg into his palm. He was balding, and the skin on his bony forehead looked stretched and sallow, like a condom pulled down over a fist.

'Helping out?'

'Yes.' Kölmel was apparently serious.

'No, of course not,' said Erskine. 'That's what I'm – what I'm here for, after all.'

'We're building a barricade on Cable Street. There's a dump round the corner. My boys'll show you. Just get whatever you can – wood, tin, anything. And put your back into it, right? Wouldn't want anyone thinking you're a double agent or anything like that, ha ha!'

'No, ha ha!'

'See you, then,' said Kölmel and gave him a pat on the shoulder.

How was it, Erskine wondered, that in the midst of all this chaos Sinner's friend still had time to play this sadistic little game? He followed one of Kölmel's henchmen south down Back Church Lane, another two at his back, then off to the right where rubbish was piled high in a fenced-off square of ground between two garment factories – mostly old splintered chairs and burst mattresses and smashed china, but also fishbones and pumpkins and pools of cooking oil and even, Erskine noticed with disgust, the rotting body of a mongrel dog. This, he thought, not brimstone, was the smell of the inferno – the perfume wafting from this crusty infected sore on the flank of the city. Climbing up the dump's nearest slope, Erskine employed a technique which he had honed to perfection during cricket matches at Winchester, which was to look both busy and unobtrusive in a way that immediately made everyone else forget you were there – and, indeed, after he'd spent a few minutes making a vague show of picking through some wooden planks, the others started off towards Cable Street with their own armfuls of debris and did not even glance back to see if he would follow. He took out his handkerchief and wiped his fingers and sat down on an upturned bath and wondered what to do next. That was when he saw Sinner, climbing down the fire escape of the factory on the other side, with a tight black shirt on and a knife between his teeth like a pirate.

Back in August, when he got back from Claramore, Sinner had sold Erskine's car to an associate of Kölmel's and that had kept him in half board for a while, but although he still often felt as if his innards were planning a daring escape, five months in Erskine's dubious care had left him looking presentable enough to get into the Caravan again, so a lot of the money had already gone on gin; and he certainly wasn't willing to spend another winter on the streets or in St Panteleimon's. Consequently in October, when he heard a rumour that somebody in Chelsea was paying cash for 'Biff Boys', he went off west the same day. He would do whatever he had to. By now, he didn't get quite so angry when he happened to see a poster for a title fight at Premierland, with names that he didn't even recognise. All that seemed a long time ago. Not that he didn't still have dreams about being in the ring.

What he found on the King's Road was a sort of military barracks crossed with a newspaper office. Everyone hurried around in black shirts, and Sinner soon realised that these must be the same Jew haters, led by the same Mosley, that he'd often heard both Frink and Erskine slagging off (for very different reasons) – but it was an easy wage, and, anyway, didn't it make more sense, if you had a choice, to take your money from a Jew-hater than from another Jew?

Finally he found someone who would stop to talk to him, a very tall man with a handlebar moustache and motorcycle goggles. He was told that they already had more than enough good recruits to keep order in their meetings, but that they might need reinforcements for the march through the East End on Sunday. Sinner explained in turn that he knew his way around the East End, he used to be a champion boxer, and he didn't mind getting his knuckles bloody for a few shillings. The man said he could come back in three days.

He did, and was given a black shirt which he didn't even have to pay for out of his wage. The other men made jokes about how he looked a bit 'Oriental', and as soon as he realised they meant Jewish, not Chinese, he just said he'd eat as many pork chops as they felt like buying him, and they all chuckled and slapped him on the back and moved on to making jokes about his height instead. As the morning passed, some of them did a bit of sparring to pass the time, and it turned out none of them had a clue how to fight. He didn't like these Blackshirts much. Erskine had been a wanker and a nobody but at least he clearly knew it.

Finally, at noon, the procession set off, but they only got as far as Tower Bridge before they had to stop. At the end of Royal Mint Street was a line of police horses like a dam holding back the roar of the local mob, a roar with an accent that Sinner remembered from Premierland. Mosley hadn't even arrived yet. After they'd hung around for nearly an hour, Albertson, one of the senior Biff Boys, had said that if they could get round by the back streets they might be able to charge in and take down the barricade from the other side: 'Those kikes won't know what hit them.' Sinner, of course, knew a route, pioneered in early childhood: down an alley, through the back of some shops, over some low rooftops from which he could almost see into his parents' window, then across the rubbish dump where he'd often played hide and seek with his sister and where, until he discovered the superior charms of Soho and the Caravan and the Hotel de Paris, he'd sometimes taken local boys. So Albertson promised Sinner an extra gold sovereign to scout the way through, and although Sinner didn't think much of the plan – they'd get torn to pieces before they brought down the barricade, which now included a lorry parked across the middle of the road – it was more easy money. One of the other blokes slipped him a knife in case of trouble, and within ten minutes he was climbing down into the dump, which was where he caught sight of a frightened Philip Erskine.

Taking the blade from between his teeth, Sinner made his way over.

'What the fuck are you doing here?'

'Hello. That's just what your friend Kölmel asked me.' Erskine wished he could have watched Sinner for just a bit longer before Sinner noticed him. He thought back to their unexpected encounter outside the Caravan Club two years ago; why did so many of their meetings have to take on the quality of nightmare?

'Kölmel?'

'He sent me here.'

'What, you mean he remembered you from after that match?' said Sinner, as if it were an oddity for anyone at all to remember Erskine. 'Always does remember,' he conceded.

Erskine gulped and said, 'But I was looking for you.'

'Why?'

'Why on earth are you wearing that uniform?'

Sinner shrugged.

'You don't mean to say you're on their side?'

'Fuck off.'

'No, of course not. You're not on anyone's side. Short of money, I suppose? And they just let you join up without anyone noticing that there might be one or two factors to disqualify you? I'm not surprised. You do have an extraordinary talent for that sort of thing. You did very well at Claramore.'

'Wasn't hard. Why ain't you in one of these yourself, then?'

'Oh, not in a million years. The Blackshirts are beyond the pale. This march is just an exercise in intimidation, because they can't be bothered with anything more serious. Mosley's moment is past and he knows it. And, as I said, I was looking for you.'

'Looking for me. Again. What the fuck for this time?'

Erskine looked at his feet. Sinner's old sarcasm seemed to be gone, just like the flyweight bounce in his walk. He almost missed it. 'We haven't seen one another since the day . . . . You know, Morton and all that. And I rather wanted to make sure that . . . .'

'Yeah?'

'I suppose perhaps I rather wanted – I felt rather compelled – to make sure you didn't despise me,' said Erskine.

'Why?'

'And also I thought I'd find out what you'd been up to all this time,' Erskine hurried to add. 'I hope you've been enjoying yourself. For my part, I've been busy with my insects. There have been some really fascinating developments. If only you could see what I've done with *Anophthalmus hitleri*.'

'Answer the bloody question,' Sinner said, lighting a cigarette. 'Why do you care what I think of you?'

'You were my experimental subject for quite a while.'

'Your "subject"?'

'I think it's natural to take an interest in one's—'

'Just fucking say it,' Sinner said.

'What?'

Sinner came closer. 'This is boring. You're always boring. Get it over with. Just fucking say you're still after my arse, and I'll let you have it right here if you want.'

Erskine coughed and licked his lips. 'I'm not going to lower myself to your—'

'Can't do it? Here's another one, might be easier. Say I fucked you and you liked it.'

'I don't think I've ever heard you quite so chatty,' Erskine mumbled.

'Come on, you cunt! Just say why you came to find me – say why you give a toss if I hate you or not – and my dick and my arse are yours for as long as you want them. Say it. Might be too late to save the maid now but it's not too late for that.'

Erskine's fingernails dug into his palms and tears began to well up in his eyes.

Then Sinner smiled. It was the first time that Erskine could ever remember seeing the boy smile, and it was one of the cruellest smiles he'd ever seen. 'Or if you like, Mr Erskine,' said Sinner, 'you can just tell me you love me.'

Erskine let out a sob that sounded more like a death rattle. Warmly, tenderly, Sinner stepped forward and put his hand on Erskine's shoulder. Erskine stared deep into Sinner's eyes. Then Sinner brought his knee up into Erskine's groin. Erskine howled and fell to his knees in the rubble and slime.

'Knew you couldn't. Only reason I said you could have me if you did is 'cause I knew you couldn't. And, yes, of course I fucking hate you, you cunt.' Sinner flicked away his cigarette so that it bounced off Erskine's shoulder. 'Bye, then,' he added, in the sing-song voice of a housewife concluding some gossip in the street.

'Seth Roach!' Sinner looked up in surprise. Two men were standing down at the edge of the dump. One was Barnaby Pock. 'Haven't seen you in a bleeding age, you little shit! Heard you'd kicked the bucket!' He noticed Sinner's shirt. 'What in fuck's name are you wearing that for?'

'Stole it off a friend of this schmuck. For a laugh.'

The two other men cheered, and started to make their way up the slope.

'You look like a real tosser, mate,' said Pock. 'Got up like that, I mean.'

'Yeah. Tired of it. Let's get the shirt off this one. I'll have that.'

'How's he ended up here?' said Pock's comrade. 'I thought they were still all back behind the flatties?'

'Fucking advance party, I bet,' said Pock.

All three men loomed over Erskine.

'No, please!' Erskine said, struggling to his feet. 'I'm on your side! I hate Mosley as much as anyone! He's a . . . he's a frivolous nightclub-going popinjay.' His father's phrase didn't seem particularly forceful in the circumstances. 'I'm only here because Kölmel sent me to help build the barricade.'

'Oi, Sinner, hear that? He knows Kölmel,' said Pock. 'How the fuck does he know Kölmel?'

'You sure he's one of the other lot?' said Pock's comrade.

'Are you taking the piss?' said Sinner. 'Listen to him. Listen to the way he talks.'

'No! I promise! I promise!' wailed Erskine refinedly.

'Boy's right,' said Pock. He stepped round behind Erskine and installed him effortlessly in a headlock. 'Get his shirt.'

While Erskine wriggled and begged, his snot soaking into Pock's dirty sleeve, they ripped his coat, jacket and shirt off him, losing most of the buttons in the process. Sinner took off his own shirt, threw it away, and put on Erskine's, loosely fastening it with a safety pin from his pocket that he usually used to pop blisters. 'I want to go and find some more of these cunts,' he said to Pock.

'What shall we do with this one?'

Sinner shrugged and turned away. Erskine watched in horror, the October cold making the hair stand up on his bare arms, still not quite able to believe that Sinner would abandon him so easily – then lifted his head and shouted, 'I still bloody own you! I'll still have your body after you're dead! And it won't be long, you leprous little thug!'

'Yeah? Well, I fucked your sister,' said Sinner, without looking back. Pock chuckled at the joke and then thumped Erskine in the kidneys.

A few minutes later, back on Royal Mint Street, Albertson was bending down to wipe a speck of mud off his shoe when the first roof tile flew past his head. He sprang back and looked around. Then a second one smashed into the pavement.

'We're under attack!' shouted one of the Biff Boys. 'Take cover!'

'Oh, for Christ's sake, we're not being shelled,' said Albertson. 'Stand tall.' But a third tile caught him in the pit of the stomach and he flopped to the ground like laundry.

'He's up there,' somebody else shouted, pointing.

'Is anyone armed?'

Somebody was caught in the head and fell backward, blood pouring from his temple. After that, there was a general retreat. Albertson, struggling to his feet, tried to throw back a chunk of brick he found in the gutter, but their attacker was hidden behind some chimneys. Several of his men were huddled against the wall of a nearby furniture warehouse, out of range of the bombardment, so he ran over to join them, two more tiles crashing at his heels.

'This is a bloody travesty. What the hell are we going to do? Can anyone see a way to get up there?'

Nobody could.

'Did anyone see his face?'

'It looked like the little blighter with the sneer. Forget his name.'

'Don't be a fool, he's one of us,' said Albertson.

'I told you he looked Jewish.'

'If we just let this bastard get away with this, and the boss hears about it . . . .'

'Hey, hey, hey, listen – I said listen – what's that?'

From directly above them, there was a faint rasp of heel on grit.

'He's right over our heads! Climbing around like a bloody tomcat. What the hell are we going to do?'

'We need a firearm,' said Albertson, staring grimly upward. 'It's the only way.' The sun was in his eyes, so he had to squint, but he thought he could see movement of some kind. He was correct. Sinner had unbuttoned his fly and stepped to the very edge of the warehouse roof.

'Oh, shitting Christ!' howled Albertson as he was blinded by a stream of piss. As he hopped backward out of its golden arc he tripped on the kerb, lost his balance, flung out both arms in the vain hope of a steadying shoulder, spun gracefully on his heel and fell face first into the road – knocking himself unconscious, breaking his nose and embossing his forehead with the geometric pattern of a studded iron manhole cover.

Which was how Seth Roach came to be almost the only Jew in London to see off a Blackshirt at the Battle of Cable Street. Hundreds would pretend otherwise – Albert Kölmel, for instance, would write to his brother Judah in New York boasting that he'd personally given Mosley a thump in the mouth – but in fact, apart from a few unlucky late-arriving fascists who took wrong turns on the way to join the procession, it was only the prophylactic ranks of mounted police who had to face the chair legs and fireworks and rotten fruit. At about four o'clock the demonstrators were sent home, without ever having pushed further than Royal Mint Street.

For a while, after descending from the rooftops, Sinner wandered through the crowds with a bottle of gin. ('Give me a little swig of that,' he'd said to its owner, a weedy, trusting butcher's apprentice he remembered from the old days in Spitalfields Market.) He knew he was back where he belonged, but something still troubled him: Erskine. It wasn't that he felt guilty for leaving him at the mercy of Pock and Pock's friend. It was the opposite: he hadn't done enough. So soon he found himself veering northwest, away from the clashes, back towards the centre of London – back towards Erskine's flat in Clerkenwell.

By the time he got there he'd drunk the entire bottle of gin and bought another from a shop in Moorgate. Mrs Minton recognised him, but when she saw how drunk he was she wouldn't let him up into Erskine's flat, so Sinner told her it didn't matter because he had a key. Actually, he just waited until Mrs Minton had grumbled her way back into her own lodgings and turned on her wireless, then went upstairs and broke down Erskine's door, bruising his shoulder.

Inside, the flat was exactly as he remembered it. On the table in the front room there was some unopened post that Mrs Minton had presumably brought in that morning. Sinner ripped open each of the three envelopes. A tailor's bill, a circular from the Royal Entomological Society, and then this:

Dear Doctor Erskine,

I have received gifts from popes, tycoons, and heads of state, but none have ever been so singular or unexpected as your kind tribute. It is a reminder that the conquests of the scientist are every bit as important to our future as the conquests of the soldier. I hope you will keep me informed of the progress of your work – perhaps one day the Third Reich will have a position for you. How is your German?

Fond regards,
Adolf Hitler
Reichschancellor

Sinner couldn't make out most of the words, and he didn't know much about Hitler, but he recognised the name, and he knew enough about Erskine to realise that he'd be thrilled to get a letter like that. So he crumpled the letter up and stuck it in his pocket before kicking over the table. He crossed the room, took the creepy painting of the dissection off the wall and flung it out through the window. Then he went into the laboratory, which was unlocked.

The tuck box housing *Anophthalmus hitleri* was gone. In its place was a tank that looked as if it might have been specially designed. The lid, the base and three of the four sides were made of steel, while the fourth side was made of thick glass reinforced by a steel grille. The tank was full of soil and chicken bones, and through the grille Sinner could see the occasional darting movements of the beetles inside. He closed the door of the laboratory, then went back to the tank, unhooked the catch of the lid, opened it, picked up the tank and tipped everything out on to the floor, just as Erskine had once made him tip it from the broken glass case into the tuck box. Immediately, several beetles shot out of the pile of soil, escaping into the corners of the room; but Erskine, to prevent a repeat of the enicocephalid calamity from his university days, had sealed up every tiny gap in the skirting board, so they had nowhere to go, and Sinner was able to go round crushing them one by one under his boot heel. Often they took two or even three hard stamps to stop moving. Afterwards, he kicked through the soil. All gone.

He celebrated with a long swig of gin, and let the empty bottle drop to the floor. He had become tremendously drunk. In fact, he hadn't felt quite so unsteady since the night of the Polish honey mead, and although he hadn't had any intention of staying here he decided now that it might be a good idea to lie down for a bit in his old bedroom. After that he would get up, go back east and ask every single person in Whitechapel, every single one of the tens of thousands of men and women and children out on the streets today, whether they had seen Anna in the last three years. And if anyone lied he would know and he would beat them as he used to beat his father.

But as he was about to stagger out of the laboratory, he noticed one last pair of insects cowering on Erskine's book-shelf. He lunged for them, catching them in his hand, and held them up in front of his face for a proper look. Immediately he felt a stinging pain, and realised with surprise that one of them had drawn blood from his index finger. Since when could a beetle break the skin? They reminded him of Erskine, somehow, as they flounced their little patterned wings and nipped irritably at his grimy hands. He thought of cutting them open to see what they looked like inside, but he'd lost the knife while he was up on the rooftops. On a whim, he stuffed them both into his mouth.

Biting down, Sinner felt black legs crunch between his teeth. Fried and salted, he thought, they would probably taste no worse than pork scratchings. But before he could bite down again his eyes widened and his jaw went stiff. He couldn't breathe. The beetles were crawling down his throat.

He groped desperately at his neck, and then he gagged hard as he felt them scratching at his tonsils like transubstantiated whooping cough. He staggered forward and leaned against the wall, trying to pump them out like a gob of phlegm, but they were much too big, and they were already moving further down into his windpipe, deeper into the dark wet warmth of him. Even half-chewed, even crippled, they carried on – that was how Erskine had bred them. He tried to make himself vomit but he couldn't, and he tried to shout for Mrs Minton but he couldn't. In fact, the only sound he could make was a wet chitinous clicking, as if the beetles themselves were talking out of his mouth; little skittering blurs appeared before his eyes, and they reminded him of beetles too. He tasted blood, and for some reason he thought he could smell fish. Hammering at his throat with his fist, he dropped slowly to his knees, and wondered if he could smash the gin bottle and dig the beetles out with a shard of glass – people had done that sort of thing in the war with shrapnel. If he let himself die he would have delivered his body to Erskine like a birthday present, and he couldn't allow that to happen. But before he could reach for the bottle his vision went black, his arms went limp and he slumped sideways on to the floor.

Seven minutes later, a twenty-two-year-old girl ran into the laboratory.

18
OCTOBER 1936

To Evelyn Erskine, the 'laws' of probability were nothing but playground cant, as tiresome as all her brother's theories of eugenics. Would she ever see Sinner again? The chances, Philip would probably say, were minuscule. Well, of course they were, but the chances were also minuscule that she should ever have met someone like Sinner in the first place, and it had still happened. So the problem was not simply that Sinner had vanished among the East End's hundred thousand Jews. That was no real obstacle – there are a hundred thousand seconds in the day, almost, and any one of them might find her bumping into Sinner in the street. The problem was the sadness of those Jews: their children dead of typhoid, their parents at the mercy of some Nazi passport clerk, their lovers NO LONGER AT THIS ADDRESS nor at any other that anybody knew. There must be so many in the East End who had missed so many others so deeply for so long that, in some stern moral sense, it just didn't seem to matter a jot that she, Evelyn Erskine, happened to miss somebody too: in this cauldron of tragedy her own little narrative took no precedence, and the reunion she desperately desired did not have the cheering inevitability of the really important things – like becoming a composer.

On top of all that, here was Mosley. When all those legions of anonymous poor were following the orders of history, of proper newspaper history that Evelyn could take no part in, it felt even more plausible that Sinner would just melt into this gigantic neighbouring world, and that the sheer earnest intensity of her desire to see him again wouldn't be quite enough to make sure that it actually happened. In other words: while, to Philip Erskine, the fascist march through the East End was the first time since Claramore that he really thought he had a chance of finding the boy, to Evelyn Erskine it was the first time since Claramore that she really thought she had a chance of losing him. And yet, despite all that, her basic optimism might still have been enough to sustain her – if only it hadn't been so badly mauled by what had happened at Claramore.

She'd grieved far more over her fiancé, eventually, than she ever would have expected. One may think one doesn't care, but one always does – she realised that now. But at least death was final, whereas what Bruiseland and her father had done hadn't ended with Morton, and might never truly end, because Tara was still in hiding.

Caroline Garlick had telephoned her only a few hours after Morton's body had been discovered on that day in August. Tara hadn't told Caroline very much, only that she needed Evelyn's help, but Evelyn could guess at least part of it, so she told Caroline to give Tara some money and to tell nobody else. Morton's funeral took place in London the following week, and after hours of begging Evelyn's parents let her stay on with Caroline afterwards instead of going back to Claramore. So the next day, finally, she had a chance to visit Tara in the boarding-house where she was staying under a false name and to learn the whole story. It was even worse than she'd imagined.

Of course Evelyn wanted Bruiseland and her father to be punished for what they'd done – but she knew that if she went to the police and they didn't believe her, she might only succeed in exposing Tara. With every hour that passed, justice seemed more impossible: it was as if Tara had her arm trapped between the gears of one of Claramore's machines and was being pulled further and further in. And so all Evelyn could do was help Tara to lead as decent a life as possible, while inwardly feeling so guilty about her inaction that she could hardly sleep. They spent many of their days together, often joined by Caroline, who was an enthusiastic accomplice and had not yet married her Scotsman. That wasn't too bad, but she didn't know what they'd do in the long run. They had to be careful to avoid any acquaintances who might recognise the fugitive maid; once, in the street, a man did remember Tara's face from a picture in the newspaper, but Evelyn just scolded him until he skulked away, convinced of his unspeakably rude mistake. At least in future, after all this practice, she expected she would have no trouble conducting a discreet infidelity.

So Tara was with her on the Sunday of the march, when Evelyn concluded, at last, that she really might never see Sinner again unless she asked Philip about him. She'd promised herself she'd never stoop that low, because she didn't want her brother even to suspect how she felt, and it took her the whole weekend to work up the resolve to pick up the telephone. Infuriatingly, he didn't answer, but she knew he never went out, so he was probably just preoccupied with his insects. Or could it even be that Sinner was living with him again, in secret? She decided to visit the flat in person that afternoon.

At five o'clock there was a smell of lemon peel in the Clerkenwell air, and everything seemed quiet until Evelyn caught sight of her brother's painting, the one modelled on Rembrandt's *The Anatomy Lesson of Dr Nicolaes Tulp*, lying on the pavement outside the flat, the frame cracked, shards of glass all around. She looked up and saw that one of the flat's windows was smashed. Puzzled, she went inside, while Tara, who obviously could not be allowed to cross paths with her brother, waited in the taxi. Upstairs, she found the front door broken down and the table overturned. Assuming there must have been a burglary, wondering if it was safe, she took a few cautious steps into the flat. 'Hello?' she called out. And then, through the open door of the laboratory, she caught sight of a body sprawled beside a heap of soil like an exhausted gravedigger.

As she ran to it, her first wild thought was that Bruiseland had come here and murdered her brother, too. But then she saw it was Sinner wearing one of her brother's shirts. His eyes were closed, and although his face looked pink and bloated he was almost as beautiful as before. She dropped to her knees and put a hand to his cheek. It was warm, but she couldn't tell if he was breathing, so she slapped his face and shook his shoulders roughly, but that only made his head loll around. There was no blood on him, except on the tip of one of his fingers. The white shirt was half off one shoulder so that one of his small nipples was uncovered; she hadn't seen him so naked even at Claramore, and some small brainless part of her felt almost embarrassed. With tears in her eyes she jumped up and sprinted out of the flat and down to the taxi, almost falling headlong down the stairs in her haste.

'You've got to come upstairs,' she said hoarsely to Tara.

'I can't.'

'You've got to. You've got to. Philip's not here.' The driver watched them in his mirror with disinterest.

Tara got out and Evelyn led her upstairs and into the laboratory.

'What's happened?' said Tara, seeing Sinner.

'I don't know. I can't tell if he's . . . .'

Tara knelt down and listened to Sinner's chest, then tried to take his pulse. She turned sadly to Evelyn and shook her head.

'Oh, Christ, can't you do anything? Or we could get a doctor?'

'It's too late, love.'

'But he just looks as if he's passed out. What can have . . . ?' Tara gestured sadly at the empty bottle of gin by Sinner's right hand, and Evelyn felt as if rotten floorboards were giving way beneath her feet. 'Oh no! No, no, no!'

Tara got up and held on tightly to Evelyn while she sobbed. After a few minutes Evelyn sniffed and said, 'We've got to get him away from here.'

'I'll go. Then you can call the police.'

'No. Not the police. We've got to get him away ourselves. Remember what he said to me. About my brother.' Evelyn had told Tara every single detail of that night in the drawing room.

They carried Sinner downstairs, Tara taking his feet and Evelyn taking him under the armpits. 'Our ridiculous friend's got himself terribly drunk, I'm afraid,' Evelyn shouted to the driver as they approached the taxi, just managing to keep her voice steady. 'Will you help us, please?' Grudgingly, the driver got out, opened the door for them, and helped them slide Sinner into the seat.

'Where to?' he said when they were all inside.

'Cable Street,' said Evelyn without thinking. It was the only street in the East End that she could name.

'You know it's that big march on today?'

'Yes.'

'You Blackshirts, then?' joked the driver.

'We're undecided,' said Evelyn.

By the time they got to the western end of Commercial Road, the streets were too choked with revellers to drive on any further.

'Wait here,' she said to the driver, and gave him some money in advance.

'Where are you going?' said Tara.

'There must be someone who can help us.'

Feeling as if this was the bravest thing she had ever done, Evelyn got out of the cab, went up to the first man she saw and said, 'Do you know Seth Roach?'

'You looking for him?' He leered, revealing brown teeth, and took her hand. 'I just seen him round the corner. Come along and I'll show you.'

She pulled her hand free and strode on. She wanted desperately to get back in the taxi and go home to Caroline's, but she'd already failed Tara and she couldn't fail Sinner too, so she tried three more passers-by, and finally found a man who said, 'Yeah, I know him. Haven't seen him, but if he's anywhere he's probably in Dabrowski's.'

'What's that?'

'Dabrowski's pub. That's where all the Premierland lads have gone.'

'Where is it?'

'Cannon Street Road,' he said – and when it was obvious that she didn't have any idea where that was, he gestured with his thumb and added, 'Few streets down on the right.'

'Thank you very much.'

After several minutes she found the pub, which had no sign. Dozens of people had overflowed into the street outside, and she endured several wolf-whistles and a pinch on the bottom as she made her way through; then, inside, there was no space to move, and a belligerent song was being sung in an interestingly atonal mode, so she had no choice but to stand where she was and shout at the top of her voice, 'Does anyone know Seth Roach?' After she'd shouted it three times the song diminished a little, and suddenly she felt as if every single person in the pub were staring at her. (She'd never been anywhere like this before, and as tremulous as she did feel, there was something exhilarating and libidinous about the crowdedness of the place, the sweat and beer and unforced jubilation all sloshing around under its low wooden ceiling. She thought of how commonplace her summer adventure with Sinner would probably seem to any of these men and women. And the bold, unruly, port-swilling boys her friends gossiped about at balls, the Wykehamists and Etonians who were 'really wild, really *too* wild': here, they wouldn't last long enough to recite their middle names.) 'Does anyone know Seth Roach?' she said again, trying to keep her voice steady. Several people shouted back what she took to be some unintelligible expletive and all her confidence fled her, until she realised with relief that it was not an expletive but a name. 'Frink? Frink?' they were saying.

At last, Frink was produced from the back of the pub.

'Yes, miss?' He held a pint of beer in each hand.

'You know Seth Roach.'

'I knew him, indeed. But I ain't seen him in over a year. You a friend of his?'

Evelyn was deeply grateful to this kind-looking man for asking that question without a hint of sarcasm or incredulity. 'He's dead,' she said.

Frink's face fell, but he didn't look very surprised by the news. 'Well. That's a sorry thing to hear. I do thank you for coming to tell me.'

'How old was he?'

'Would have been eighteen, if I remember right. Does his mother know?'

Evelyn had never thought about Sinner having parents, any more than one thinks about a thunderstorm having parents. 'No. But I need your help.'

'With the funeral? I'll put in what I can,' said Frink, but a bit sceptically this time – Evelyn didn't look poor.

'It's not that,' said Evelyn, and she did her best to explain about Sinner's terrible debt to her brother. He listened with a frown. 'Is there anything you can do to help us?' she finished. 'To help him?'

'You mean, bury a body so no one can find it?' said Frink. 'That's not my line of work, miss. Never has been. I'm sorry.'

'You must know somebody.'

'It's a dirty business.'

'He hasn't been murdered or anything like that.' She recalled with shock that the word 'murdered' referred to something that was now actually within the range of her experience.

'Still, it's not just a matter of—'

'Listen to me. I have him in a taxi at the end of the road.'

'You what?'

'If you don't help us, then my friend and I will have to do it ourselves. And something will go wrong, and someone will find out, and I don't know what will happen to the two of us, but more importantly my brother will get Sinner, and if only you knew how desperately Sinner didn't want that to happen . . . .'

Frink stopped her. 'All right. All right. I do know someone. And as luck would have it – pretty bad luck, I'd say – he's here. But he's not a bloke you want to get involved with. You understand me?'

'Yes.'

'It's on your own head.'

'Yes.'

'Come on, then.'

Frink led her through the crowd to the back room of the pub, which, having no bar of its own, was not quite as crowded. Inside, a buxom girl in a torn dress giggled as she danced a parody of a waltz with a stocky man in a suit. Frink tapped the man on the shoulder.

'All right, Albert. There's a lady here for you to meet.'

'Happier words were never spoken,' said Kölmel. After apologising with exaggerated politeness to the buxom girl, he turned to Evelyn. 'What's your name, precious?' he said.

'Evelyn Erskine.' His gaze alone was ten times worse than the pinch on the bottom outside the pub. Even the most loath-some boys at Lady Molly's dances merely looked at her as if they wanted her, but Kölmel looked at her as if she already belonged to him and he was proud of it. She imagined it must work on quite a lot of women.

'Erskine?' he repeated.

'Yes.'

Kölmel smiled and started to say something, but then stopped, as if he'd decided to hold that particular information in reserve for the moment. Instead he said, 'What can I do for you?'

Three hours later, she was climbing up the treacherous slope of the rubbish dump on Back Church Lane. Darkness had fallen, with not much of a moon, and she was almost glad that she couldn't see where she was putting her feet. She carried a spade, and beside her, carrying a mallet, was Tara, and behind them, bearing Sinner's body rolled up in a blanket, were Frink and Kölmel.

'You serious about this place?' said Frink, who had a scar, Evelyn had noticed earlier, on the palm of his right hand. 'I thought we'd go out somewhere in the middle of nowhere. This is in the middle of . . . everything.'

'Yes, I'm fucking serious. Don't mean to be indiscreet, but I used to use this place all the time in the old days. You go out in the middle of nowhere, you usually get nicked on the way.'

'Kids play here, you know.'

'Don't worry, I bury 'em deep. Kids shouldn't be here, anyway. Unhygienic.'

Earlier, a handful of cash from Evelyn and a quiet word from Kölmel had been enough to make sure that the taxi driver wouldn't tell anyone about the drunkard in his car who never seemed to snore or sober up. Now, with a combination of mallet and spade, Frink and Kölmel began to gouge a space out of the festering debris. Occasionally there would be a clang as they hit a bed frame or a bicycle or some other big skein of rusty metal, and they would have to put down their tools to haul it out of the way. The two men kept digging in this strange soil until their heads were level with Evelyn and Tara's feet, and then for quite a while afterwards. Finally, when Kölmel was satisfied that the hole was deep enough, they climbed up out of it, panting with exertion, and got ready to hoist Sinner's body down into the stinking entropic unconscious of the city. Their trousers were splattered with some sort of poisonous black ichor.

'No, please, wait,' said Evelyn.

'What's the matter, precious?' said Kölmel. 'No use blubbing. You know the old Yid curse? *"Vi tsu derleb ikh im shoyn tsu bagrobn."* "I hope I outlive you long enough to bury you." That's good sense.'

'I just want to . . . .' Evelyn knelt down beside Sinner and pulled the blanket aside. She checked his fingers for rings and his chest for a locket or a good-luck charm, but there was nothing, so she went through his pockets, praying for even the most trivial souvenir. All she found was a crumpled-up piece of paper, and it was too dark to make out what was written on it, so she stuffed it into her purse. If she could have taken a lock of hair without the others seeing, she thought, she would have. But then she felt pathetic, because the urge reminded her of Morton, who had saved a ribbon that had fallen from her hair the very first time they met, and had often reminisced about how it was obvious even then that they would fall in love, when in fact she knew perfectly well he had only started talking to her because he'd just been humiliated by a prettier girl whose name she couldn't now remember, and had only picked up the lost ribbon because it was an easy way to start flirting. Suddenly, Evelyn felt desperate that her memories of Sinner should never get a squirt of disinfectant or a coat of paint; that in ten years' time she should not think of their time together as any less trivial, their conversations any less stilted, their coupling any less clumsy, his sentiments any less obscure, his death any less contemptible, than they really were; that all those fascinating dissonances not be transmuted into bland harmonies; that she should never give in to time, which was not the great healer, as everyone said, but the great bowdleriser; that as one of only four people in the world who knew where Sinner would rest, she should not betray the jagged truth of his life by writing herself into a beautiful tragic romance.

But perhaps there was no danger of that. 'Anyone want

to say anything soppy about him, then, before he goes?' said Kölmel. He looked around for a moment, snorted, and spat on the ground. 'Thought not. The boy always was a bit of a putz.'

19

Back Church Lane was a curved street of ugly brown-brick offices and warehouses. 'I just don't see the point,' I said to the Welshman as we drove down it, looking for the address. The dusk was seamed with glowing aeroplane contrails, and, to the west, skyscrapers blocked out most of the soft band between the upper blue and the lower gold that is the closest the sky ever comes to evading the notion of determinate hue. 'It's been seventy years,' I went on, as we passed an incongruously grand wooden doorway flanked by ornamental marble columns and, above, the inscription BROWNE & EAGLE LIM.D, which I recognised as an old wool company. 'There won't still be a rubbish dump there. There'll be flats or a car park or something. We can't just demolish whatever's there.'

But when we got there, we didn't find flats or a car park. Nor did we find the old rubbish dump. Instead, there was a building site. And attached to the wooden fencing around the site, next to the usual warnings about hard hats being worn and children not playing nearby, was a familiar placard:

GRUBLOCK HOMES
It is our tomorrow that commands our today

The slogan was an unattributed quotation from the preface of Nietzsche's *Human, All Too Human*. Grublock's marketing department had loved it. I recalled, now, seeing a computer mock-up of this project on Grublock's desk: it was to be a block of luxury flats with a rippling turquoise façade and a vegetable garden on the roof, full of young bankers who didn't mind living in a grotty bit of Whitechapel if it meant they were only fifteen minutes' walk from work.

'This is extremely convenient,' said the Welshman. He took my mobile phone out of his pocket.

'Have you had that the whole time?'

'Yes, I took it from your flat. You are going to telephone someone in Grublock's organisation who will be able to disable the alarm systems on this building site. I presume you can do that?'

I nodded and he handed me the phone.

I knew this was my last chance. Whether we found Sinner's body or not, my usefulness to the Welshman would have run out. To my enormous relief, he'd left Tara alive when we politely departed her house in Roachmorton, but I had seen far too much. He would definitely kill me. The fact was, I had nothing to lose. So instead of calling Grublock's head of security systems I called Stuart.

'Kevin?' he said.

'Hello, is that Teymur?'

'Are you still in trouble?'

'Yes, this is Kevin Broom. I'm at the Grublock Homes site on Back Church Lane, and I need you to – hello?' I'd discreetly pressed the button to end the call. I looked at my phone in fake puzzlement and then dialled again, this time the real number.

'Teymur here.'

'Hi, yes, this is Kevin Broom again. We must have got disconnected.'

'Pardon?'

'As I was saying, I'm at the Grublock Homes site on Back Church Lane, and I need to gain access. Will you turn off the alarms, please? I'm sorry to call you so late.'

'What's this about?'

'I've got a job to do for Horace.'

'Oh, are you in touch with Mr Grublock? None of us can get hold of him. I've been wondering about sending some-body up to check in person, but after what happened last time I did that . . . .'

'No, there's really no need. I'd just be grateful if you could sort out this alarm.'

'But you'll need the keys to get on to the site, anyway.'

'We've got them.'

'You've got them? From where?'

'I'm in a bit of a hurry, Teymur.'

'Right, sorry. Just give me five minutes and it'll be done.'

I relayed this to the Welshman. We waited fifteen minutes, to be sure, then we got out of the car and the Welshman picked the padlock on the gate to the site.

Inside, we saw that they were only just beginning to lay the foundations after clearing away the remains of whatever building had stood here before. 'We'll use that,' said the Welshman, pointing to a big yellow digger. Its claw looked like a coffin ripped in half. 'The rubbish will have been compressed over time, so we shouldn't need to dig down more than ten or fifteen feet.'

'You'll need the key to start it.'

'No, I won't. Now, the old woman told us they dug the grave in the middle of the far end of the dump. And if she's right, the gangster wasn't using this place so often by the time they buried the boxer, so it should be the first skeleton we find, or at least one of the first. When we think we're getting close, you can go in with a spade.'

'It'll take us for ever.'

'No, it'll just take us all night. And we've got all night. I needn't tell you that if you try to run I shall bite your head off with the digger. Remember, we're looking for a foot with four toes.'

So we began. After two hours the Welshman had excavated a crater of almost lunar magnitude, and there was an ammoniac gnawing at our sinuses that told us we'd reached the upper strata of the old rubbish dump. Standing at the edge of the hole, I watched closely for fragments of bone. Another hour later, my ears aching from the thumps and snarls of the digger, I saw one. It turned out to be part of the spongy pelvis of a dog or cat. Not long after that, the bones of a human foot fell from the claws of the machine. I yelled to the Welshman and he got out to look at it. But it was a right foot with five toes: spooky, but not Sinner's. We seemed as likely, I thought to myself, to find a hoard of gold coins or the lost manuscript of Archimedes' *On Sphere-Making*, but we carried on; and then, finally, as midnight was nearing and I was beginning to lose concentration, the digger ripped away a twisted old bicycle and beneath it, cracked and brown but still unmistakeable, was part of a human ribcage. Again I shouted to the Welshman to stop; then, carefully, I scraped away some more rubble with the spade. From what was left of the skeleton, I could see that it was a great deal shorter than my own. That didn't mean it wasn't just a woman's or a child's, of course; but a few minutes later I found the detached right foot. Four toes, like a cartoon character. Seth Roach.

The Welshman made me sit down on the ground beside the skeleton and and then briskly handcuffed my hands behind my back.

'I still don't understand what you're looking for,' I said. 'Is this what Hitler was talking about in the letter?'

'No.'

'What, then?'

'The beetle.'

So Grublock had been telling the truth! 'What beetle?'

'*Anophthalmus hitleri.*'

I had no idea what that was. 'What makes you think it's here?' I said.

'Be quiet, please.'

'Look, I know you're probably going to kill me after this, whether you find it or not.'

'That's correct.'

'I just want to know what all this has been about.'

The Welshman looked at me and sighed, then he said, 'Two

weeks ago, the individual who is now my employer became aware that a private detective was making enquiries about *Anophthalmus hitleri*. For a long time the consensus has been that there is not a single specimen of the organism, alive or dead, anywhere in the world – but if a serious collector like Horace Grublock believed that somehow, somewhere, some examples might really have been preserved, then that in itself seemed a good enough reason to pursue the possibility. So the aforementioned individual contracted me to find the beetle before Grublock did. Unfortunately, Zroszak had already made excellent progress.'

'So you killed him and searched his flat.'

'Yes. It seemed simplest to pick up where he left off, rather than start from the beginning.'

'But you didn't find much. Then you saw me go inside. And you thought I might have found something you missed. But actually the letter from Hitler didn't tell you anything you didn't already know.'

'No.'

'And I wasn't much help either.'

'No. Except perhaps at Claramore, and with the spinster.'

'So why were you looking for Seth Roach's body?'

'Zroszak seemed convinced that two of the beetles had been buried along with the boxer. That was in his notes. He didn't really explain his reasoning. I believe he had access to some notebooks of Philip Erskine's and some letters of Evelyn Erskine's which I was not able to find.'

'And you thought Seth Roach must have died at Claramore.'

'It seemed likeliest. I was wrong.'

'Do you really think the beetles will still be here? With him? After all this time?'

'We shall see,' said the Welshman. 'The chemical and microbiological conditions in a place like this are unpredictable. The beetles were bred to be hardy. It's just possible that they may never have decomposed. They may even have been fossilised in some way.' Finishing his explanation, he knelt down beside the skeleton. He brushed some filth away from the skull. And then Seth Roach vomited on him.

Black and flickering, the vomit raced up the Welshman's arm, spread across his chest and swirled up to his chin. He tried to scream and straight away it filled his mouth. Falling on his back, he clawed clumsily at himself, but could barely tear open a gap in the flow, and soon every inch of him was tarred. I heard a sound like thousands of tongues clicking in quiet disapproval; I could see flashes of blood and then, worse, flashes of white beneath the boiling slick of black. At first, his whole body thrashed back and forth, but then it was only his hands and feet that shook, and before long even those went limp. Within seconds there was almost nothing left of him but bones, hair, clothes and shoes. Then the beetles came for me.

They shot across the ground, jumped on to my feet and carried on up each of my legs. There was something not quite right about the way they moved, like a cheap animated film. I clamped my mouth shut so they couldn't get down my throat. I wished the Welshman had already shot me so I didn't have to die like this.

But then the beetles stopped.

Some had got as far as my groin, which was drenched, of course, in urine. Others had got as far as my armpits, which were almost as damp. There was something almost nervous in the way they milled around the fetid arches of my body, pricking my skin through my clothes with their tiny needle legs – this, I thought, must be what the angels feel like to the pin. One or two detached from the mass, spread their swastika wings, fluttered up in front of my face, gave me an eyeless glare and descended to rejoin their fellows. Then, all at once, in an instant, like a black tablecloth being whipped from a table, they withdrew. I watched the last few hop back into Sinner's eye sockets. There was silence. Steam, just visible in the dim light from the streetlamps on Back Church Lane, rose from the Welshman's hollow carcass. I fainted.

At about five in the morning, I was awoken by something licking my face. I opened my eyes. A fox. I jerked my head away, and, startled, it trotted a few steps back. Mangy and thin, it had sinews like twisted telephone wires, a stink like a petrol station forecourt, and a coat the colour of a traffic cone left in a skip full of rainwater. It was – if I'm not making myself clear – impossibly beautiful. For perhaps a full minute, the animal stared at me with a strange scepticism and a boy's eyes. Then it darted away and up over the fence. I breathed out, and so did the dawn.

A couple of hours later the first yawning Grublock Homes workmen arrived at the site. When they saw the skeletons they wanted to call the police, but I managed to talk them into calling Teymur first. With the mobile phone held to my ear, I explained everything. I don't think Teymur believed me when I told him that Grublock was dead, but he still gave the order to the workmen to let me go. (One little-discussed advantage of building sites is the fantastic selection of ways to break a pair of handcuffs.) Before I left, I borrowed some gloves and searched through the clothes that still clung raggedly to the Welshman's remains. In his left inside jacket pocket was the letter from Hitler.

It wasn't until much later – after all the research and investigation and speculation that has gone into writing this story – that I understood what must have happened. Deep in Sinner's throat, almost dead, those final two specimens of *Anophthalmus hitleri*, bred to be indomitable, had managed one last desperate, damaged, awkward fuck; and Millicent Bruiseland, luckily, wasn't there to interrupt them. Buried ten feet beneath the surface of the rubbish dump, the resulting larvae thrived on the boxer's flesh. And after those ferocious offspring had reduced Sinner to a skeleton and gnawed the marrow from his femurs, they made do with the toxic borscht of cooking oil and mushy vegetables and bacon fat that pooled in every cranny. Occasionally, they might feast on a dead dog or cat or pigeon, and perhaps, when they were really lucky, one of Albert Kölmel's younger, more reckless rivals might decide to bury another human body. Later, in Whitechapel's rather more prosperous years, when a warehouse was built on top of the old site of the dump, they tunnelled up through the floorboards and punctured the tins of baked beans. Weeks or months might go by without food, but – thanks, again, to Erskine – they were resilient enough to survive. Often, they would simply cannibalise each other. Eighty years later, although these grandchildren of Fluek had spread throughout the dump and into the foundations of the adjacent buildings, a miniature London Underground, Seth Roach's skull was still the epicentre of their colony, so when the Welshman exposed it to the light for the first time since its original interment they devoured him. And the same thing would have happened to me – if not for my trimethylaminuria. Even beetles have standards.

When I got home, the first thing I did was wake up my computer. Stuart was online, and immediately he popped up on my chat program.

STUART: omfg are you ok?
KEVIN: yeah
STUART: did the police come?
KEVIN: no
STUART: what? why not? What happened, then?

I told him, from the beginning. Once or twice I broke off, because there were certain details I wanted to check on the Nazi memorabilia collectors' forums. When I was finished, he said:

STUART: that's insane

KEVIN: i know

STUART: so did you ever find out who hired him?

KEVIN: no

at first i believed grublock that it was the japanese

then i sort of believed him when he said it was him, anonymously

then i thought maybe old man erskine

for a minute i even wondered if it might be tara southall

but none of those theories stood up

in a way, the biggest mystery is his thule society tattoo

i'd sort of forgotten about it until just now, but i think, by the end, it had actually begun to smudge

STUART: so it wasn't a real tattoo?

KEVIN: no

but that's not such a surprise – it was pretty obvious he wasn't really from the thule society

STUART: why?

KEVIN: come on, stuart

it's unrealistic

whatever all those websites might say, they disbanded in the 1920s

STUART: that's what they want you to think

KEVIN: no, stuart, they did

what's weird is, why would you even pretend to be from the thule society? what's the point? who is it going to work on? because there must be only about a dozen people in london who might recognise that symbol

even grublock probably wouldn't

of course, i would

but why would anyone make such a big effort to fool me, specifically, into thinking the ariosophists were involved?

STUART: yeah i see what you mean

KEVIN: but that's a bit of a dead end

we can't ask him

he got eaten by beetles

STUART: which is pretty awesome btw

you have to tell me more about that at some point

KEVIN: yeah i will

anyway, so i was thinking about the other thing i didn't really understand

it was only two nights ago but it seems like ages

when i posted on the forum about philip erskine, and someone replied asking me about seth roach

'nbeauman'

who was that?

they never replied again

in retrospect it was less like they wanted to help and more like they wanted to see how much i already knew

bit creepy

STUART: we should hack into the account

KEVIN: yeah, could do

but there's not really any need

i had another look at his previous posts

i think he's just a sockpuppet

STUART: whose?

Everyone on the forum, including me, had at least one 'sock-puppet' account – some probably had five or six. If you were losing an argument badly and needed reinforcements you would log out of your real account, log into your sock-puppet account, and post something like 'yeah kevin's right, any fuckwit knows that.' It didn't really help, but sometimes there was nothing else to be done.

KEVIN: stuart, why did the police never arrive?

STUART: what?

KEVIN: when i was in the service station, you said you'd call them

then again when i was at the building site

but they never came

STUART: i think maybe they thought i was a prank call

KEVIN: you never called them
STUART: i did!
KEVIN: you already know whose sockpuppet nbeauman is
STUART: no
KEVIN: like i said, i looked at his posts

and the only time nbeauman ever posts on the forum is when you are losing an argument, stuart

There was no response for a while, then, after a bit:

STUART: really?
KEVIN: yes
STUART: well, that's weird
KEVIN: it's not weird

you knew about seth roach before i did

you must have been looking for anophthalmus hitleri yourself

you'd heard that grublock was convinced it was real

so you hired the welsh guy

and you guessed i'd get dragged into it, because i work for grublock

so you told him to put on that thule society symbol because you knew that i would know what it meant, and i'd think he was an ariosophist, not just a gun-for-hire, and then i'd never suspect it was you

STUART: kevin, that's ridiculous

you have too much imagination

come on, you're my best friend
KEVIN: we've never actually met
STUART: what does that matter?
KEVIN: i know

but it's the only anophthalmus hitleri in the world. the swastika wings, the name, the personal commendation from hitler, the sheer rarity – the fact that it eats human flesh! – it's not just priceless, it's practically mythical. even i hadn't heard of it until all this started

are you saying you wouldn't betray your best friend for
that?
   you would
   i would
   we all would
   it's our hobby and it's our life
   the only difference is, most of us can't afford to hire a
proper operative like that welsh guy
   but you can
   plus, you love all that stuff
   assassins, mercenaries, special agents
   you wouldn't have been able to resist

Stuart didn't reply at all this time, so I typed:

KEVIN: why 'nbeauman' anyway? who is that?
STUART: oh
   all my sockpuppets are randomly generated
   otherwise i wouldn't be able to resist putting in some
geeky reference, and it would be too easy to guess it was me
   i'm really sorry, kevin.

Then he went offline.
   A few days later, I had Sinner buried at the Jewish cemetery
in Edmonton. I have no personal interest in ritual, but I felt I
had to do something after my complicity in the unsettlement
of his resting place. When I thought back to the rubbish
dump on Back Church Lane I was reminded of its gargan-
tuan great-nephew, the Waste Isolation Pilot Plant in New
Mexico, a frequent locus of Stuart's conspiracy theories. In a
salt mine near the town of Carlsbad, the US government is (so
they claim) burying thousands of drums of radioactive pluto-
nium: the absolute worst of the worst, the nuclear equivalent
of serial killers in isolation cells at a high-security prison.
The waste will still be dangerous for hundreds of thousands
of years, and the greatest challenge of the project is not the

brute engineering, but the question of how to mark the site in a way that will be intelligible to the inquisitive North Americans of the distant future, be they cavemen or cyborgs. Those descendants must be warned away. But the Egyptians tried the same thing with the pyramids, and look how that turned out. So some anthropologists say we shouldn't mark the site at all. Like Sinner, they hope an unmarked grave may never be disturbed. And probably, like Sinner, they're wrong. Anyway, it's almost irrelevant whether or not their procedures work as intended: if you fear that something will mutate you, then, really, it has already mutated you.

I'd telephoned Tara Southall to see if she wanted to come, and she told me she would send flowers but London was too far. So I was the only mourner on that warm Tuesday. Or at least I thought I was, at first. After the rabbi had finished the ceremony I thanked him, and he left me alone at the grave. That was when I noticed, some distance away, a pale, chubby man in a wheelchair, squinting at me. I didn't recognise his face because I'd never even seen a photo, but of course I knew immediately who it was. I wondered how he'd found out about the burial.

But I didn't go over to speak to him. Instead, I ran to catch up with the rabbi.

'Rabbi,' I said. 'I have a confession to make.'

He stopped. There was a pleasant breeze, and instinctively I moved sideways a few steps to make sure I was downwind. 'You're mixing up your faiths,' he said, smiling.

'I know, I know, but – look, I have a hobby and it's something terrible. I collect Nazi stuff. Lots of it. I'm not a Nazi, I promise, but I have this huge collection. I've never been in a proper Jewish place before and suddenly I feel like such a—'

'Memorabilia of the Third Reich?'

'Yes.'

He patted my arm. 'You needn't worry. I'm a collector myself.'

'What?'

'Well, not quite a collector. But I have a little box of trinkets at home. Quite a lot of European Jews do. I inherited it from my father. It's rather like taking a trophy from a dead enemy. A scalp, if you like.'

'Oh.'

'I'm sure you have your reasons too. But, of course, if it has begun to distress you, you should get rid of it.'

I spent the rest of the day wondering whether I should do as he suggested. It wasn't really that I was distressed – I didn't meet many Jews in my daily life, so I didn't often have to feel so weird – but somehow the excitement of those objects wasn't quite as electric after all that had happened since Thursday. Still, by the following morning I'd decided that I would keep everything. What else would I do with my days? (Also, I'd made friends with Stuart on the forums. Now that we weren't speaking I didn't really have anyone else, so I thought perhaps I should try to make another friend in the same way. Or even two. And I certainly wasn't going to go back to the trimethylaminuria forums to do it.)

But then I got a phone call from Teymur. That afternoon I had been reading a copy of *The Perception of Harmony: A Life of Philip Erskine*, which had just arrived in the post from an online secondhand bookshop. (The title turned out to be from an essay by Le Corbusier: 'Architecture is the art above all others which achieves a state of platonic grandeur, mathematical order, speculation, the perception of harmony that lies in emotional relationships.') Erskine had died, I learned, in a California health spa in 1981. He was divorced from his wife. Friends of his, interviewed by the biographer, seemed to think he had been working on an autobiography, but no manuscript was ever found. The book made no mention of Seth Roach.

'It looks like the company's being bought up by some investors from Japan,' Teymur told me. 'I'm afraid there'll be no one to give you errands any more.'

'That's all right.'

'That's not what I'm calling about, though. It transpires that Mr Grublock had left some instructions about you in the event of his death.'

'Really?' I hadn't been invited to Grublock's funeral.

'Yes. The number of instructions he left about various things was staggering, by the way. We're still going through them. You're to have his "collection". All of it, apparently. I don't even know which collection that means. He had several. I suppose it's wine or something. But, anyway, the head porter at his building says it's being boxed up and shipped to you.'

'Oh. Thanks, Teymur.'

I hung up. I should have been thrilled by the news. But, really, although I was surprised and touched by Grublock's totally unanticipated generosity, I felt a bit dejected. What did that leave of my hobby? (It reminded me of the day I finally completed my 78,000-word prose prequel to John Carpenter's *The Thing* and found it strangely hard to celebrate.) Suddenly, I had one of the greatest Nazi memorabilia collections in the world – why would I spend hour after hour making negligible augmentations? And I couldn't even brag about it on the forums – no one would believe me. (Was this how Grublock used to feel about everything in his life? Was this why he was so insatiable?)

It was time for a new pursuit, I decided. Boxing stuff, maybe. I quite fancied a pair of Seth Roach's boxing gloves. So from Grublock's collection I'd keep only the Goebbels Gottafchen Goethe, and from my own the letter from Hitler to Philip Erskine. The rest could go. I thought of donating it all to the rabbi from the cemetery, but I thought he might take the gesture the wrong way. Also, I wanted a nicer flat.

But selling it off would bog me down for months. Unless I could sell it all at once. To someone with a lot of money. To someone I was already in touch with. To someone I knew so well, in fact, that I could guess the exact percentage by which he would try to cheat me.

I'm embarrassed to admit how relieved I felt to have an excuse to open my chat program and unblock Stuart. Before I even had the chance to tell him what had happened, he typed:

STUART: did you see on the news? they've discovered a cure for trimethylaminuria
they can fix it with gene therapy
KEVIN: what?
are you serious?
STUART: lol
no
why would that get on the news? no one would care
i had you fooled though, right?
KEVIN: yeah
ha ha
hey, i've got something cool to tell you
but first do you want to hear more about the guy being eaten by beetles?

Acknowledgements

Thanks to everyone at *Dazed* and *Another*; to James Sturz, Dan Stone, and the staff of the London Library for their help with my research; to Jane, Felicity, Daisy and Sarah at Lutyens and Rubinstein; to Jocasta, Henry, James and Laurance at Sceptre; to Hermione, Olaf and Sam for their comments on the first draft; to Agata, Archie, Bea, Fran, Josh, Livy, Victoria and Will, and especially to Raoul, Jess and Harry, for all their support; and to my parents, to whom this book is dedicated. A complete bibliography is available on my website www.nedbeauman.co.uk

NED BEAUMAN

was born in 1985 and lives in London. He has written for *Dazed & Confused*, *AnOther* and the *Guardian*. This is his first novel.